Abandon Hope

A Cutters Notch Novel

By Michael DeCamp

First published by Dog Ear Publishing
4011 Vincennes Rd
Indianapolis, IN 46268
www.dogearpublishing.net

ISBN: 978-1-4575-5810-8

This book is printed on acid-free paper.

This book is a work of fiction. Some of the places in this book are real, however, events, and situations in this book are purely fictional and any resemblance to actual persons, living or dead, is coincidental.

Printed in the United States of America

Acknowledgements

One thing I've learned from this project is that writing and publishing a book is no easy task. It takes a team to make a book happen. The author gets the accolades, but behind him or her is a myriad of other people who aided the effort. In my case, I'd like to thank and publicly acknowledge the following people for being instrumental in moving this project along:

1. My wife, Nancy, is a steady source of encouragement. "Creative people need to be creating," she would say, urging me to write.
2. My friend, John Wright, who told me I should finish. For some reason, he was the right person at the right time to move me along.
3. My Beta Readers, who poked some holes in my work and helped me find the mistakes I could no longer see. Thank you Lynnetta Pierce, Brian Holeman, Dan Holeman, Patti Scott, Brandi Clark, Amber DeCamp, Amy Lenz, Dan Redkey, Kathy Nelson, Anni Carter, Lee Ann Lasher, Kristina Seifert, and Sally Marini. Special thanks to Sally for teaching me how to properly use an ellipse.
4. My friend, Royce Cole, for schooling me on police jargon.
5. My agent, Sarah Joy Freese, for believing in my work and teaching me about the process.
6. Finally, the two twin boys who swiped my wife's retainer in 1989, and then snuck it back into our house without a word. They planted the seed of the story in my mind. It took twenty years to germinate, but it finally bloomed. They were the origin of the "Dimensional Bandits."

I also have great appreciation for you, the reader. Everyone has different tastes in stories, but I hope you enjoy this one. I sure enjoyed discovering it as I let it unfold in my imagination.

Mike

Prologue

The heavy steel gate rumbled closed behind Kenny Burton as he stepped out into the warm afternoon sun. In his right hand, he carried his meager belongings in a canvas bag. He was wearing jeans for the first time in a couple of years. He had grown accustomed to his orange jumpsuit, but he welcomed back the Levi's like an old friend, although they were a bit roomier around the waist than the last time he had worn them. A fly buzzed around his face as he turned in a circle to take in the world, and he sucked in the first taste of free air he had enjoyed in two years. Waving the insect aside, he turned back and took one last, long look at the place that had been his cold and bitter home for most of the last twenty-four months. *Adios,* he thought.

"Behave yourself," said the stern voice of the burly guard standing on the other side of the prison's gate. The man was old enough to be Kenny's grandpa, but still big and strong enough to take down the toughest of the bozos still inside those walls. "Don't come back here, son."

The Pendleton Reformatory had been built in 1923 and had continuously operated as one of Indiana's maximum security state prisons ever since. Large and utilitarian, the dark-brown bricks of the various wings, each with a red roof, stood in the sunlight like a rash of giant pimples on the Hoosier landscape—and Kenny Burton had just been popped out. Good behavior had paid off with a quicker-than-expected parole.

"Don't worry," Kenny replied, "I'm ready to live on the straight and narrow." Then he glanced up to the guard with the rifle in the tower, gave him a grin and a half-hearted salute, and walked away.

There was an old Ford Gran Torino waiting for him in the parking lot. His mom had come to get him as requested and was driving his car. Relief settled over him because he had been a little concerned that he might have to walk back to Muncie—the first several miles anyway. People tend to avoid hitchhikers near prisons.

The old car was dark green with a white racing stripe down the side, and his mom had been driving it since his incarceration. Rust spots had broken out on the fenders and eaten holes in the finish, but the engine still sounded good. He pulled open the passenger door, tossed his bag in the back, and jumped in.

"Good to see you, honey," she said as she leaned over to give him a little peck on his scruffy cheek.

Kenny took the kiss but didn't immediately reply. Instead, he leaned his head back, sucked in another dose of freedom, and listened to the big engine rumble. The vibration felt good as it worked its way up from the soles of his feet. He felt a chill drift across his arms and slink past his neck. *The air conditioner still works, too,* he thought.

He kept his head reclined against the headrest as his mother put the transmission into drive and wheeled the car out onto Highway 67. She left a little rubber on the pavement as she gunned the muscle car into traffic. *I'm probably going to need new tires.* He turned slightly to glare at the woman who had given him life.

"Want a burger?" she asked. "I could get you a sandwich at the Hardee's in Pendleton."

Instead of answering her question, the freed man sat up, angled toward his mother, and said the first words he had spoken to her in a year: "Where are they, Mom? Where's my wife and her little brat? Where's Megan and Hope?"

ONE

ope Spencer stepped off of her front porch, onto the sidewalk, and into the bright sunshine carrying the basketball she had won in a tournament the previous winter. Her mother usually nagged her about playing with it. "It's a keepsake," she often said, "You should keep it in your room so it stays nice." Hope thought that was dumb. She would normally reply that a good basketball is simply wasted if all it does is sit on a shelf, and today was no different from those previous days. As she stepped off into grass that was still wet from the previous night's rain, she bounced the ball one last time on the sidewalk and then tucked it under one arm as she trotted on to join her friends.

Stopping halfway to the court, Hope looked around. She felt watched. The deep forest surrounded her neighborhood and some days it gave her comfort because of the life teeming in its recesses and the birds flitting in and out of the towering limbs. Other days, however, it gave her an uneasy feeling. The shadows under the canopy seemed to hide secrets, dangerous secrets. Hope grimaced. This was an uneasy-feeling kind of day.

Hope's friends yelled to her and she waved back. "I'm just being stupid," she said out loud, but low enough that no one could hear, "a couple of three-pointers and I'll feel better."

* * *

As she waved at her friends waiting for her on the basketball court, a set of eyes was watching her. The person behind those eyes was shrouded in shadow, well-hidden and unnoticed. The person marveled at Hope's strength and beauty, and yet still wanted to slice her throat so that her life would drain out through her slender neck. *Soon*, thought the owner of the eyes, *very soon*.

* * *

Hope took a shot at the goal before she even reached the court. It rimmed out, but the action had the desired effect. That feeling of lurking danger evaporated from her mind as she released the ball and watched it sail across the pale blue sky. Being active took her mind away from the paranoia that came with the secrets she carried, so she had poured herself into sports.

Josh flung the ball back to her. "Try again," he said. "I bet you drain it on the second shot." She put it right back up and it zipped through the rim, nothing but net.

* * *

The eyes turned away, disgusted and hungry. *Time to go hunting.*

* * *

September in southern Indiana can be gorgeous, and this year was no exception. The heat of the summer had begun to settle into the cooler air of autumn. The leaves had only just started to turn as the days had shortened and the air at night had taken on a chilly edge. Midday could still be warm but without the overbearing humidity of July and August.

Seen from above, Cutters Notch, Indiana, is a sleepy little town nestled deep inside the ancient timber of the Hoosier National Forest. Imagine soaring like a crow just above the treetops as you follow Highway 257 through the twists and turns as it traverses the rolling hills. The road crosses the brisk-flowing streams and slips in and out of the shadows of the deep woods. Here and there are old farms with broken-down barns and dilapidated silos. Small, random lakes reflect the sun. You're cruising along, skimming the upper branches of the mighty old oaks, the majestic sycamores, and the towering walnuts. Lost in the splendor of the natural beauty, you're intrigued when, suddenly, the sea of green parts and Cutters Notch emerges like a whale breaching the surface of the ocean.

The tiny community sits below a bluff that rises into the air fifty feet above the tallest tree. It takes its name from the notch that the miners cut into the side of that bluff, creating an angled cliff with sheer walls—one heading to the east and the other to the southwest. Once the focus of commercial activity, those tall limestone walls are now peppered with brush and young trees, just a lonely reminder of the hopes and dreams of another generation.

There, below the precipice, is the Notch Inn—an old motel, sometimes open but more often closed. It had been built in the style of the motor inns of the 1950s. Behind it, down a gravel road, through the trees, and along the base of the notch, is the last remaining active limestone quarry in this once-thriving community of stonecutters: Robbins Stone. Here and there, you might spot a lonely man or woman toiling in the rocks. On the far side of the massive pit is a cemetery of abandoned cars and trucks—some very old, some of a more recent vintage.

Farther into town is a row of large older homes that once housed the wealthy owners of the multiple limestone mines that brought prosperity to the area in the early part of the 1900s. Now, they are just big, old houses that are cheap to buy but expensive to maintain. Multiple stories. Basements. Tall wooden pillars supporting once-impressive balconies. In days gone by, they were bright and majestic. Now they are faded and hidden behind overgrown shrubbery. In the middle of the row stands one that has been burned out and left to the elements. Blackened wood encircles the broken windows, and the roof has caved into what was once a massive attic.

At the crossroads of Highway 257 and Robbins Creek Road sits the one last vestige of success in the little town: the Cutters Notch General Store and Gas Station. Open seven days a week from 6 a.m. until they roll up the sidewalks at 9 p.m., it sees a constant flow of traffic from both locals picking up supplies and tourists grabbing a Coke, chips, and a bathroom break. Old-timers gather there every morning for a cup of coffee, to shoot the bull, and to catch up on the gossip.

Diagonally across from "The General" sits what's left of the old Cutters Notch Bank. It closed in the mid-80s, and now the only money that passes through the place is carried in the pockets of teenagers. They slip in at night to smoke, drink, and break any number of other laws in the dank darkness of the big crypt-like stone structure with the giant stone columns on the front.

Next door, to the west, stands another large deserted building: the Cutters Notch School. Once the home to all grades from kindergarten through high school, it was closed down during a massive school consolidation in the 1970s. Now it stands alone, an ominous red-brick and gray-limestone memory of a bygone era in the middle of a large lot, overgrown with weeds. Three stories plus a basement. The windows in the top have all been broken out—mostly the result of sharpshooters with slingshots. The windows and doors below are all boarded up with weathered plywood that is cracked, curled, and peeling.

With the rundown houses, closed businesses, vacant lots, abandoned buildings, and rusted-out old vehicles that dot the landscape of this simple little village, you would think that the whole place is in danger of being deserted. If you gained a bit more altitude, however, and flew over a few more treetops just to the south of town, crossing over Robbins Creek where it flows under Robbins Creek Road, very quickly you would happen upon a small cul-de-sac known as Basketball Court.

The terrifying and dangerous adventure of three young friends began there on a warm late-September Saturday.

* * *

Everyone knows that basketball is a dominating sport in the culture of Indiana. Nowhere is that truer than in the rural southern half. It was early fall in Cutters Notch. The air was cooling off, and the leaves were just beginning to change. Hope Spencer, thirteen, Josh Gillis, twelve, and Danny Flannery, also twelve, had been shooting hoops at the neighborhood court.

Basketball Court is a short street that ends in a small circle where six houses stand huddled together. The lonely neighborhood is isolated inside several thousand acres of forest, which surrounds them on all sides. Five homes are ranch-style and had been built fifteen years prior to this particular day. The sixth is an old farmhouse sitting at the mouth of the neighborhood. At the junction where the cul-de-sac adjoins Robbins Creek Road, the street splits, leaving a small plot of turf with the basketball court that provided the inspiration for its official name. The Robbins family, who built the tiny development, placed it there for the enjoyment of the neighborhood children.

Josh put up a jumper from twenty feet away, but it clanged off the rim. Danny started for the rebound, but Hope was quicker. That was the story of his life. Being a bit chunky and heavy on his feet, Danny had no leap in him. Often, he was left watching as the others ran layups or snagged rebounds. He didn't mind, though. They were his friends. He loved them, and they loved him, even though they would never say so out loud.

Despite the cooler air, the kids had gotten hot and thirsty during their game, so a trip to the Cutters Notch General Store and Gas Station was in order. It was about a mile north of their neighborhood, at the intersection of Robbins Creek Road and Highway 257. There was nothing in between but forest on both sides of a road overhung with trees that plunged it into deep shadows, even at midday.

"I kicked your stinky bu-utts!" claimed Hope with a sing-song voice as she skillfully dribbled in and out between her legs. She was just a little older than both of her friends, but she was a good two inches taller.

"Yeah, well I kept slipping 'cause my shoes are old," Josh said. He was the more athletic of the two boys, but he couldn't quite match Hope's skill level. At least not yet. But he would never admit that. He had too much pride and too much drive. Where Hope had the skill, he had the determination.

"Oh, here we go with the excuses," Hope laughed. She was bouncing the ball on the road as they rounded the corner out of their court and onto the county road, being careful to avoid the occasional puddle from the previous night's rain. August had been hot and dry, but September had broken the drought with regular showers.

"I'm not making excuses! I got a new pair at the Converse store in Edinburgh, but I went to put them on this morning, and they were gone." Most of the kids preferred Nike shoes, but Josh went for Converse because his dad wore them, and his dad had been a star player in high school. "It's bugging me 'cause I know I left them by my bed last night."

"I know what you mean," Hope responded. "I can't find my green socks anywhere. I had them laid out, ready to go and everything. I hate it when stuff just disappears."

"I hate that house," Danny said randomly. He was pointing at the old, white, weather-beaten two-story at the corner, where their court emptied onto the road. Hidden by tall shrubs and surrounded by towering sugar maples, it was dappled in fluttering shade. Behind the house, the forest receded enough to allow for a detached garage and faded red barn. A small pasture meandered off toward the trees to the right of the barn, its wooden fences neglected and broken in multiple places. "It creeps me out, and that old Robbins dude is the weirdest."

"Ah, he's a nice old guy," said Hope with a friendly smile. "My mom talks to him all the time when he's out in the back trimming his bushes. I think he's sweet."

Josh piped up, "I dunno, Hope. He creeps me out too."

Almost on cue, Willie Robbins stepped out from behind some of his hedges with a pair of shears in hand. He gave them kind of a crooked smile. Stringy white hair hung unkempt off the sides of his head, and sweat streaked down across his wrinkled cheeks. There was mud on the knees of his jeans, and he had green clippings clinging to his arms all the way up to where his elbows sprouted out of an old AC/DC concert T-shirt.

"Hi, Mr. Robbins!" Hope called out, waving with her right hand as she bounced the ball with her left.

Willie waved the shears in their direction, smiled, and returned to his chores.

"You guys are just babies," she said as she threw the basketball at Danny. "I'll race you to the creek!" With that, she sprinted away toward the bridge at Robbins Creek, located about halfway to the store. Her strawberry-blonde hair was flowing out behind her from under her knit hat. "The last one on the bridge has to buy me a Coke!"

The boys took off after her, but having the head start and the longer legs, she beat them easily. She turned and put both hands up so they could give her a high-five as they ran onto the steel grating that formed the bridge surface. The water produced a dull roar as it rushed underneath, propelled along by the previous night's runoff. The noise almost drowned out Danny's gasps as he recovered from the run.

They purchased their drinks at the store and stopped on the bridge again on their way back to throw some stones in the water. It was an aging, steel-frame bridge that was showing large patches of rust through its old green paint. Sitting on the edge with their feet dangling, they joked and laughed and sipped their sodas. Josh was trying to hit a stick that had lodged itself in between some rocks in the stream, but he kept falling short by a couple of feet. He kept stealing glances at Hope on the sly as she giggled and goofed off. He was twelve years old and feelings were awakening that he didn't yet realize were there.

A couple of cars rumbled over the bridge behind them. The first one, headed north toward town, was the old Ford Explorer driven by the elderly couple that lived at the very rear of the cul-de-sac. Earl Hicks was driving, and his wife, Faye, was in the passenger seat with a long cigarette pinched between her fingers. They seemed okay to the three friends, but they kept to themselves almost as much as old man Robbins did. Sometimes, when she left her bedroom window open in the evenings, Hope could hear Faye yelling at Earl late at night. It was disturbing, but that angry voice was off-set by the sweet smile the old woman would show during the day as she worked her flowerbeds and tended to her potted plants.

The other vehicle was a plain Chevy Astro van headed south to someplace unknown, driven by someone also unknown. There were no windows on the sides, and its white paint was scratched, dented, and showing signs of rust near the wheel wells. It slowed down as it passed the kids on the bridge. The friends did not look up to see the man watching them as he rolled past.

Suddenly, Danny jumped up. "Hey, I gotta go! I forgot my mom wants me to go to the store with her over in French Lick. It's grocery day!"

"You move pretty fast when you're going to the store," Josh jabbed.

Danny ignored the friendly tease and smiled. "Well, it is kinda fun. I like to go check out the books and magazines. Especially the ones about the movie monsters!"

Hope turned her head to look up at her slightly nerdy friend. "I don't like monsters." Then she dropped her gaze. "Some monsters are real people," she mumbled.

Danny didn't understand how close his friend was coming to revealing her true self, and he blathered on, "I just love to read the stories about how they make them up. You know, turn the actors into the creatures. There's pictures and stuff. It's just cool!"

Josh was more intuitive, but he didn't ask questions. He just looked at Hope and wondered. He wanted to give her a hug, but twelve-year-old boys didn't do that, so instead, he grabbed the ball out of her hands.

"Hey!" she said and then smiled at him. Mission accomplished.

Hope and Josh had just gotten up to leave with Danny when Hope's cell phone rang. She stopped to answer it, and the boys paused to wait for her. When she got off the phone, she seemed a little frustrated. Sighing, she turned to look back north toward town. "I've got to go back to the store," she said.

"Why?" asked the boys in unison.

"Mom wants a gallon of milk. I guess we ran out this morning. You guys go on. I'll see you tonight."

"I can go back with you," Josh said. "I don't need to be nowhere." Outwardly, he was trying to play it cool, but inside he was nearly ready to explode with the possibility of getting some extra time with her alone. Danny was his best friend, but lately he'd found himself just wanting to be with Hope.

"Naw. No need. I'm just gonna run back there and grab the milk. Then I've gotta get it home quick before it gets warm."

"Okay, I guess I'll catch you in a couple hours," Josh replied, holding in his disappointment with superhuman effort. "Let's all watch a movie tonight," he suggested. Any time with Hope was good time.

"Sounds good" was Danny's reply. "Can we watch a monster one? Maybe about aliens?"

Hope punched him in the arm, smiled, and turned away toward the General Store. "See ya tonight," she said over her shoulder.

With that, the boys turned for home, and Hope started jogging back to the store, dribbling the basketball with her left hand again for practice. It was 1:35 p.m.

At 3:45 p.m., Danny was at the grocery in French Lick flipping through a monster magazine, Josh was watching an old Clint Eastwood Western on the sofa with his dad, and Hope's mother was calling the police. Hope had not made it home with the milk.

* * *

When Maggie Spencer hung up the phone after calling the police, she was scared and alone. Being a twenty-nine-year-old single mother of a teenage girl was not easy. Hiding from an abusive ex-husband who did not want to let go was even harder. Now, her Hope was missing.

She had called Hope earlier and sent her to the General for some milk. But afterward, Maggie had gotten distracted with the laundry. Flipping, folding, and hanging gave her quiet time to think. Her life had been hard and had taken a horrifying turn not all that long ago. The pain of that experience sat on her heart, and she struggled to work through the crippling fear that kept her in Cutters Notch. She allowed her chores to consume her. The combination of bleach, laundry detergent, and folding clothes provided her with such a complete distraction from her anxiety that she hadn't noticed that two hours had passed without Hope's return. Then she'd tried Hope's cell and had gotten no answer. She had waited five minutes and tried again. Again, no answer. Finally, she had called over to Josh's house. His mom told her that Josh had come home a couple of hours ago and that she had seen Danny and his mom leave in the car, but she had not seen Hope.

As Maggie waited now for the sheriff, her mind went to her ex-husband. "It couldn't be him. He's in jail," she whispered to the walls. Sweat plastered her dyed-black curls to her forehead and then trickled past her delicate blue eyes before streaking her mascara across her angular cheeks. Pacing the floor, she worked through the possibilities. Maybe Hope had gotten distracted with another friend ... but she always answered her phone. Maybe she had dropped the phone in the creek ... but, she'd have come home by now. Maybe Kenny ...

"No!" Maggie screamed. "It can't be him."

Without realizing what she was doing, her tongue moved delicately over the scar inside her lower lip, and her left hand went to rub at her lower back, as her right hand tried Hope's number one more time. Five rings, and the voicemail again. A cold feeling gripped the pit of Maggie's stomach as she stood at the front picture window, staring desperately out into the empty neighborhood.

Her mind was abuzz with fear. *Could it be Kenny? It couldn't be … could it? Oh, Hope! Oh, please, no!*

Maggie was near hysterics waiting for the Sheriff's Department car to arrive when she spotted a patrol vehicle pull past the basketball court. Rushing out the front door to meet the sheriff, she was initially disappointed to see that it was her neighbor, Rick Anders, pulling into his own driveway in his Indiana State Police cruiser.

Through the summer, she had been enamored with Rick. He was alone too. She knew that he had been married, but she was too timid and still shell-shocked from her own recent domestic trauma to pry into his life. That didn't stop her from noticing his cute smile or his muscular physique as he worked in his yard. They had chatted a few times, but it had been nothing of substance.

Her initial reaction of disappointment in seeing her neighbor and not the sheriff was quickly replaced with a strange mixture of relief and desperation. *He's a cop!* She bounded off the stoop and ran to him, not bothering to avoid the flower beds and landscaping—her extreme need driving out her previous timid fear.

* * *

Rick did not see Maggie at first. His mind was in other places as he backed into the drive and stepped out of his cruiser. It had been a long shift, with two drunk drivers and one really bad accident out on Highway 37. All of that had been followed by a couple of hours of paperwork back at the post in Jasper. It was the accident that was bothering him—a head-on collision caused when a truck crossed the median and hit a minivan. Everyone in the van had been killed. Being a state trooper meant that you were usually the first official on the scene, the first to provide any kind of medical treatment, and the one responsible for the investigation, family notification, and paperwork.

Rick was not one who could easily block his emotions; he could not help but be affected by the pain of others as they learned the fate of loved ones. Empathy was both his gift and his curse. For most of his thirty years, he had relied on his faith to give him the strength to push on, but lately that had been wavering. It was getting pretty tough. Disappointment had bored a hole in his heart, and most of his optimism had leaked out. He was discouraged with life and mad at God.

"Rick! Rick!"

He turned and looked over the roof of his car to see his neighbor, Maggie, running through his mums, kicking up mulch and smashing what was left of his summer's work. Her wavy black hair was flowing out behind her like an ebony mane. He thought she was truly pretty, and even though she kept to herself most of the time, he had enjoyed the few glimpses he'd caught as the warm months had brought her outside some. If it weren't so painful, he had even thought maybe he would ask her over for dinner. But every time he started over to knock on her door, something in the house would remind him—remind him of how his ex-wife had wrapped his heart around her little finger before dipping it in kerosene and setting it afire.

"Maggie, what are you—"

"Rick! Hope's missing!"

"What?"

"I sent her for milk two hours ago! She didn't come back, and she's not answering her cell."

"She's probably over at Josh or Danny's," Rick reasoned. He glanced back around the court toward the boys' homes.

"I checked. Josh is watching TV with his dad, and Danny's over in French Lick with his mom. Rick, I'm really scared."

He could see the fear in her eyes. She was breathing hard, and her chest was heaving inside her gray Ball State sweatshirt. Even now, when she seemed so upset—her hands balled up into fists, and her mascara all over her face—he was taken with her beauty. Pushing those thoughts aside, he used his training to focus his mind.

"Okay, Maggie. Let me put my gear in the house, and we'll start looking."

Ten minutes later, at about four o'clock, they were walking up the road, Maggie hanging on his right arm. He liked that but couldn't allow himself to think about it. They had almost reached the bridge when a deputy sheriff's car approached from the direction of the town. Rick waved him over.

A moment later, the car stopped on the bridge, and the deputy rolled down his window. "Did you call about the missing girl?" the deputy asked Maggie.

"Yeah," she said with fearful anxiety tearing at the edges of her words. "My daughter didn't come home from the store up there." She pointed in the direction from which the sheriff had just arrived.

"Okay, ma'am. Where was she when you last had contact?"

"She was right here on this bridge. I called her and asked her to go to the store to get me some milk. She told me she was here throwing rocks with her friends. That was over two hours ago."

"Have you tried contacting the friends? Maybe she's still with them."

"Yes, of course! Do you think I'm stupid?" she yelled. "Something's wrong! I can just tell." At that, Maggie couldn't hold it any longer and began to cry. Rick pulled her to his chest to hold her until she calmed.

The deputy noticed Rick's uniform. "How'd you guys hear about this?"

"I'm her neighbor," Rick replied. "I just got home from my shift."

"Good timing."

"Sometimes luck is all we have."

When Maggie calmed down, she said, "It could be my ex-husband. I think he's in jail, but I haven't heard any news about him for a while."

"So, he's violent?" asked Rick.

"That's why he's my *ex*-husband."

The deputy took down her information and suggested that they continue to look around. Since Rick and Maggie had already walked the road to that point, they all decided to start looking at the bridge and work their way back toward Cutters Notch. While the deputy turned his car around, Maggie walked to the west side of the bridge, and Rick to the east. Occasional leaves drifted down and skittered along the pavement. The rays from the late September sun had begun to fall across the tree-tops, and shadows were stretching out in long lines on the road.

They were walking north, scanning the creek bank and woods as the sheriff's car drove up between them. That was when Rick saw the ball: Hope's basketball was sitting in the stream about twenty yards down the creek, lodged in the fork of a rotting old tree. With the stream flowing over it, the ball almost looked like a rock.

"Maggie! Come here!" he called. "Is that Hope's ball?"

As she rushed to Rick's side of the bridge, the deputy got out of his car, and they both reached the railing together.

"Oh, Rick! I'm pretty sure it is!"

The deputy scanned along the creek and pointed. "I think I see a milk container in the weeds over there." The white plastic container was cracked, and the milk had leaked in a mini stream down toward the water.

Rick trotted back south, around the end of the bridge and down into the weeds. Cockleburs grabbed at his trousers, and stickers snagged at his sleeves. He made his way through the thorns, dandelions, and overgrown grass and reached the milk jug. He bent over for a second, and when he stood up, he was holding Hope's phone.

With that, an Amber Alert was sounded, and the search was on.

* * *

Hope opened her eyes. Her head was swimming as her mind swirled back to consciousness. At first, she couldn't figure out what had happened. She definitely did not know where she was. Her head ached, and the hair on the back of her head felt moist. She tried to move and realized she was bound to a chair. Although her eyes were open, she couldn't see anything. The place was as dark as that cave over in the state park she had visited in July. It was as cold as that cave too.

She didn't know how she had gotten where she was, wherever that may be. The last thing she remembered was walking over the bridge, holding her basketball in her right hand and the milk with her left. She had heard a vehicle approach, then ... *Lights out.*

She hadn't seen who'd hit her. She hadn't seen her ball bounce over the lip of the bridge or the milk and her phone get tossed into the weeds. One moment she had been strolling along, listening to the birds and feeling the chill of autumn begin to nip at her nose, and the next minute she had been strapped to a chair in the dark.

Could it be him?

She tried to focus into the blackness, but there was nothing to see but a sliver of light down low and the hint of a pale rectangle up high to the left. *Window?* She tried again to move her hands, her feet, her elbows—anything—but she realized that duct tape was wrapped in a myriad of ways around her body. She tried to scream, but the only sound she made was a muffled *"huuuumpf."*

Panic rose. She bellowed her muffled scream again—over and over. Feeling the blood rushing into her neck and face, she continued her silent screaming until she began to see stars in the darkness, millions and millions of swirling stars. And then, the bliss of unconsciousness returned.

* * *

Hope had not been able to see the heavy oak door just five feet in front of her; she had been unaware that beyond it, preparations were being made. An old wood stove was being fired, and the edge of a chill was slowly starting to give way to warmth. Smoke from the kindling still hovered just overhead. Utensils were being laid out on an old, beaten-up navy-issue oak desk that was serving as a table in the middle of the room.

A large metal spoon. A huge stainless-steel pot. A pair of tongs.

Clear plastic tarps were draped over the desk, as well as a ragged sofa and an aged easy chair. Both the sofa and chair sported faded-brown fake-leather upholstery that had stuffing poking out in multiple places.

Just as in Hope's room, there was a window in this room, too, also up high. But no light seeped in, just a hint of grayness as the day slipped toward night. Eventually, even the grayness ebbed away. It was swallowed up as darkness slipped in to fill the void the sun left behind.

The window in the prep room was surrounded by pegboard, which was studded with tools of various shapes and functions. Dirty, old tools. A rusty hammer. A wood saw with broken teeth. A pipe wrench missing its lower jaw. An old hoist chain dangling from a large nail.

Just to the right, an old calendar hung, showing Santa sipping a Coke in December 1973.

Over by the door was a cleaning bucket with a mop. Several sponges, bottles of bleach, and some rubber gloves sat at the ready in a box next to the wall.

The muffled sounds from the next room could not be heard over the sound of the electric grinder as it sharpened first the large carving knife and then the smaller fillet knives. They would not be needed for a few more hours, but they needed to be prepared and ready. They needed to be ready so that when the time was right to start the cooking process, no time need be wasted. It was meticulous, exhausting work, but efficiency helped.

TWO

By five o'clock, the search was in full swing. The investigation, involving several agencies, was under the control of the burly and imposing county sheriff, James Buckworth Dunlap. All but a handful of his deputies were on the scene. Rick's commanding officer at the Indiana State Police had made him the official state police liaison for the evening. The FBI was on standby should the investigation cross the state line, and they had indicated that an agent would be sent to observe in the morning.

As it stood, J.B. Dunlap was in charge. He was giving orders and creating teams to head in various directions to look into the multitude of possible scenarios. Some would start a search of the woods until they ran out of daylight. Some would canvass the farms, homes, and businesses for any helpful tips. Josh and Danny's dads had been sent with flyers to stop at every convenience store, gas station, and fast food restaurant within a thirty-mile radius: a job that would take most of the night.

Overall, the searchers faced an enormous task with endless possible trails to follow.

* * *

When Danny and his mom returned from the store, they pulled into the driveway, and the boy jumped out and ran over to Josh, who was outside watching all the activity. Blue police lights were flickering, reflecting off of the windows and creating a blue hue to the fading evening.

"What the heck's going on, Josh?"

"Didn't your mom check her phone?" Josh replied with a little attitude in his voice.

"No. She accidentally left it at home."

"Hope's missing!"

The chubby boy's heart leapt into his throat. "What? Whadaya mean, Hope's missing?" His face flushed with worry.

"She's missing." Josh's voice cracked a little, but he bit his lip to force his emotion back. "She didn't come home from the store." *I should have gone with her*, he thought.

Right after the Amber Alert had been sounded, Josh's neighbor, Rick Anders, had come over to talk to Josh. He had wanted to know about what Hope had said and which way she had been going when Josh had last seen her. Josh had tried to remember every detail and help all he could, but all he could think of was that he should have stayed with her. He should have gone back to the store with her. It was his fault.

"Geesh! We've got to help them look," Danny moaned. "I bet that old dude, Robbins has her!"

"I know, but my folks won't let me outta their sight," Josh complained. "And I told Rick about the old man, but he just scribbled it down in a notebook and kept asking me questions."

"We've gotta find her!" Danny exclaimed. "Why won't they let us help?"

"Danny, they're worried that we could be next," Josh replied, "It's stupid, but it's what they think."

They sat down on some big rocks in Josh's front yard and just stared at the flashing blue lights for a long time. Neither could think of anything to say, and the truth of it was, despite what Josh had said about their parents' fears being stupid, they were both scared. They were worried about their friend, and they wondered how close they had come to being where she was—wherever that might be. As they sat there, the sun dipped down behind the forest. Darkness draped their homes, while fear and a touch of guilt draped their hearts.

"Come inside now!" Josh's mom called out.

"What are we gonna do, Mom?" Josh asked as the boys walked through the door. "We need to help them find her!"

Cindy Gillis put her arms around her son. "Don't worry, honey," she said, "Mr. Anders and Sheriff Dunlap will find her." She could see the concern in their eyes as she tried to comfort them. "You boys need to stay close. We're going to stay here while your dads are out canvassing the area and searching."

"But we want to help search!" Danny blurted out. "We can't sit around here while Hope is … is …"

Cindy released her son and turned to his best friend. "I know, Danny," she said, "I know. But we need to keep you and Josh safe, and—"

"Mom, we're fine!" Josh interrupted. "It's Hope that needs help!" The boy was nearly screaming.

Cindy's patience was starting to wear thin. "I understand, but you're not going anywhere, and that's final!" she replied. "Do you understand?"

Both boys reluctantly nodded.

Josh's mom was scared and worried, too, but she didn't show it. She stayed calm and explained that the authorities couldn't focus on finding Hope if he and Danny were underfoot and in the way. Further, she and Danny's mom would be worried sick unless they knew where the boys were all the time. Inside, she was fraying around the edges, but outside she was cool, collected, and focused. The only outward sign of her anxiety was a slight tremor in her hands and the thin layer of patience. She kept them busy to camouflage the shaking, and she felt better when Danny's mom came over to join her vigil.

The idea of sitting around the house and waiting didn't satisfy the boys, but they resigned themselves to the situation. They would wait. They would sit there and do nothing. They would let the adults do all the searching. They would do all of that, at least until later—when their parents were asleep. A quick glance passed between them, and their minds were in sync. From the determination they saw in each other's eyes, they each knew they would have to mount their own search. After all, they had a prime suspect, one they had discussed while out there sitting on the rock, and they were determined to check it out. Old Willie Robbins' house would be their first stop.

* * *

The heavy door creaked open, and the sliver of light widened into full bloom. A figure stepped inside, but Hope couldn't see its face because it was backlit by the glow from the other room. It walked toward her and said something. She didn't comprehend what it said because she was still somewhat dazed from the blow to her head. That, coupled with her overwhelming fear of the situation, made her senses fuzzy.

The figure stopped right in front of her. It had something in its right hand. "Are you awake yet?" said a voice that seemed far away.

The light pouring in from the other room formed a halo around the figure's head, giving it the impression of a dark angel speaking into the abyss.

"Hey! Wake up!" It seemed closer now and not so angelic.

The figure smacked Hope hard on her cheek with its left hand, causing pain to flare in her face and jaw. She came fully aware again. She wanted to rub away the sting, but she couldn't move. Wiggling, she tried again to twist free, but it was no use.

"Are you awake now?" it asked. The voice clarified the figure into a man. It had a gravelly, sort of familiar sound. Not deep. Not high pitched. Just a touch too low to be feminine, but with a coarseness that defined it as truly masculine.

With his hand, he picked at the duct tape over her mouth, then yanked it free. She could feel adhesive clinging to her lips.

"What do you want? Let me go!" Hope screamed at him. The removal of the tape from her face gave her a renewed hope, so once again, she squirmed and struggled, but she simply could not move.

Calmly he said, "Oh, you're not goin' anywhere. As for what I want, well, right now ..." He paused and chuckled. "I just want you to drink this." He held up a glass in his right hand. Bubbles sparkled in the clear liquid and clung to the sides of the crystal.

"I'm not drinkin' nothin'."

"Oh, you'll drink it—one way or another." The man chuckled again. "Don't make this hard. Besides, you'll like it. You've got to be thirsty, and it don't taste too bad. At least, I don't think it does."

He raised the glass to her lips, but she struggled to move her head away, keeping her lips clamped shut. The more he pressed, the more she refused to open up. The man grabbed the top of her head with his left hand, gripping it like an eagle's talon might grip a helpless rabbit. Again, he pressed the glass to her lips. Again, she kept them clamped shut.

"Okay." He leaned down in front of her face and said, "Have it your way. We'll do it hard." His breath tickled her nose. It smelled like a combination of beer, tobacco, and onions. The odor was familiar, raising memories of another time and another nightmare.

He let go and turned. "Bring the funnel in here!" he called out.

Momentarily, another figure stepped into the angelic light. It didn't speak, and Hope couldn't make out any more detail of this one than she could of the first. It walked around behind her, handed the funnel to the man, and then grabbed the hair at the sides of her face and jerked her head back, pulling at the roots until she was facing a ceiling she couldn't see.

The man forced open her mouth and inserted the funnel through her teeth. He shoved it down deep, past her tongue. He then poured a warm fluid into her mouth, and she had no choice but to swallow. Its taste wasn't unpleasant, and surprisingly, the man had been right: It did taste pretty good. Even so, Hope wished with all her heart that she could spit it back out. Spit it out and all over the two people who were doing this to her. She wanted to drown them in their own liquid concoction, whatever it was.

"There. See?" the man said. Then he leaned into her again, and with a tone that sounded almost cheerful, added, "That wasn't so bad, was it?" At this, he chuckled one more time as if he'd just heard a funny joke. "And in a few minutes, you'll forget this whole thing."

"What was it?" Hope asked weakly. A tear wandered down past her nose and settled in the corner of her mouth. It tasted salty.

"A special mixture," he answered. "Part sedative and part preparation."

"Preparation for what?" she asked.

The light from the other room illuminated the fear in her eyes, but the man gave no reply. Instead, he patted her on the head and let his coarse hand slide down around her cheek in an almost fatherly way. Then his companion grabbed him by the arm and drew him back into the other room. The door closed, and again, Hope was buried in darkness. She screamed for help. She screamed and she screamed, but no one could hear her except for the two dark angels, and they had no intention of helping.

Soon, the sedative began to work, and she faded back to sleep, a sweet and brief escape.

* * *

Three sets of eyes looked into the room. They had watched as the two larger ones had cruelly forced the little female to drink something. They didn't like what they saw. It was upsetting to them, making them squirm and moan. They had seen this before, several times. They knew what was coming, and their sorrow was deep.

"Bad, awful, terrible," moaned the one on the right, twisting his ears.

"Horrible, monstrous, detestable," groaned the one on the left through the hands he had used to cover his mouth.

After a long silence, the one in the middle pulled the green socks he was wearing up over his bony knees and said defiantly, "We are going to stop this. This cannot happen again!"

The other two turned simultaneously and stared at their friend in the middle with a mixture of respect and surprise. They had known him all of their lives, and yet, there still were times when he could take them off their guard. He was too spontaneous and too unpredictable. And they loved him for it.

"But what can we do?" asked the one on the right.

"We have no control," said the one on the left. "We are here, and they are there."

"I am creating a plan," said their leader as he retied the oversized shoes he wore over the green socks—looping the strings around his legs and doubling the knots. "Follow me!" He then deftly swung down through the branches and landed lightly on the ground next to the old tree's trunk. Waiting for his companions, he patted the giant tree softly, like a child might pat his father's leg.

The other two were following close behind, and soon they were all on the ground. Gavin, the leader, headed off down the trail at a trot, leading through the thick brush that had grown up between the ancient trees. Gronek and Smakal hurried to catch up.

"Where are you going? What are you planning?" asked Gronek.

"Slow down and let us catch up!" called out Smakal.

"There is no time to waste! We are going to go get her friends!" Gavin called back to them as he shoved his way through a wild huckleberry. "Keep up with me!"

As they hurried through the trees, the limbs swayed and the colorful leaves rustled. On the wind, a voice followed after them. It was deep and rumbling. They heard it as they hopped over a forest stream, and it seemed to envelop them as a blanket on a cold night. It said, "Good luck, little ones. May the Mighty One give you courage as well as strength." Then it added, "But watch yourselves. There is a force behind their evil deeds."

The three were both encouraged and frightened by the voice. The ancient trees were powerful beings, and they did not speak often, nor did they speak lightly. When they *did* speak, the three knew to carefully heed what was said. They knew they indeed must act.

* * *

Rick stepped out of the command-post trailer that had been stationed on the basketball court. Throwing his arms wide, he twisted and stretched. He was tired. It had been a very long day—and an emotional one, at that. He knew, however, that it was far from over, even at 10 p.m. Still, he had to take a break.

Glancing around, he saw a county cruiser stationed at the entrance to the addition, with a second one parked alongside the trailer. Two deputies were leaning against the one nearest the command-post, smoking and chatting about the weather or the Colts or something. They were so engrossed that they barely noticed him. One finally looked up and gave him a little wave. He waved back but walked away toward the other end of the ball court and stopped under the backboard.

After a moment, he decided to walk up to his house, get a soda, and sit on his back deck for a few minutes to think. He would have rather had a beer, but he needed a clear mind, and the caffeine in the cola would help at least a little. He could have had coffee in the trailer, but it was bitter, and he really wanted something cold.

As he stepped off the playing surface onto the road, he paused and sucked in a deep draw of the cool night air. The chill rushed into his lungs and acted like a shot of amphetamine. It had been a painful year since his wife had left. Now this. He wasn't sure how much more he could take. Hope was just a neighbor girl, but somehow, he had let his heart get attached over the last several months.

"Where are you, God?" he asked the sky. "Are you paying attention to the mess my life's become?" He paused and looked as his feet, feeling guilty at his selfish words. After a moment, he looked up again and asked, "Do you know that a little girl is gone? Do you care?"

He pushed the thoughts of his own pain from his mind and turned toward his house. The wind was picking up, and he thought maybe he should get a heavier jacket while he was home.

As he passed Willie Robbins' house, the huge row of shrubs that encased the property swayed violently in the breeze. The burning bushes had turned crimson, but Rick couldn't see that in the dark. All he could make out was their massive shapes moving quickly this way and that, all enveloped in one giant, hypnotic dance in the dark. Overlooking the spectacle was the old farmhouse, poking like a spire into the sky above the botanical melee.

As he passed the driveway where it wound down and split the greenery, Rick noticed an unfamiliar vehicle tucked in toward the back of the house. It was a Chevy van. It had been backed in and was up beside the house. A detached garage sat in the shadows just beyond it.

He stopped in his tracks, looked at the van, and considered whether something so visible and close by could be related to the situation at hand. *Could it be that obvious?* he wondered. Willie seemed harmless enough, but you never really knew what was inside a man. Rick had seen that often enough in his years as a trooper. With those experiences, he decided the vehicle warranted further investigation.

As he walked up the driveway, he realized that he hadn't seen Willie all evening—even though there had been police vehicles, flashing lights, and even a couple of TV news crews swarming for hours. The neighbors had been out watching, searching, and praying, but Willie had been scarce. That seemed odd, but then again, Willie was an odd person. And there was no law against being strange.

Even so, Rick walked slowly up the gravel drive. He had a radio, and he was armed, but he was alone. He felt a tingle in his spine and a pit in his stomach. It would be better if he had backup, but he decided he'd just look around first. He didn't want to overreact.

The front of the house was dark, and even the spotlights at the command post couldn't much penetrate the old man's botanical barrier, but Rick could see a back porchlight burning, reflecting off the overhanging trees beyond the house. Fallen leaves blew past his feet and crinkled as they skittered over the gravel. The wind ruffled through his close-cropped hair and nipped at his ears. A sudden chill caused him to shudder, but he shook it off and walked on.

As he passed the side of the house, he looked at the darkened windows on the side. He then scanned the basement windows and noticed something odd. There was some sort of black material covering the glass panes in the basement casements, and just a sliver of light was slipping out around the edges. The hair stood up on the back of his neck, and an internal alarm began to sound in his head.

At that moment, he heard the back door open, so he quickly ducked behind a shrub and watched as an older man unloaded something from the back of the van. Hoisting it over his shoulder, he carried it back toward the rear entrance. It wasn't Willie. This man had his hair pulled back into a short ponytail, and he was bigger than Rick's neighbor.

When he was sure the man had gone inside, Rick headed back to the command post. His break would have to wait.

* * *

She heard the door open again. It seemed so far away. There was a sliding sound, so she lifted her head and tried to open her eyes. A switch was flipped, and a light seemed to wash around her. She had been in total darkness for so long that the light, dim as it was, was overwhelming.

"Put it over there behind the screen," a voice said.

Was that the same voice? Hope couldn't tell. She couldn't concentrate enough to figure it out. It seemed familiar somehow, like an echo in her memories. She forced her eyes open and realized that her head had fallen back. She was looking at the ceiling. *Weird.* She knew she was looking up, but all she could see was the floor. *How?* Disoriented, she tried to think. She could see the person sliding something into the corner, but she was seeing the top of a head.

"Mussssst be aaaa mirror," she mumbled, and then her head rolled around so that she was looking at her own lap, where her hands were duct-taped to her legs. A string of drool slipped from her mouth and landed on her arm. Slurping what she could, she tried to rub the slime off on her shoulder. Then her stomach rumbled.

"Cut her loose," the voice said.

"Are you sure she's ready?" another replied.

Footsteps. Blurry shapes moving around her.

"Yeah. Besides, she's gonna need to go pretty soon."

"Should we give her some water?"

"Absolutely. It will help flush out her system."

Someone stopped in front of Hope holding a knife. The blade slid under the duct tape and began to slice it loose. In a couple of minutes, she was free of the restraints. She could feel the tape being peeled off her legs and arms. Blood was flowing again into areas that had been oxygen deprived, but she still couldn't seem to move around. It was like her muscles wouldn't do what she told them.

A moment later she was drinking a cup of water. She didn't remember starting to drink it, but it was cool, and she was thirsty. Once she had drunk it all, she handed it back. "Thank you," she said, and then wondered why. Then her stomach rumbled again.

The door closed once more, and she could tell she was alone, but this time there was still some light. Blinking her eyes, Hope could just make out the shape of a table lamp in the corner. They had left it on. She thought it looked like the one she'd had in her bedroom back in Muncie, but that was impossible. That one had been broken.

Her stomach rumbled more. She fell back to sleep, draped loosely over the chair with her head lolling backward.

THREE

"Let's go," Josh whispered.

"Now?" was Danny's reply. "Our moms are still awake. I can hear them talking." He was fidgeting nervously with the little green plastic army guys arranged on a small table in the corner of Josh's room. They were set up in a mock battle scene behind makeshift forts of Lincoln Logs, Tinker Toys, and rocks from the yard. Sometimes, the boys would create miniature catapults and pelt each other's side with marbles until every man was down and one of the armies was declared the winner. Somehow, Josh always seemed to win.

"I know, but we can't wait any longer. Besides, I don't think they're gonna go to sleep. They're too upset." He was sitting on the side of his bed, leaning back on his hands and kicking his feet up and down for no apparent reason.

"But what if they look in here and see we're gone?" Danny worried. "They'll freak!"

"We've got at least an hour," Josh said. "That's plenty of time to check out the old dude's house. Either we'll find Hope and no one will care that we snuck out, or we'll be back before they even know we're gone."

Danny didn't speak for a few seconds. Instead, he stared at his feet. Josh's plan seemed logical, but Danny was stuck between his concern for Hope and his fear of getting caught. An hour or two earlier, he had been eager to search, but now that he'd had time to think about it, his fear was in the driver's seat. "I dunno …"

"Fine," said Josh, as he hopped up on his feet. "I'll go by myself."

Turning his back on his indecisive buddy, he walked over and quietly slid his window open. There was no screen; he had torn it earlier in the summer, and his dad had not yet fixed it. When the window was fully open, he crawled up on the ledge. "I'll be back before you know it."

"Wait, I'm goin'," Danny whispered, lumbering over to join his friend at the window. "Let's just hurry, okay?"

"That's the plan, my friend. That's the plan."

They slipped out into Josh's backyard and belly-crawled past the patio doors. They could see their mothers and Hope's mother sitting on the family room sofa. Hope's mom was crying, and their mothers were sitting on either side of her, doing their best to console her. She was bent over, sobbing into her hands with her black hair hanging loose on both sides.

As they were about to reach Josh's back fence, a wet slimy thing washed across Danny's neck. "*Uhhhhgh!*" Danny moaned and rolled over on his back.

"*Shh!*"

"Sorry, your old dog just licked my whole neck," he said, wiping the slime off onto his sleeve.

Josh's dog, Sheba, was about as old as they were. She didn't move very fast, and she didn't make much noise, but she did like to show her affection. A couple of years ago, she would have jumped right on top of Danny's belly when he rolled over, but she just didn't quite have that kind of energy anymore. Instead, she sat down on her haunches and let her tongue loll out of the side of her mouth.

"Come on. Let's get over the fence," said Josh.

They scampered over the chain-link fence that separated the suburban home from the wilds of the forest. It really was like two worlds separated by galvanized steel wire. Once they were on the other side, their reality became infused with various creaks, cracks, whistles, and rustling brush. The moon gave them plenty of light, but it was still very creepy as it reflected off the moisture that the dew had deposited on the leaves and grasses. The wind was gusting, blowing the trees around and pushing wisps of clouds across the moonlit night sky. Josh didn't seem to notice or care, but Danny was nervous as a beetle in an insecticide factory. He kept glancing around, expecting a bear or a cougar to pounce on them at any second.

"What do we do now, Josh?" he asked.

"We're gonna sneak around the back of all the houses until we get to Willie's house, and then we'll see what we can see."

"Can't we sneak around the front?" Danny pleaded, already wishing he'd stayed back in Josh's room.

"No! Are you crazy? There's way too many people out there. They'd see us for sure. Come on, let's go."

Josh led the way, and Danny followed. Josh's house was on the south edge of the cul-de-sac. They would have to go past Danny's house, then the Hicks' yard, Rick Anders' yard, and then finally, Hope's yard before ending up in old man Robbins' small side pasture. The forest would be on their right the entire way.

Behind Danny's house, the ground sloped down to the woods, so the boys slid down the hill to allow the ground to help conceal them. It would get a little mucky if they went too far, so they tried to stay about mid-hill. They relaxed a bit behind the Hicks' yard, because it had a high privacy fence with a wide, double-hinged gate. Still, they stayed on their hands and knees as they crossed an old overgrown, double-rutted path that led off into the woods. The boys had made a few short explorations on the old road before, but they had been saving a deeper exploration for later on in the coming fall. More light would be filtering through the trees then, and there would be fewer mosquitoes.

Danny stuck his knee in some mud in one of the ruts. "Crap!" he mumbled grumpily.

"*Shh*," Josh whispered again.

They passed Rick Anders' house, and it was all dark. They figured he was still out looking for Hope. Since they knew that Hope's house was empty, too, they sped up and rushed past both homes without much caution. Soon, they found themselves in the targeted pasture. The Robbins' house was just up ahead. There was a light on in the back.

Josh dropped back down on his belly. Danny followed suit, imagining he was an infantryman like the little plastic guys in Josh's room—and wishing he was back there. Doing the army crawl, they made their way stealthily up toward the house. Despite the light, there did not seem to be anyone moving around. They reached the garage without a hitch and then snuck along the back side to get a better look at the back door.

"I think we need to sneak inside," said Josh.

"Are you nuts?" Danny blurted. "No, no, no! We'd get caught for sure!"

"But how're we gonna find her if we don't go inside?" Josh reasoned.

Thinking about it for a moment, Danny finally gave in. "*Ugh*! Okay, let's go."

As they began to make the turn around the corner of the garage toward the house, two sets of hands came from behind and pulled them backward into the darkness. The boys each had a gloved hand over their mouth and a strong arm wrapped around their torso. They were secured with no hope of escape.

* * *

Gronek and Smakal closely followed Gavin through the trees and brush. They dodged several ancient oaks and skirted around dozens of younger maples and sycamores, eventually coming up on an open path where the forest seemed to hold back at an even spacing along the entire length. There were two trails in the path, with grass growing between them. Gavin ran up the trail on the right, with the other two on his heels. The wind was in their faces, but they were swift, and it barely slowed them at all.

"What are you going to do when we get there?" Gronek inquired as they ran.

"I am still working that out" was Gavin's reply.

"Are you going to reveal yourself to them?" Smakal asked as he leapt over a fallen tree limb.

"I see no other way."

"But you will frighten them horribly," said Gronek, dodging a thorny bush.

"I know. But we need their help. They are the only ones we can go to. The older ones either will not believe we are real, or they will not be able to see us anyway."

The three reached the end of the path, and the trees fell away, leaving a circular clearing with an opening on one end. There were a few small trees scattered around and some shrubs formed into unnatural shapes. The grasses were strangely short. Odd square and rectangular depressions ringed the clearing, some very deep and some a bit shallow. Here and there, small squares of light hung like pictures in midair.

"Which one do we go to?" Smakal asked.

"They will be at the brave one's home, I believe." Gavin was guessing. "Let us go there first."

As they walked into what was Josh's backyard in another place, Sheba whimpered and wagged her tail briskly. Gronek stopped and patted her on the head. "It is good to see you again, little friend."

Sheba returned the affection by licking his hand and then trotted alongside him.

"Let us look into this shimmer first," said Gavin, as he pointed toward a rectangular panel of light hanging in the air directly in front of them. "Be careful not to fall into the hole below it," he added, meaning the deep, square depression in the ground just below the shimmer. In that other place, it was a basement with a house sitting on top of it. In *this* place, it was just an odd hole in the earth. "That one is very deep. You could be injured if you fell to the bottom."

As they stepped up to the strange light hanging in the air, they could not see in; it was too high. It dangled just a couple of inches above their heads. As they looked under it, all they could see was the hole in the earth where Josh's basement would be. It truly was deep, and the moon formed angular shadows across the bottom.

"Hold me up," Gavin instructed. "But for all that is mighty, be careful not to drop me!"

Gronek and Smakal grabbed Gavin's legs and hoisted him up so he could see into the shimmer. He studied it for a few moments and then motioned for them to put him down.

They both simply let go. Tumbling down, Gavin nearly stumbled over the edge before his companions grabbed his arms.

As if nothing had happened, he said, "It is the mothers. They are sad and crying."

"Where are the young ones?" asked Smakal. "Are they with them?"

"No. Perhaps they are in the boy's room where he sleeps," said Gavin as he pointed to his right about ten feet, to another shimmering square in the air. "It is over there."

That shimmer was not as high, and they could all peer inside. Gavin stood in the middle, with Gronek and Smakal on each side, all three standing on the tips of their toes. The room, however, was empty. There was a light on, and there were many items scattered around on the bed and floor: balls, socks, T-shirts, small cards with pictures on one side … But, there were no boys to be seen.

"Where could they be!" Gronek exclaimed.

"What do we do now?" Smakal asked.

"We wait," said Gavin. "There is nothing else we can do. We wait until they return."

Sheba licked Gronek's hand again, sat up, and stared at the trio with the moon reflecting off of her big, bright, brown eyes.

* * *

Rick Anders and Sheriff Dunlap left the command post and crossed over to the mouth of Willie Robbins' driveway. Rick had worked with Dunlap for the last several hours, and despite a few eccentricities (like the pearl-handled Colt .45 revolver he carried instead of a standard service weapon), Rick found him quite competent. He liked the big man. They had seemed to click well together very quickly.

Without hesitating, they started walking quickly over the crunching gravel as the wind whistled and the moon cast eerie shadows, its beams passing through the trees. They walked quietly but without any stealth. Rick watched as the units that the sheriff had sent out moved to their positions on the perimeter.

The two men had a simple plan: Knock on the door, ask to check out the house and property, then see what the reaction was like. If they didn't like the feel of things and old Willie wouldn't let them in, then they'd have to request a search warrant and wait for someone to find a judge to sign it. But maybe Rick's suspicions were nothing, and he'd let them in to look around.

They were headed to the back door because the front of the house was dark. Besides, the back door was where Rick had seen the activity— a man going in and out. They were almost even with the front corner of the old house when the sheriff's radio crackled: "Unit Three to Unit One."

Tilting his large, round head to the mic clipped to his shoulder, the sheriff replied, "Go ahead, Three."

"We have two juveniles in custody behind the garage."

Rick and the sheriff stopped short and looked at one another. Rick just shook his head in disbelief. "What do they think they're doing?" he wondered out loud.

"You know who these two are?" Dunlap asked.

"It has to be Josh and Danny," he said with a bit of a chuckle. He had to admire their determination. "They're Hope's friends. They must have slipped out and snuck over to check out Willie's place. He's Josh's personal prime suspect."

"It's just as well then," said the sheriff. "I wanted to talk to them anyway." He grabbed his shoulder mic and said, "Unit Three, hold them at your position until we have made safe contact with the house. Then escort them to the command post."

"10-4."

The two men continued their walk to the back of the house. As they passed the clapboard side, they scanned the basement windows. There were two sets, two panes in each. Paint was peeling and chipping from the frames. Both sets had dark material lining the glass, but only one had light slipping out around the edges. As they approached the back of the house, the porch light was still on, but the door was closed and nothing was moving. A myriad of bugs buzzed around the naked bulb above the door.

Rick took the lead while the sheriff covered him from a couple of steps back and to the right. He stepped up to the door and rapped hard.

"State Police!" Rick shouted. "Mr. Robbins, open up!" His right hand went instinctively to his holster, which wasn't there. He'd left it on the table at home. He felt a little naked and a lot vulnerable, but he hadn't really expected to be banging on a potential perp's door in his own neighborhood.

They waited a few seconds. They thought they heard some movement, but no one came to the door. Rick banged again. "State Police! Open up!"

This time they heard steps approach from the other side. The sheriff lowered his hand to his own service pistol. Rick stepped back as the door slowly cracked open and was stopped by a nearly useless chain strung across the gap on the inside.

"How can I help you?" The voice of Willie Robbins slipped through the dark crack. "Rick? Is that you?"

"It is, Mr. Robbins," Rick said with a calm, almost friendly voice. "Could you step outside? The sheriff and I would like a word."

"The sheriff is with you?" he asked. "Well, I guess so, but it is kinda chilly out there."

"It won't take long," the sheriff replied. "Or we could come inside, if you prefer."

First, Willie closed the door to release the chain, and then he opened the wooden screen door. "That's okay. I'll come on out for a minute," he said as he stepped through. Released, the screen creaked as it swung closed on its own and slapped into place. The older man was wearing cheap canvas tennis shoes, blue jeans with dirt on the front, and a long-sleeve T-shirt with some faded-out logo. He stuck his hands deep into his pockets and waited for the two men at his door to speak.

"Mr. Robbins ..." Rick started.

"Call me Willie, Rick. We are neighbors, after all."

"Willie, do you have any idea why we're at your door tonight?"

"Well, not really. Seems kinda odd."

"Are you aware that Hope Spencer was apparently kidnapped this afternoon?"

A strange look appeared on the old man's face. Rick couldn't tell if it was fear, amazement, or shock. Maybe a combination. Maybe guilt.

"No." Willie shook his head. "I sure didn't. What happened?"

"That's what we're trying to find out," Rick replied. "We're mounting an all-out search for her and have been all evening. Didn't you wonder about all the activity in front of your house?"

"Well, I really hadn't noticed," he said. "A friend of mine came by this afternoon. We've been in the basement for several hours working on a project, and you know my bushes pretty well block out the road."

"In the basement, you say?" asked Sheriff Dunlap.

"Yep. We've been down there since well before dark."

"I saw your friend carry something into the house just a short while ago," Rick said.

"That's right. He brought me some stuff down from Bedford."

"What kind of stuff, Mr. Robbins?" asked the sheriff.

"Just some stuff. What's that got to do with sweet little Hope?"

The man did look genuinely concerned, but was he concerned for the girl or concerned about being caught? Rick couldn't tell.

A gust of wind rushed by. The old man shivered, and Rick wished he had that heavier jacket. "Willie, we're searching all the homes, garages, barns, and other buildings in the whole area. We'd like to take a look around your place, as well."

"I suppose that'd be okay, Rick." The old man glanced beyond the two police officers, scanning his property. "The side garage door is unlocked, and the barn door doesn't even latch. Have a look for yourself." Obviously a bit cold, he crossed his arms over his chest. Or was it a sign of defensiveness?

The sheriff spoke up. "Actually, we want to take a look *inside* your house. Can we do that, Mr. Robbins?"

Willie looked him straight in the eye and held the gaze for what seemed like five minutes but was probably only about ten seconds before responding, "Do you have a warrant, Sheriff Dunlap?"

"Now, Willie," Rick responded, "we didn't think we'd need a warrant. We just want to clear your house before we move on to the next one. Eliminate all the possibilities, ya know?"

"Maybe so, Rick," said Willie, "but I think maybe I don't want you walkin' all over my house. I ain't got that sweet little girl. Such a sweetheart," he said, shaking his head. "You'd be wasting your time. Time better spent elsewhere, I'd say."

"You don't mind us walking all over your garage or your barn," noted Dunlap, "but you just don't feel the same openness about your house. Is that right, Mr. Robbins?"

"Yep. That about sums it up, I reckon. If you want in the house, then you gotta go get yourself a warrant."

Rick looked past Willie into the open doorway, hoping to spot something in plain view that would give him the right to enter without a warrant—probable cause. But it was to no avail. Behind the door was just a dark entryway. An old pair of boots sat on the landing. There was nothing ominous or illegal in sight.

"Okay. If that's the way you're going to be about it, then that's what we'll do. We'll be back shortly, and I can't speak for Trooper Anders here, but I don't plan to be nearly as friendly on the second visit," warned the sheriff.

"You gotta do what you gotta do, sheriff, and I gotta do what I gotta do." With that, Willie Robbins stepped back inside. "I'm tellin' ya, don't waste your precious time on me." He shut his door, and the two men heard the deadbolt latch.

"Well, let's get rolling on that warrant then," said Rick.

The sheriff nodded, and they turned toward the driveway, intending to head back to the command post. As they did, four figures stepped out from behind the garage. Two were tall and dressed in dark clothing, and two were much shorter and dressed in a hodgepodge of young teen garb.

"Aren't you goin' in?" Josh urgently asked Rick. The boy squirmed, but the hands holding him kept their grip.

"We can't," he calmly replied. "We don't have a warrant, and Mr. Robbins won't let us in without one."

"But, she's in there. I just know she is," Josh continued. "Bust in and get her before he hurts her!"

"We don't know for a fact that she's in there, son," said the sheriff. "But we're gonna find out. I can promise you that. And if she is, we'll get her out safe and sound. Don't you worry. Now, let's go have a talk." Hiking up his trousers by yanking on his utility belt, he led the way back down Willie's winding driveway, kicking up stones and fallen leaves in his wake.

***

Slowly, Hope began to regain her senses. Her stomach was rumbling now. It felt like a stream was gurgling through her gut. Whatever they had given her, it must have made her bowels loosen up. She doubled over with a cramp. She had to *go*, and she needed to do it now—right now.

Weakly, she struggled to her feet and stumbled over to the door. She tried to pound on it, but instead, all of her effort resulted in only a light tapping. Placing her ear near the hinges, she could hear an electric motor and a grinding noise. She recognized the sound. Her dad had mounted an electric grinder to a workbench in their old garage in Muncie, and she could still remember him sharpening his tools—his knives—on that machine. She tried knocking again, but the noise she made increased only slightly. She doubted anyone could have heard it over the noise of the grinder.

"Help me, please. I need help. I need a toilet. Please help me."

"Go behind the screen," a man's voice came through the door. Again, it was somehow familiar. "There's a portable potty chair back there. You can use that."

She turned and looked around. There it was in the corner, one of those screens like in the old movies, like one that a saloon girl might go behind to change clothes. Hope staggered toward it, holding her stomach. It was all she could do to hold back the pressure. It was almost like her bowels knew that the toilet was just ahead. As she crossed the room, she thought about the voice through the door. She recognized it. It seemed familiar, but she couldn't place it. It was like a memory or a dream long forgotten.

She made it around the screen and found the pot just in time. Yanking her britches down, she quickly took a seat. Once the emergency had passed, she found some paper her captors had left for her, and she cleaned herself up as best she could. The smell was horrible, but there was no way to flush.

Hope got up and started back toward the door, but she made it no more than four or five feet when the rumbles hit her again, so she quickly returned to the potty chair. There were three more similar trips before she started to regain some stability. The chair's bucket was getting full.

Having been put down first by a knock on the head and then by a strong drug, much of the emotion had been drained from her mind, just as the fluids had drained from her body. She sat down on the chair that she had been bound to and looked around. She was strangely calm now. No screams. No crying. She simply looked around and surveyed the situation.

"Where am I?" she wondered out loud. "What do they want, and what am I going to do about it?" The girl had a determination about her—a will forged in a furnace of fire and hammered out on an anvil of personal pain. Normally, she held it in and only revealed it on the basketball court, but now it was emerging, pouring from her in a much more important way. Whatever her captors wanted, whatever they were thinking they were going to do with her, she decided she wasn't going to make it easy for them. She would fight. Oh yes—she would fight.

* * *

The boys were now sitting at a small table in a tiny room at one end of the mobile command post. The sheriff was sitting across from them, and Rick leaned against the wall. This had not turned out at all like Josh had planned, and Danny had the shakes. Josh, despite their predicament, was sitting up confidently.

"So, how soon are you going to be able to check out the house?" he asked.

"Look, boys, I don't know what you were thinking, sneaking around the Robbins' place like that, but you need to leave the police work to us. Got it?" said Sheriff Dunlap.

"We just wanted to help," Josh said sort of meekly. "She's our best friend." *And I love her*, he thought but wouldn't say it out loud.

"We know that," Rick said. "But you've got to realize that as much as you want to help, you are still kids. You don't have the training, experience, or maturity to do what we are doing. What if you'd gotten hurt?" he asked. "Or worse yet, what if you'd been grabbed, then how could we focus on finding Hope?"

Danny couldn't raise his eyes from his hands. Tears were slowly descending his cheeks, and his nose was running a little. His legs were shaking. Josh, on the other hand, was looking the men in their eyes, his fists balled up on the small brown folding table.

"You can't expect us to just sit in our bedrooms!" Josh exclaimed. "We want to help!"

"Okay. You know, I think you're right," said the sheriff. "You can help Hope right now by telling us what you saw this afternoon. Anything you can remember might help. Any detail, even if you think it doesn't matter, might point us in the right direction."

"I told Mr. Anders what I knew earlier. Besides, I thought you knew the right direction?" Josh replied. "You don't think the old dude has her? You're not gonna check out his house?"

"I didn't say that," Dunlap said with a more friendly tone that seemed a little forced. "But we can't jump to conclusions either. We have to consider all the facts."

"We heard what he said to you. Why wouldn't he let you in if he didn't have her?" the determined boy pressed him.

Rick responded, "We don't know yet. It does look very suspicious, but we still have to make sure we have all the details straight. And we have to get a warrant. So who's wasting time now? Can you please tell us about this afternoon? The sheriff wants to hear it in your own words, so tell him what you told me."

"There's really nothin' much to tell. We walked down to the General, got some drinks, and then threw rocks in the creek. There wasn't nobody around 'cept the usual people," Josh explained. "Old Mister Robbins waved his hedge clippers at us when we headed to the store. He's creepy, and he looked at us kinda funny. I know he's got her!"

"Who's the 'usual people'?" asked Rick as he rubbed the back of his neck.

"You know, the lady at the store. That's about it."

"There was the cars," Danny whispered. He was still looking down at his hands, and tears were still making little lines in the dirt on his face.

"What was that?" asked Rick. Danny had not been there when Rick had spoken to Josh earlier in the evening; he hadn't yet returned from the store with his mother, so this was new information.

Danny looked up from his hands, wiped his cheeks on his sleeve, and gathered himself. He was still shaking, but he seemed to feel better because he had something to add. Maybe it was nothing, but he remembered something that Josh had forgotten, and it provided just a tiny ember of encouragement. That ember gave his courage a new flicker of energy.

"There was two cars that passed us," he said.

"There was?" Josh said. "I don't remember no cars." *I remember Hope, though. Her pretty eyes, her smile.* He could feel his heart aching in his chest.

"Well, I do. I saw the Hicks. They were headed towards town. I remember them 'cause Mrs. Hicks always has a really long cigarette pointed up toward the sky when she's riding in the car. It's like she's pointing at God or something."

"And there was another car?" asked the sheriff. "Did you recognize that one too?"

"Uh, well, it was a van, I guess." Danny suddenly looked excited. "Hey! Yeah, it was that van sittin' in ole Mister Robbins' driveway, I betcha!"

"Did you notice anything about it when it went by? Did it do anything unusual?" asked Rick. "Anything at all?"

Danny thought about it for a few seconds. "Well, I guess it slowed down a little bit when it went by, but that's all." He wished he had more, but that was it.

Danny was just starting to feel a little better when he put one of his hands down on the top of one leg and felt the mud caked there. His heart sank. "Man, I'm in so much stinkin' trouble. Mom's gonna kill me."

Rick misunderstood and said, "Danny, you're not in any trouble. We needed to talk to you anyway."

"You don't understand. My mom is gonna kill me. I got mud all over my pants."

Both the trooper and the sheriff broke out in laughter. It lasted only a moment, but the comic relief was refreshing. "Did you fall in the muck in the woods?" asked the sheriff, still chuckling. "You really have to watch your step, even in the daytime."

"Naw," said Josh. "We didn't go in the woods. He crawled through it when we crossed the old road behind the Hicks' house." Josh wasn't laughing.

"You mean that old road that's all overgrown—the one that dead-ends at their back fence?" asked Rick.

"Yep. That's the one," Josh replied.

"Well, you're probably right, Danny. Your mom is gonna be pretty mad," Dunlap said. "But maybe it will help when we tell her how much you helped get the warrant."

"Really, sheriff?" said Danny with a broad smile. *Maybe she'll even be proud of me?*

"Really," the big man replied. "Now, let's get you back home."

"We need to go to my house, not Danny's."

"To your house it is, then," the sheriff said to Josh as he stood up. Walking to the door, he held it open as Rick led the boys through and down the three steps to the ground.

Rick grabbed each boy around the neck in a lighthearted headlock. "Now, let's get you knuckleheads home."

The moon brightened the cul-de-sac, and four shadows stretched out ahead of them as they walked past the goal post, across the street, and up Josh's driveway.

FOUR

"I believe that people are approaching the house," said Gavin. They were sitting in a small circle in the grass. Sheba was making the rounds, giving each of the three a chance to share her affection.

"What house?" asked Smakal.

"How can you tell?" asked Gronek.

"I can see the dust swirling around on the ground," Gavin said. "See?" He pointed under the shimmer and across the open pit.

The other two looked in the direction that Gavin had pointed, and sure enough, the dust was swirling around and getting closer. A rock skipped into the air and tumbled into the grass. They all stood up and watched.

"Hold me up again," Gavin instructed as he approached the first higher shimmer.

The dust stopped swirling as it reached the grassy area on the other side of the big rectangular hole in the ground. Gronek and Smakal hoisted Gavin up to look into the dimensional window. He stood with one foot on the shoulder of each of his companions and then teetered uneasily in their grasp. "Hold me steady!" he shouted.

"Sorry."

"Sorry."

They each replied, one after the other.

As he peered inside, he saw the three women turn their heads toward the door, and the one who lived there jumped up and ran to it.

When the door opened, Gavin could see the young males standing there. The one they called Danny looked scared and had mud all over the front of his pants. There were two large human males standing behind them. They both had on uniforms, and one wore a large weapon. Gavin recognized the one behind Danny as the man who lived next to the young female—the female they needed to rescue.

Gavin had acquired a couple of the strange little rocks that the man put into the weapon he often carried. They were fascinating, but he did not see that weapon now.

Danny's mother came over, pulled Danny inside and hugged him, but the mother of the one named Josh jerked him through the door by the arm. The large uniformed male that Gavin did not know stepped in and raised both hands and seemed to be trying to calm the females. Both mothers pointed in unison toward the room for sleeping, and Danny and Josh walked slowly that way with their heads hung low. The women were both speaking with much gesturing toward the boys as they went. When the young ones entered the next room, Gavin hopped down from his companions' shoulders, landing nimbly despite the oversized shoes on his feet.

"They are back!" he exclaimed. "They are back in the sleeping room."

All three of them scampered over to the other shimmer and peered inside. Just the tops of their heads, their eyes, and their noses rose above the edge. They had to be careful because if the light was low enough, they could be seen if they leaned too close.

"Are you going to enter?" asked Gronek. "Are you going to reveal yourself now?"

"Let us watch for a moment," Gavin replied. The truth was that he was a bit afraid to go inside. He had not revealed himself to a human in a very, very long time. First encounters often did not go well. Now that the time was at hand, Gavin needed to gather his nerve.

Then he thought of the girl, the one they called Hope, and he knew he had no choice.

"Maybe we should not," Smakal offered. "They may scream and run. Or they may try to hurt you."

This was in no way helpful to Gavin, but he had made up his mind.

Sheba wandered up to Gavin's side, licked his long fingers, and nudged his leg. It was as if she were sensing his hesitation and wanted to spur him on.

"I must do this," he finally said. "There is no other way if we wish to stop them and rescue the young one." Gavin stepped forward and pressed his nose to the shimmer.

* * *

Hope sat quietly in the chair and looked around. She needed to consider her options and not give in to her sense of futility. Desperation threatened her determination to fight. She knew she must not surrender to despair—despair that prowled around in weeds planted in her mind. Those weeds had been sown there during a previous night of horror: a night not long before. *Monster night.*

She looked, she listened, she thought.

The single lamp that her captors had left lit on the table in the corner did brighten the room, but dehydration and the residual effects of the sedative made it difficult to focus. Still, the drug was wearing off. She was young, and she was an athlete. The resilience born of youth began to revive her, and her mind eventually began to brighten. As she looked around, there were few options available to her. Very few, in fact. But that didn't mean there weren't *any.*

She noticed the window first. She could see it was high on the wall, so she pulled the chair over, which added about eighteen inches to her sixty inches of height. As she stepped up on the seat, she got woozy and nearly fell. Instead, she leaned against the wall and waited for the feeling to pass. A few seconds later, she looked back up at the window. With her arms extended, she could just grab the sill. Her energy was coming back as her mind cleared, but still, it was a struggle to pull herself up. In the end, it was wasted energy, though, as she found the window had been secured with nails.

She moved the chair back to the center of the room and sat down again. She needed to rest. Again, she looked around. The room was plain. Her chair, the table in the corner, and the screen with the portable toilet behind her were the only furnishings. The walls were covered with old, dark paneling, which was broken in several places, revealing concrete blocks behind it. She could see splotches of adhesive that had been used to secure the façade to the blocks. Two power outlets sprouted from metal conduit that was secured to the wall with clips and bolts. Everything was dirty and seemed moist; it stunk mildly of mildew.

She looked at the floor and saw that it was covered in old blue linoleum with some sort of marble design. Completely intact from wall to wall, it was in remarkably good shape, considering the rest of the room. Despite the musty dirt on the walls, the floor seemed to have been recently mopped.

Hope looked up at the ceiling again. She had been right; there was a large mirror there. She estimated that it covered over half of the ceiling's area and was positioned exactly in the center. Around the outer edges of the mirror, she could see painted plaster—blue, like the floor.

Other than the window, the only way in or out of the room was the door, which she could now see was solid wood with heavy brass hinges securing it to the frame. It was not something she could break through. She didn't have much to lose though, so she walked over and tried the knob. It was plain brass and looked old. No lock was apparent. Even though it turned, the door wouldn't budge. They had secured it from the other side.

No escape, she thought. *No way out! And he'll be coming. Again!*

She sat back down and put her head in her hands. She was tired. She was thirsty. She was weak. She had no way of escape. Deeply and terribly afraid, she was tempted to cry again, but something inside rebelled against her despair.

Let him come! Let him try!

Mustering her determination, she pulled it together and decided that if she couldn't get out, then she would give them a good fight when they came back in. She would show them that they had picked on the wrong girl. She was her mother's daughter.

* * *

On the other side of the wooden door, the preparations continued. The knives were sufficiently sharp and were laid out on a small, wheeled cart, which was positioned next to the plastic-draped navy-issue desk.

The captors carried in two galvanized-steel garbage cans lined with extra-large plastic bags, which they positioned next to the desk. They would drop the scraps inside, things they couldn't or wouldn't eat—things like hair, the stomach, and various bones. Their practice had become to deposit these things in the cans for easy disposal. It facilitated a quick and efficient cleanup.

Under the pegboard in the rear of the room, they had placed a very large cooler with wheels on one end and a handle on the other. When they were done with the night's work, it would take both of them to load it up. Girls didn't weigh that much, but when you added the ice and considered the size of the container, it was just too much and too awkward for one person to handle.

This project was a great deal of work, but they would be stocked with meat for months to come—tender, succulent meat. People love the taste of veal because young meat is especially delicious, but to them, this particular type of veal was beyond description.

"We should have gotten some milk to give the girl," said one captor to the other with a smile. "You know that's what they feed the calves they raise for veal." A grin broke across the captor's face as the anticipation of the first cookout of next spring came to mind. *Maybe we shouldn't wait for spring. Maybe we could make up some breakfast sausages for this coming week.* The grin broadened into a full smile. *Now you're thinking!*

"You did remember to bring the meat grinder? Right?" one asked the other. The voice contained a certain edge of criticism.

"Yes. It's on the bench over by the wall" was the compliant reply.

* * *

Gavin's nose had almost broken the surface when Gronek and Smakal jerked him back.

"Are we coming with you?" Gronek blurted.

Smakal asked, "What if the mothers come in?"

Before Gavin could answer either question, and almost on cue, the bedroom door swung open, and the women entered.

Gavin looked both frustrated and relieved. "Let's wait awhile and see what happens. When they leave the room, I will go in alone. You will stay here and wait for my return."

Gronek and Smakal nodded with relief. They all three then turned to watch through the shimmer as the mothers scolded the boys. If they had not been on such an important mission, they would have found the images quite entertaining. The boys were sitting on the edge of the sleeping platform, looking at their feet. The mothers stood over them with angry faces, each with one hand on a hip and the other hand pointing here and there and then back again. The women's mouths were moving nonstop, but the boys mostly just sat there and listened, nodding to show understanding. The one named Josh attempted to speak up twice, but each time, his mother promptly shut him down.

The three observers could not hear the words, but the images told the tale well enough.

The verbal barrage continued for almost five minutes before the women pointed to the bed and then returned to the other room to rejoin Hope's mother. Through the shimmering window, the three continued to watch for a few more minutes. They had to be sure that the angry mothers weren't going to return. The next step in Gavin's plan was critical. If it failed, the girl would be lost.

Gavin looked at his two friends. It was his plan, and he was their leader, but still … He remembered the words of the Great Oak: "May the Mighty One give you courage and strength." Courage and strength. Courage? *Yes, courage.* Sheba again nudged his leg and then shoved her cold nose under his long, slender fingers. The time had come once more for action. She knew it. He knew it too. He leaned forward, and his nose touched the shimmer.

* * *

"Sheriff, I'll be back in a few minutes," Rick said as they stood in the middle of the cul-de-sac. "I need to take some time to gather my thoughts, and I need a heavier jacket. I'll be at home if you need me. Radio me if the warrant arrives."

"Will do," said Sheriff Dunlap, "but I suspect it'll be awhile. The county judge is in Florida. We'll have to track someone down."

That was one of the issues with living in what many would call the backwoods of Indiana. Way out in the sticks. The infrastructure was sparse, and the government was even more so. That was why some folks liked it.

Rick nodded his understanding, and the two of them parted, going their respective ways. Rick passed his smashed mums and walked into his house. The sheriff passed under the basketball net and walked around the end of the mobile command post, up the three metal steps, and into a small den of electronics, maps, and coffee machines.

Inside his home, Rick lifted his service jacket off of the hook behind the door and slipped his arms inside. He grabbed his utility belt and service pistol off of a small table and hooked it around his slim waist. He felt clothed again.

It was reckless of him to leave his weapon sitting on a table in the open, but since his family had disintegrated, he had begun to let a few things slide. He liked it on that little table—where he could see it. At odd times, he found himself sitting on a chair nearby and simply staring at it—at the possible relief those small pieces of lead carried.

Walking into the kitchen, he picked a Diet Coke out of the refrigerator door. He thought about the beer on the shelf below the soda, but then thought better of it. His house was quiet. Way too quiet. There was no one to greet him. No wife. No son. Not even a dog.

He stopped in the dining room for a moment. It was unlit. His hand skimmed the table and then rested on the back of the chair where his son used to sit. So many meals. So many laughs. And yet also, so many angry words. He could almost feel the darkness of the house creeping into his soul. He was getting depressed, and depression typically didn't end well for police officers.

Closing his eyes, he thought of his only son. The giggles. The love of dinosaurs and Buzz Lightyear. The beautiful eyes. Then Rick tried to picture his ex-wife's face. The face he'd fallen for so many years ago. The face that had stolen his heart and then broken it to pieces. For a reason that he could not understand, he couldn't picture her. Her image wouldn't clarify. The only face that came to mind belonged to his neighbor—to Maggie.

I can't go there. Not now. Not tonight!

He shook off the sadness and walked out onto his back deck to look at the stars and drink his soda to the sounds of the woods. He sat on one of the swivel chairs that surrounded his plexiglass patio table. Leaning forward with his elbows on his knees, he rubbed his face with both hands. Hopelessness slithered in and snuggled up next to his heart. He shivered despite the jacket.

These things so seldom end well.

He wasn't sure if his thought had been about Hope or his own life. Maybe he'd meant both.

As he sat there, he looked over at the home of Earl and Faye Hicks. It was completely dark, but that wasn't all that unusual. They seemed to be gone almost as much as they were home. "I guess you can go places when you're retired," Rick mumbled to himself.

The only place I'm likely to go is hell—in a handbasket.

The Hicks were only slightly more sociable than Willie Robbins. They would occasionally join a cookout, but that was very rare. Generally, they kept to themselves. They had never invited Rick over, and as far as he knew, they hadn't extended an invitation to anyone else, either. Mostly, they stayed behind their privacy fence.

Rick hated that fence. It made him feel closed in, and more importantly, it blocked part of his view of the woods. No one else in the neighborhood had a privacy fence.

As he sat there wishing destruction on the neighbor's fence, something started to gnaw at the back of his mind like a mouse on a leftover cob of field corn. Something was bothering him, but he couldn't quite figure out what it was. He was tired, so maybe it was just the weariness and the stress, but he didn't think so. There was something else, a minor detail that was tickling his senses.

"What is it?" he asked himself as he ran his fingers through his close-cropped brown hair. "Come on, *think*."

He took a big gulp of Diet Coke and stood up. Drawn to the woods, he stepped off the deck into the grass. He found the forest to be magical and full of mystery, especially at night. It was why he had bought this house and brought his family here. It was the only reason he had stayed when his family left him here alone.

He walked to where the back of his lawn butted up against the blockade that was the Hicks' fence, and he looked out into the shifting shadows. The moon was filtering through the trees. He stood there, staring. He was staring into the darkness of the forest and also into the darkness that had enclosed his own heart—the abyss.

A gust of wind blew through the tunnel formed by the woods and the privacy fence. Catching inside Rick's jacket, the breeze caused it to billow out like a parachute. He pulled it closed, zipped it, and found himself walking along the ridge behind the fence. He didn't remember starting to walk. Instead, he just became aware that he was walking. He had reached the gate and was about to turn around when he realized he was standing at the old road—the one the boys had crossed earlier in their journey to old man Robbins' house.

He couldn't see the road very well in the moonlight, but the last time he had walked back there, it had been quite overgrown with weeds, briars, small trees, and various other kinds of brush. The ruts of the old road had been barely discernable at the time, but Rick couldn't remember exactly how long ago that had been. He scratched his head. *Was it last year?* he wondered. *No,* he decided. *It's probably been two years.* He knew it was before his family had left. After they had gone, he had spent most of his time working.

He looked down at the road and walked a few feet toward the woods. He stepped into a soft spot and pulled out a muddy shoe. "Crap!" he said, echoing the words a boy had said in the same spot just a short while earlier. Frustrated, he let out a few other choice words and turned back toward the fence. That was when he realized that it was not the Hicks' *fence* that lined up with the road; it was their *gate*. He wasn't sure why, but he found that to be curious.

"Anders?" his radio crackled.

Rick jumped with the sound but responded, "Anders, go ahead."

"Anders, the warrant will be here in thirty minutes."

"I'm headed your way," he said and pushed the road, the gate, and his sorrows out of his mind as he made the brisk walk back to the command post. Back to the one thing that usually kept him sane—his work.

* * *

When their moms left the room, Josh and Danny simultaneously flopped back on Josh's bed. Despite Sheriff Dunlap's supportive words, their mothers had gone completely nuts on them. The word "grounded" was used frequently, and they were warned about what would happen when their fathers returned. Josh's Xbox 360 was gone indefinitely.

Dejected, they both just lay there for several minutes in silence.

Finally, Josh sat up. "What are we so unhappy about? All that's happened to us is we got grounded and stuff. Hope's the one in real trouble."

"Yeah" was all that Danny could muster, but he sat up too.

Josh began to fidget with a baseball he had sitting on his headboard. He tossed it up in the air with his right hand and caught it with his left. He was thinking, plotting really. *They've got to sleep sometime; I'm going back out.* He might be grounded, but that had never stopped him before.

Danny stood up and leaned against Josh's chest of drawers. He had his right hand in his pocket, and his left hung on to one of the drawer pulls. "I just hope we helped some," he said. "That would make it worth it."

"Help some? Are you crazy? Danny, you helped a bunch! You got them what they needed for a warrant. They'll get into that old perv's house and get Hope out before you know it." *I hope.*

"Do you think she'll be okay?" Danny asked with a glum voice. "I mean, who knows what he might do to her—or what he's already done to her."

Josh thought about that for a minute. *He better not hurt her. I'll kill him.* Then he looked back over at Danny and said, "She's got to be okay, Danny. She's gotta be." At that, a tear snuck out of his eye and trickled down his cheek. Quickly, he turned away and wiped it off onto his sleeve.

When Danny saw Josh's tear, he turned away himself, afraid that his own tears would start. If they did, he had no idea when they might stop. Pulling his lower lip in between his teeth, he bit down until the pain in his mouth overcame the anxiety in his heart. Besides being pudgy and a little nerdy, he also tended to be a bit emotional. The other kids would call him a baby whenever he cried, so even though Josh had his own tears and was his best friend, Danny was afraid that Josh would make fun of him if his tears began to flow.

They needed a distraction. Video games were out of the question. Danny looked around, and his eyes landed on Josh's comic book collection stacked neatly on his dresser. His friend liked the classics like Superman, Spiderman, and The Fantastic Four. That seemed promising, so he started over to pick one up when he noticed something odd.

Something kind of pointed was sticking out of the mirror above the dresser. Not only that, but there was a round shape that seemed to be behind it and yet, somehow inside the mirror. *Did Josh glue something to his mirror?* Curious, he looked closer, and the shape had two large eyes that looked back at him—and blinked.

"Oh, holy crap! Josh, what's that?" Danny yelled and scampered back around the bed to where Josh was sitting, all the while pointing at the mirror.

"What? What's wrong? Did you see a mouse or something?" They lived next to the forest, and mice were commonplace.

"Look. Look at your mirror! There's something coming through it, or out of it, or … I don't know. Just *look*!" Danny was frantic.

Josh knew his buddy could have an overactive imagination, but he turned and looked anyway. Then he leapt to his feet. Danny was right. There was something coming out of his mirror. He could see a nose and part of a face. It was bulging out like a balloon being inflated. As he stared, the eyes came clear, and then a hand popped in and gripped the edge of the mirror, as someone would if they were trying to pull themselves out of a hole. The glass of the mirror rippled like a still pond when someone drops in a stone.

Danny was frozen in place. He felt like his feet were nailed down. He wanted to run, and he wanted to scream, but he found that he had no ability to do either. He could only stand there with his mouth hanging open.

Josh didn't have that issue and started to run for the door. Instead, he bumped into Danny and almost fell down. Quickly, he regained his balance and began to push his friend toward the exit, but Danny was just slightly more moveable than an oversized, lumpy bag of potatoes.

"Come on!" Josh urged him. "Let's get outta here!"

Danny barely registered a response. Terror had locked up his brain. Fear had hijacked his body, and he couldn't shake it. Josh pushed him again and again. Finally, he started to move, but now the thing's whole head and shoulders were inside. Just before they reached the door, they heard a voice: "Do not be frightened, young ones. I have come to help your friend. Please, do not run."

* * *

At the same moment that Gavin's head popped through Josh's mirror, Hope got back up from the chair and walked around like a big caged cat. She put her hands up and behind her head so she could get more air, like her coach had told her to do after she ran the 440 in a track meet. The soiled air reeked, but the extra oxygen she sucked in still helped her think. Her hair felt sticky. She probed a little with her fingers and felt a small gash under her matted hair. It wasn't bleeding anymore, but it ached and stung at her touch.

"I have to figure out something," she mumbled. "There has got to be something here I can use."

Her eyes went back to the lamp. *Maybe I could pull it loose, hide behind the door, and bang it over one of their heads the next time they come in.* Then she realized that if she pulled it loose, the light would go out, and they would be expecting something when they came in. That wouldn't work.

She looked back at the screen with the portable toilet behind it. The screen wasn't heavy enough to make any difference, just cloth on a plastic frame. Then an idea arose in her mind. *I'll dump my poop on them and then run past as they choke on it.* But, she wondered, would that be enough to get away? *I doubt it. Even if I don't get away,* she thought, *it'll be worth it to see the disgust on their faces. Maybe they will choke on it!*

The humor of the idea gave her a little more energy, so she walked back and pulled the white plastic container out of the toilet. Carrying it over, she positioned herself to the side of the door opposite the lamp so she would be more in the shadows when they came in.

Oh, yeah! They might get me, but I'm gonna enjoy this part.

The stink was terrible, but she crouched down on her heels next to the pail to wait. That was when she thought of the chair—the one she had been taped to in the middle of the room. It was obviously oak, and it was sturdy, but she really hadn't looked at it closely. It was still there, in the same place in the middle of the room where she had replaced it after trying the window.

Hmm.

The chair was just a small upright piece of furniture with braces underneath the seat that connected the legs. *Could I break the chair and get one of those pieces out?* She decided it was worth a shot, but she had to hurry because her captors could come back at any second. She sensed the timer of her life was quickly ticking down to zero.

She walked over, picked the chair up over her head, and started to throw it against the floor, but thought better of it. *They'll hear me if I do that. Then they'll be in here on me before I can blink.* If she was going to break the chair, she had to find a quiet way to do it, so she turned it over and took a closer look. She fiddled with a couple of the braces, and they were solid, but when she tried a third, it moved. *Loose. Oh, yeah!* She tried to turn it, and it rotated in its joints.

"Okay, how do I get it out?" she mumbled again.

She considered the problem, and then sat the chair down sideways on the floor. *Maybe … just maybe.* She plopped down on her bottom beside it and wedged her feet against one leg, pushing while she pulled on the opposing leg with all her strength. It took some effort, but finally, with a *-crack!-*, the legs broke free and the brace she was after clinked onto the floor. The others each still had one side stuck into the broken legs.

Gotcha!

She grabbed the brace she had worked so hard for and stood up. Looking it over, she rolled it around in her hands and felt its weight. It wasn't very long, maybe fourteen or fifteen inches. It was blunt on one end, but the other side had a jagged point. *Perfect!* Maybe a poke to the eyes or a poke to the groin would make a difference. Holding it in her preferred hand, she returned to her spot by the door and leaned her back against the wall.

Hope closed her eyes to focus her mind. With her hands, she could feel one weapon, and with her nose, she could smell the other. Just like preparing for a free-throw in a big basketball game, she worked through her moves, visualizing each one she would make when the door opened. *Dump and poke, dump and poke.* Satisfied that she had worked it through, she started to tap the brace on her hand. She tapped, she tapped, she tapped—and she waited.

* * *

Hope? When Josh heard the voice of the thing coming through his mirror say that it had come to help Hope, he hesitated, and without his friend's urging from behind, Danny stopped dead in his tracks. In that instant of hesitation, the creature from the mirror, moving with incredible speed, jumped down from the mirror and positioned itself between the boys and the bedroom door. It raised the palms of its hands out to emphasize that Josh and Danny really needed to stop. Josh noticed that it had four unusually long fingers and two equally long thumbs on each hand, all splayed outward like a spindly handheld fan without the webbing.

Danny reversed positions with Josh, pushing him to the front and then backing up to the opposite wall. He wanted to scream, but he had no voice. "Uh …" was the only sound that could pass through his lips.

His knees buckled, and he slid down to the floor, staring bug-eyed with his mouth still agape.

"What did you just say?" Josh demanded.

"Do you plan to hit me with that orb?" Gavin asked, pointing one long, slender finger.

"Huh? Oh." Josh still had the baseball in his hand and had raised it, cocking his arm. He was unconsciously ready to fire a fastball at whatever this strange, talking, mirror-entering thing was. Keeping his only weapon at the ready, he said, "That depends. Look. I don't know who or what you are. What do you know about Hope? How did you get in my room?"

Gavin smiled, and his mouth seemed to stretch from one slightly pointy ear to the other, revealing a row of yellowish teeth. "You saw me come through. I came in through the shimmer."

"You came in through the what? What's a 'shimmer'?" the boy asked.

"Young one, a shimmer is a doorway between your world and mine. In any case, a shimmer is what it is on my side. On your side, it is a mirror. I entered through your mirror."

Josh, having not yet shed the innocence of youth, accepted the explanation easily as he stared at the strange creature standing in front of his bedroom door. This being was small, maybe three and a half feet tall. His eyes seemed too big for his face, and his ears were just a little pointed. Josh couldn't tell in the dim light if the being had any hair, because he wore what looked like a very old Cincinnati Reds baseball cap. His body was covered in a one-piece suit of leaves, maybe sycamore, and on his legs were long green tube socks. When Josh's eyes managed to fall to the thing's feet, he saw his very own new—and previously missing—basketball shoes.

Josh registered the fact that whatever this thing was, it had pilfered his new shoes, but that issue was surpassed by two vastly more important points. First, he was dealing with a being that had come into his room through his mirror. Second, that being had said that it knew where Hope was.

His shoes would have to wait.

"You must come with me so that we can rescue her from her awful fate!" Gavin blurted. "Come! Come quickly! We must hurry before it is too late. They will not tarry long."

"What is that old dude gonna do to her? Is she okay?"

"What he is going to do will not be an issue if we can rescue her first. She was restrained and afraid when I last saw her, but she was alive and not in imminent danger. They were still preparing. Those preparations, however, do not take long, and her danger rises with each passing moment. We must hurry!"

Josh was no longer afraid, so he lowered the baseball in his hand. He could see genuine concern in the crazy creature's eyes. As wacky as the situation was, with a small elf-like creature crawling through his mirror, Josh sensed that this being intended no harm. "Okay. Let's go! Can you go through the window with us, or do you have to go back out through the mirror?"

"We must all go through the mirror," Gavin replied.

Josh, who was already headed to the window, stopped in midstride and processed what he'd heard. *Through the mirror? I can crawl through my own mirror? Mom didn't say I couldn't go through the mirror.* He considered that loophole in his mom's instructions, and then he said, "Cool. Let's do it. Come on!" he said as he motioned to Danny.

Suddenly, Danny found his voice. "Are you freakin' nuts? You want me to crawl through a mirror? Go through a mirror, and go with some little freaking gnome or something?" He was beside himself. "We don't even know what it is, and you're gonna go crawling through a mirror with it? Nope! Not me. No way." He shook his head vigorously from side to side. "Nope. Nope. Nope."

"Daniel ..." Gavin began.

"How do you know my name?" Danny demanded.

"Daniel, allow me to introduce myself. I am Gavin Allwind of the Trees. I know you because we often follow your antics and those of your friends by gazing at you though various mirrors."

We? There's more than one? Danny thought. *And, they peep through my mirror?*

Josh grabbed Danny by both shoulders and stared him in the eyes. "Danny! Look at me! I'm tellin' you that I'm going with him. I don't know how, and I don't know why, but I trust him." *Maybe I'm nuts?* "He says that he knows where Hope is, and he says we need to come with him to save her." *Maybe I am crazy, but I'm going to save her!* "Do you hear me? We need to save her!" *We have to.*

Danny hedged. He hated this feeling of being stuck. Again, he was so very afraid. Afraid of creatures from mirrors. Afraid of the unknown. Afraid of the dark. Even afraid of what others thought of him. But he also wanted to save his friend. *Hope needs me, and I'm afraid!* Again, his feet felt nailed down. The only things about him that seemed free to move around were his fear and the guilt that his fear spawned.

"Danny, we can't abandon her. We can't abandon Hope." Josh pulled on him hard. "Come on!"

Danny's love for his missing friend overcame his anxiety, and the nails in his feet evaporated. Free from the fear-inspired shackles of guilt, he looked Josh in the eyes and said, "Josh, this is scaring the livin' crap outta me, but I'm with you. Let's go get her."

It then occurred to Josh that they had a problem: Their mothers would be checking on them regularly after their earlier escapade, and he was sure they were a long way from being asleep. Soon after the boys left, their absence would be discovered, and their moms would freak out. "Gavin, what about our moms? When they find out we're gone again, they'll lose it."

"Ah, yes. Good point, my young one. I have just the solution, however." Reaching under his leafy shirt, he pulled out a small pouch with a leather cinch at the top. Quickly, he opened it up and poured the contents, a sparkling powder, out in his odd, oversized hand. "I will cause them to sleep with the Slumber Dust."

"What is Slumber Dust? You're not going to hurt them, are you?" asked Danny.

"It will cause no harm, my young friend. It will only cause them to sleep soundly for a few hours, and if they see me, they will not remember—or they will perceive me only as a dream," Gavin explained. "It is a special powder made from a particular flower pollen in our dimension. We use it whenever we want to visit your world and ensure that we are not discovered."

Gavin returned the empty pouch to his shirt, turned, and opened the bedroom door. "Wait here for just a moment," he said and quickly slipped out. In only seconds, he returned. "They are asleep already and will not awaken for some time. We do need to hurry, however, for the sake of your Hope." At that, he hopped up on the dresser and motioned for them to join him. The boys quickly complied, knocking aside comic books and baseball cards.

"You cannot pass through without being in contact with me. Lean forward. Touch your noses to the mirror." As they did so, Gavin positioned himself in the middle and placed one arm around each boy, then leaned forward into his dimension. Instantly, they fell through. Landing on the grass, they looked up at two more friendly faces with huge smiles, yellow teeth, and pointy ears.

* * *

As the boys were meeting Gavin in Josh's bedroom, Maggie Spencer sat between their mothers on the sofa in the other room. Her two neighbors, the mothers of Hope's friends, sat on each side of her. Annie Flannery, Danny's mom, was a robust woman with bright-red hair. She was slightly younger than Maggie but well insulated and bore a flushed complexion. Cindy Gillis, Josh's mom, on the other hand, was very much the opposite. She was slight, athletic, and blonde, which seemed to match her tanned skin well. They both leaned into Maggie with their arms draped over her shoulders.

The room connected to an eat-in kitchen and was adorned with the typical middle-class American furnishings. Two lamps sat on small side tables. In the corner, a television was on but muted. A mirror hung the on the back wall, flanked by family pictures, and a coffee table sat just in front of the women, a plate of sugar cookies positioned in the middle. They were untouched, except for two that Annie had snagged when Cindy had first placed them there.

Her tears had stopped for the moment, but Maggie was still slumped over with her hands over her face. She had alternated all evening between sobbing, hysterics, and anger. *It has to be Kenny! But how?*

She didn't really know these women. Sure, they lived across from her and they'd shared a neighborhood cookout or two, but Maggie had become a recluse. Most of the time, she stayed in the house, only venturing into the yard on rare occasions to mow or pull weeds. The only words that had passed between the three women had been about the weather or where the kids were at any given moment. Maggie was hiding, and she couldn't afford friends. Friends knew too much. Friends could be tricked—tricked by smooth-talking, violent ex-husbands.

Her heart had leapt with excitement a few minutes before when Rick and the sheriff had come to the door, but then she'd slipped back into despair when she'd realized they were only returning the boys. She wished she had someone to comfort her. Someone strong. Someone she could count on. *Rick?*

Pushing that unwelcome urge out of her mind, she leaned back and took a deep breath, caressing the tiny scar under her lip with her tongue. She was tired. So very tired. Tired from the fear and desperation of what may have happened to Hope and tired from the fear and desperation of being in hiding. It had been several months since she had moved into that little ranch house across the court after her dad had sent her packing—*even he let me down*—several months of fearful loneliness.

She had run to her father after that night, the night that Hope called *monster night*. But her dad had still been angry with her for marrying Kenny to begin with, and when she'd arrived on her dad's doorstep, all he would do was give her some cash. That, and give her his blessing to take her maiden name back. "You made your bed," he'd said. So she'd started using her middle name again and returned to her father's family name. Megan Margaret Burton had dyed her strawberry-blonde hair black and had become Maggie Spencer, single mother alone and on the run. After bouncing around from one friend's house to another, and when the divorce was final, she found Cutters Notch in an old road atlas. Without telling anyone, she gathered what few things she had and moved herself and her daughter to a new place and, hopefully, a new start.

From down the hall now, she heard one of the boys make a muffled shout.

"I'm gonna tan that boy's butt!" said Cindy, and she started to get up.

"Oh, let 'em be," said Annie. "They ain't hurtin' nothin' now. They're worried, too, so let 'em wrestle and get their minds off it."

Cindy sat back down beside Maggie and began to rub her back. *A little lower would be good, and I'll give you about an hour to stop.* But Maggie wouldn't say that out loud. They would want to know why, and she just didn't want to go there. Not right now. Maybe not ever. They didn't need to know her personal problems.

It was nice to be around these women though. They seemed like good people. They seemed to genuinely care about her. *Kenny cared too. At first.* It was nice to have the comfort and support, but Maggie dared not let her guard down. It was too dangerous. Too easy to get hurt.

Oh, Rick, please bring her home!

It was a few minutes later when Cindy said, "I'm gonna make some coffee. You girls want some?"

"That sounds wonderful, Cindy. Can I help you?" asked Annie.

"No need. I've got it."

Again Cindy started to rise, but this time she didn't quite make it to her feet. There was movement from the hall, and all three women turned to see which one of the boys had developed the courage to venture out. Rather than seeing the stubborn eyes of a boy, however, they saw an odd-shaped face and a sudden fog of sparkles that flew over their heads and twinkled down on their hair like falling stars. And then they slept …

In Maggie's dreams, Rick was walking away from her. He was holding Hope's hand, and they were strolling across the sand of a warm, tropical beach. Seagulls soared and swooped overhead, enveloped in the backdrop of a bright-blue sky. Waves casually washed up around their feet and then shrank back. The sun was low over the water.

"Rick!" Maggie called. "Rick! Hope! Wait for me."

They didn't respond. She was falling behind and could not catch up.

"*Rick*! *Hope*! Please wait for me."

They turned to look at her, and everything changed. Hope's eyes were full of fear. Rick wasn't holding her hand. Instead, he had his hand clasped tight around her neck.

"What are you doing?" Maggie asked in anger. "Let her go!"

Rick changed. His face shifted from the friendly smile and genuine eyes of her neighbor to the scowling mouth and angry eyes of her former husband.

"*Kenny!*" she screamed. "*No!*"

She began to run, yet somehow the sand kept shifting under her feet, and she couldn't make any headway. Kenny, however, had no issue with the sand. He could run. He slung Hope over his shoulder and took off, getting farther and farther ahead.

Maggie screamed, but it didn't slow them down. She was losing Hope. Her Hope was disappearing—not quite gone but shrinking smaller and smaller into the horizon.

FIVE

$\mathcal{T}$wo odd hands immediately sprung forward in a friendly invitation to shake hands. "I am Gronek Allwind of the Trees," said the owner of one. "I am Smakal Allwind of the Trees," said the owner of the other.

Gronek wore a ragged pair of striped shorts below his leaf shirt, and an old pair of penny loafers adorned his feet; a single penny still rested in the tiny pocket of the one on his left foot. He didn't wear a hat, so the boys could see a short tuft of bristly hair pointing skyward from the top of his head. The other, Smakal, had on a pair of Danny's old Star Wars pajama bottoms and a pair of his mom's pink house slippers. He also had a shirt made of leaves, but he wore an old cowboy hat on his head with a drawstring cinched up under his chin. It made the tips of his ears bend forward.

On this side of the mirror, all three of these strange little beings had a bit of a green glow flowing out of their skin in tiny waves.

Josh grabbed Gronek's hand and allowed him to pull him up, but Danny refused. He got up awkwardly on his own.

"We are very pleased to finally meet you in person," said Gronek. The little fellow was smiling and hopping from foot to foot in excitement.

"It's nice to meet you too," said Josh with just a hint of hesitation. "Where are we?"

Both boys were gazing around in amazement. Just a moment ago, they had been in Josh's bedroom. Now they were … well, somewhere else. As they slowly turned in circles, they couldn't believe their eyes.

"You are in your own backyard," said Smakal.

They were standing next to a big rectangular hole in the ground, and in front of them was a shimmering light hanging in midair. Beyond the light and across the hole, Josh could see other holes of various sizes, all with square corners. There were lots of other shimmers too. Most of these dimensional doors were square or rectangular, but there were occasional ovals. Some were large like the one they had passed through, but others were small—tiny, even. On the other side of the crater where the house should have been, there were two small shimmers in midair, a few feet apart. Another one was suspended in between and just above the other two. The shimmers were hanging in the air above a rectangular groove in the ground that ran at a right angle to the hole. *Are those the mirrors on Mom's car?* Josh wondered.

Danny grabbed Josh's arm and pointed at something else. Looking in the direction where Danny's house would ordinarily be, he saw a bunch of plants that were floating in midair. The soil was formed into upside-down cones that hung just below the greenery on top.

"Those are my mom's potted plants," Danny said with amazement in his voice. "I recognize them. This place is crazy weird!"

"I'll tell you what's weird," said Josh. "You are!" He laughed. "Danny, you're glowing."

"Huh?" the pudgy boy said.

"Your face is glowing all sorts of creamy white." Even as he said it, Josh could see the glow change to a dull pink. *He's embarrassed; I embarrassed him.*

"Yeah, well, you're glowing too. I guess we both are." Danny's pink complexion shifted back to tan, then returned to cream.

Josh lifted his hand up for a look, and it was true. His hand had a creamy light blooming from each of his slender fingers. "Wow!"

Besides the holes with right angles, the lights and plants that were floating in midair, and the green and cream glowing faces, there were other odd sights all around them. While it had been nighttime and fully dark when they had come through the mirror, this place was aglow with a myriad of colors that seemed to bloom from the various trees and plants. The boys continued to turn in circles, amazed by the forest. Light illuminated everything; shadows didn't seem to exist. The whole world was twinkling, flashing, and flowing together with every color imaginable, merging to illuminate the sky and the ground all around.

While Josh and Danny recognized some things—like the plants and the trees that grew in their yards—nothing else from their neighborhood was anywhere to be seen. The basketball goal was gone, but they could see the depression in the ground where the court should have been. The houses were all gone. No mailboxes. No light poles. Even the driveways and the streets were missing, leaving grooved, open ground running in various angles. Everything was earth, rocks, and glowing plants.

"Are they going to be alright?" Smakal asked as he watched them slowly turn and stare with their mouths stretched into giant grins.

"Yes, is there something we should do to help them?" asked Gronek.

Gavin could see their surprise, as well, and guessed as to their questions. "This is the world of the Trees. The Arboreal Realm. Only those earthen things that retain their natural state appear here, along with all plant life. Even natural items such as rocks or wood, if they have been tooled into an unnatural state, disappear from this place. Artificial materials do not exist here unless carried in by such as us. The light that you see in the trees and in our faces is the aura of the life force bestowed on all life by the Mighty One. During the day, when the sun is high, it is less obvious, but aura is always there as long as there is life." Even as he spoke, a twinkling leaf broke free of a nearby limb and drifted down toward their feet. Its light dimmed as it sank, until the twinkling faded into a faint, slow blink. After a moment, it ended altogether.

"There is very little animal life here," he continued, "but there is some."

As if on cue, Sheba waddled out from behind a bush and trotted up to Josh. She sat at his feet and gave a little bark before the boy noticed his canine buddy. Her aura twinkled around her in waves and sparkled in her eyes.

"Sheba!" he shouted. "Wow, you're here too!" Josh dropped down on his knees and gave the dog a playful rub around the ears. "How did you get here, girl?"

Sheba leaned forward and slobbered on his cheek, then sat back with a satisfied look, her tongue hanging out of one side of her mouth.

Gavin again explained, "She exists in both places. Sometimes, an animal will have extra senses that allow it to pass in and through both dimensions at the same time. It is fairly common for a family dog to have that sense."

"Really? Wow!" Josh was amazed.

"Have you not ever seen Sheba barking at what appears to be nothing and wondered what she saw?" Gronek asked.

"Well, sure. I have," Danny replied. "But I always assumed it was something in the trees or bushes. A squirrel or a chipmunk. Maybe a bird."

"Sometimes that is true," said Smakal. "But sometimes it is something in this realm that has her attention."

"Like what?" Danny asked.

The three strange little fellows looked from one to another, each unsure how to answer that question—unsure if they should answer.

"We should make haste and be on our way," urged Gavin in an effective dodge. "We have a mission."

"Right, yeah. We should get going," said Josh. His adventurous blood was pumping. "Let's go get Hope!"

"Which way?" said Danny. "I'm all turned around and confused in this place." His blood was pumping hard, too, but more from fear than adventure. He loved monsters and scary stuff but only when it was on TV or at the movies. Now, he was living it.

"I will lead the way. Gronek and Smakal, you must carry them."

"Carry us? That's silly. You guys are too small for that," Josh reasoned.

The oddly dressed little men all laughed together.

"We are small," replied Gavin, "but we are exceedingly strong and much faster than you. If you walk, it will take us much longer to reach our destination."

With that, Gronek and Smakal motioned for the boys to climb onto their backs. The boys complied, with Josh crawling onto Gronek and Danny onto Smakal. Each boy wrapped his legs around his new friend's waist and draped his arms around its neck. Before they had time to really settle in, they were off at breakneck speed into the trees.

* * *

While the boys were meeting their new friends, Rick Anders and Sheriff Dunlap were again walking up Willie Robbins' gravel driveway. This time they moved without any hesitation. Deputies fanned out to cover all the other potential exits. The sheriff quickly climbed the steps and took the lead at the door, with Rick on his heels. A third man carried a ramrod, should it be necessary.

Dunlap pounded on the door. "Robbins! Sheriff's Department! Open up now!"

The sheriff gave the door one more pounding then stepped back. He was about to have his man break down the door when the latch clicked. It was slowly pulled open from the inside, revealing Willie's pale features.

"Hello, Sheriff Dunlap. Rick. Come on in," the old man said. Willie stepped into full view and then backed off, holding the door open for them. A bare incandescent bulb lit the small entryway, shining off of Willie's sweaty forehead. There was a smudge of dirt on the side of his nose.

"Robbins, we've got that search warrant," said the sheriff as he placed his foot across the threshold to discourage Willie from any last-minute change of heart. He placed his right hand on the door and used his left to provide the document for inspection.

"No doubt," Willie replied. "I don't need to look at it. Come on in. Let me know if you have any questions, but as I said before, you won't find that sweet little girl in my house. You're wasting your time."

"If that's so," replied Rick, surprised at the old man's changed demeanor, "why didn't you just let us look earlier and save us all a great deal of trouble?"

"I'm sure you'll figure that out for yourself, if you insist on searching."

Ignoring Willie's strange, newly compliant attitude, they escorted him down the hallway. It was decorated with several vintage posters of rock bands like the Rolling Stones and the Grateful Dead. Some of the posters seemed to be autographed.

When they entered the living room, they found Willie's friend seated on the sofa. A man in his mid-fifties, he wore dirty jeans and an old T-shirt. It featured Bob Seger and the Silver Bullet Band. His thinning gray hair was slicked back and gathered in a ponytail. His face was covered with stubble. Smiling, he greeted them with an odd chuckle, "Dudes! How are ya?"

The sheriff and Rick looked at each. Rick shrugged.

"You two stay right here," Dunlap told Robbins and his guest. Getting the attention of a deputy, he ordered the man to stand guard. Then he sent three men upstairs while he and Rick headed to the basement. Two other deputies were checking the rooms and closets on the main floor—opening doors, sliding back hangers, and checking any cubbyholes large enough to hide a person.

When they reached the head of the stairs, they could see that the basement was already lit. Rick pointed to the steps. "Dirt on the risers."

"I see it," said Dunlap.

Scanning down the wooden steps, the men could see a trail of soil that ran from top to bottom and then off onto the floor below. Otherwise, the passage down was very clean, no cobwebs and no old handprints.

They descended with their guns drawn, Rick followed by Dunlap. Careful to avoid stepping into the dirt, they hugged the walls. When they stepped onto the concrete floor at the bottom, they looked around and saw a typical basement. As with the stairwell, it was also strangely clean with the exception of the dirt trail. To their right and behind the stairs was the utility area with an old oil furnace and a water heater. Pipes and tubes ran off in various directions. A far corner held a sump pump. Across the room was an old workbench with a vise mounted to one end and an electric grinder attached to the other. Several knives were laid out in a row across the top. A small shovel leaned against one side. Above the bench was a pegboard with miscellaneous tools hung here and there. Sometime in the past, someone had taken the time to outline where each one belonged, but now the tools were in disarray. They seemed to be hung wherever Willie could make them fit.

There was a window to the left of the pegboard—the same window Rick had seen from the outside. It had a dark-colored plastic film taped over it.

Between the workbench and the furnace, on the wall that connected one side of the house with the other, was a large, old oak hutch. It was beat up, but it must have been something in its day because it had a great deal of ornate trim. Some of the doors still had the stained glass panes that must have adorned all of them in a bygone era. Instead of fine china and crystal, it now held boxes of nails and screws, and a great many gardening tools. Opening one of the doors in the bottom, Rick found a collection of plastic and clay pots.

"The trail of dirt ends at the hutch," Rick noted. "But I don't see any bags of soil or anything else that could have caused the mess. Do you?"

"Nope, and I'm finding it a bit odd," replied the burly sheriff.

There were two bare bulbs lighting the room. A moth flickered around one, giving off oversized, fluttering shadows.

Holstering his pistol, the sheriff walked over to the large piece of beaten-up antique furniture. First, he paused to admire the old craftsmanship. "I love old furniture like this. I do a little restoration on the side." Then, he examined the floor around its base. "Looks to me like it was just recently moved to this spot," he said. "There's scrape marks on the floor." With that, he peeked behind the hutch. "There's a door back there! Come on. Let's move this thing."

It took them both, but they slid it to one side, revealing an old six-panel wooden door. It was painted green but had a million tiny holes in it. The holes were everywhere except right in the center, where a dart board must have once hung. That area contained a perfectly round spot with no holes at all. There was a small thumb bolt and a brass doorknob.

The thumb bolt was engaged, so Rick unlocked it and tried the knob. The latch popped free, and the door seemed to groan with pain as it creaked open. There was a little light from one corner but not enough to see well. "Smells a little ripe in here," he said as he reached inside. He felt around on the wall inside for a switch. Nothing. Stepping back and scanning the wall on either side of the door, he found a switch behind the spot where they had moved the hutch.

When Rick flicked on the lights, he and the sheriff could at once see why Willie Robbins had not wanted them to search the house.

* * *

Despite the fear and the anger that had generated such strength of will just a few minutes earlier, Hope now began to feel the energy leak from her body as she crouched beside the old wooden door. She fought it. She battled valiantly to keep her mind sharp and her eyes open. She tried to consider the possible scenarios for when the door opened. She walked through various strategies for the use of her makeshift weapons. She even tried slapping herself in the face and pinching her own arms as hard as she could. She fought, but ultimately she lost her battle with sleep. It snuck up, captured her mind, and overcame her will. It carried her off into another scary place that seemed as real as the one she truly occupied.

When her mind brightened into the dream that took over her reality, she recognized where she was at once. She found herself in a place that she both missed terribly and loathed deeply. It had been the location of some of her most pleasant—and most horrifying—memories.

It was her old bedroom but not the one in Cutters Notch. Rather, it was the one in Muncie, tucked into the back corner of the house where she had grown up, in more ways than one. It was the place where she had lived from the time she had been born until they'd moved to Cutters Notch last year to get away from Kenny—to hide.

She could see her old toys, her old posters, her dolls, and her trophies—all of the things she had lost when they had fled. Her mother had been too distraught to even return to the place long enough to pack up some clothes. There was Hope's bed with her lavender spread. On the wall, pictures of her best friends were tacked here and there. *I miss them,* she thought. She had loved that place, and she had loved those things, but she had been forced to leave them all behind.

She plopped down on the bed. She could feel the softness of her favorite pillow and the pleats of the bedcover under the skin of her arms.

She looked to her left, at the wall of pictures. *I didn't even get to say good-bye.*

She felt a warm, fuzzy face nuzzle up next to her as she reclined on her bed. It was Bart, her old, lazy golden retriever. He licked her ear and gave her a canine smile. His familiar dog-breath mounted a nostalgic assault on her face.

"Hey! It's great to see you again, old boy," she said with a joyful laugh. "Wow! I've missed you so much!" Hope wrapped her arms around her dog and shoved her face into his fur.

"It's great to see you, too," Bart replied. "And I've missed you more." Then, he licked her again.

Being a dream, it seemed quite natural for Bart to be speaking. Hope gave it no thought. It was as if dogs always spoke.

"You need to be careful," Bart said in a hushed tone. "He's home tonight." Then he closed his mouth, tucked his ears, and whimpered.

Fear struck her like a punch in the gut. *Oh no! It can't be!* Now she could hear him. He was close, in the next room. He was talking to her mom. No. That's not right. He was *yelling* at her mom. *How did he find us?* She could hear what they were saying, and as much as she tried, she couldn't *stop* hearing it.

"But, Kenny, she's your daughter," Megan said. "You can't do that! Please don't do that!"

"Are you sure she's mine?" Kenny asked with a suspicious tone. "She don't look nothin' like me. I think maybe you got yourself knocked up by one of those slugs you worked with, and you're just trying to make me pay." The big man suddenly shivered all over. "And why's it always so freakin' cold in here?" he asked as he walked over to check the thermostat.

"Kenny, honey, she's yours. I swear! There's never been anyone else but you. Please, just come over and sit down, and I'll get you a burger and a beer. I'll fry you up some—"

"Keeennyyy, hoooneeey," he mimicked. "Why you callin' me 'honey'? I'm not your honey. I'm your money train, baby. I go out and kill myself in that hot foundry, and what are you doin' all day? Hmm?"

He looked up into the corner above the refrigerator, his head cocked like he was listening to something. After a moment, he said, "Yeah, I bet I know. You're either sitting on your rear or hookin' up with one of the neighbor boys." He pulled open the refrigerator and got himself a beer. Popping the top, he chugged it down, then grabbed a second can.

Hope realized that this wasn't just the same house that they had lived in before they'd fled—it was the same night too. It was *that* night. *Monster night.*

"That's just the booze talking," Hope's mom said, realizing that he had stopped and had a few on the way home. "You know you're the only one for me. I love you, and I always have. Hope loves you too." She tried to put her arms around him to ease his paranoia. He brushed her off and shoved her back.

"Love me? Love me, do you? Well, let's just see how much you love me. Bring that girl out here, and let's see how much you love me." He pulled his pocketknife from his pocket and opened the slim four-inch blade.

"Ken, no. Please. Please stop and think. She's your little girl. You've rocked her to sleep."

"Get her out here, Megan!" he shouted. "*Get her out here now!*" He slammed his beer on the table, causing it to foam and spew from the top.

"I won't do it."

"You get her out here, or I'll drag her out here myself."

Kenny laid the knife on the table and lurched to his feet, flinging a kitchen chair across the room. Stumbling slightly, he started toward Hope's bedroom, but Megan jumped in the way. She blocked him and tried to wrap her arms around him again. He hit her with the back of his hand so hard that her feet left the floor. She flew backward into their old Panasonic television, shattering the tube. Glass shards cut into her back and blood seeped through the fabric of her blouse. She had a metallic taste in her mouth.

In her room, Hope slunk back into the far corner of her bedroom. She knew what was coming because she had already lived it. Hindsight is 20/20, but when it is also foresight, it can be terrifying.

She hugged her buddy, Bart. "Bart, we've got to get out of here."

"There is no way out. You know that." Bart seemed awfully calm. "We have to go *through* it." His tongue drooped out of the side of his mouth.

"Maybe we could jump out the window," Hope suggested.

"What window?" Bart answered.

Hope turned and looked, and sure enough, her window was gone. It had been replaced by a door that opened into a tiny little room with a tiny lamp, a tiny privacy screen, and a tiny wooden chair sitting square in the middle.

She heard footsteps approaching, Kenny's steel-toe work boots on the hardwood floor. It was weird. On the one hand, she was shut up in her bedroom. On the other hand, she could also see what her parents were doing in the other room. Her dream body was in one room while her dream spirit floated in the other.

Her mother ignored the pain in her back and the blood spilling from her mouth. With her tongue, she felt a cut on the inside of her lower lip. Regardless, she leapt to her feet and lunged at Kenny from behind. She hit him hard in the back and shoved him face-first into Hope's bedroom door. The door broke, and he fell into the room, landing on the floor. The large man was still. He didn't move, and he didn't make a sound.

Hope looked at her mother, and a sense of déjà vu hit her, but this was not just a feeling; she had truly lived this already. She knew what was next.

Thinking that Kenny was out cold, Megan motioned for Hope to escape and slip past his prone body. Even as Hope tried to say, "No, he's not really knocked out," she felt her feet moving to get up. She tried to stop herself, but she was no longer in control. Fate was taking the wheel. She tried to scream for her mom to help, but nothing came out.

Just as she was about to step over Kenny—as she knew he would—her drunken father popped up onto his knees. His face was right in front of hers. He had a weird smile and blood oozing between his teeth. His black-rimmed safety glasses, that he wore constantly because he was too cheap to get a regular pair, had a cracked lens over one eye and hung crookedly over his nose. *His eyes*. Hope would never forget those eyes. There was anger there, but even more, there was true hatred glowing from inside him. Somehow, her daddy ... her daddy hated her.

"Now I've got you, you little maggot!" He grabbed her by her arms and shook her hard. "Come to your loving daddy, Moneybags, you little leech. Do you know what you do with leeches? Hmm?" he said as he continued to shake her back and forth. Blood mixed with spit spewed from his mouth. "Well, let me tell you so you know what's comin'. You peel them off your butt and you squish 'em. Now that's what I'm gonna do. I'm gonna squish you like the leech you are!"

He put his hands on each side of Hope's face and pressed, like he was going to smash her cheekbones into her brain. "Let's see if we can get those eyes to pop out!"

Before he could put any force behind it, Megan grabbed him from behind and yanked him back by the hair. Kenny fell back awkwardly over his own legs, and Hope heard one of his knees pop. Screaming in pain, he tried to get back up. That was when Bart roared into action. Hope screamed at him to stop because she knew what was coming. She screamed, but still no sound came out, and she could do nothing to stop the reenactment. Fate would have its way.

Bart rushed forward and sunk his formidable teeth into Kenny's right forearm. He pulled the man hard, jerking from side to side. Kenny cried out again in pain and then gave his full attention to the dog. As big and strong as Bart was, he was no match for a man who was six foot four, weighed in at 265 pounds, and made his living pouring molten iron at a casting foundry. The man gritted his teeth and rose to his feet with the dog hanging from his arm.

Kenny was quiet for a few seconds, watching Hope's buddy jerk the arm in his teeth as he dangled in the air, listening to the dog's angry growls. Kenny cocked his head to one side and raised an eyebrow like he was thinking about what to do about this sudden turn of events. Ulti-mately, he twisted the attacked arm around so that he got ahold of Bart's fur. Then he slammed Hope's defender into the door jamb with so much power that not only did Bart's spine snap but so did the wood that framed the jamb.

Bart released his grip on Kenny's arm and fell to the floor in a lump. He whimpered twice, and his head shook as he gasped for one last breath. Then, Bart was gone. Again.

Hope finally found her voice as the grief of losing her friend again became too much. She screamed. Giving in to the inevitable course of the nightmare, she rushed at her father with her fists flailing in anger just as she had done before. Just as before, he grabbed her by the arms and lifted her into the air like he had done with Bart. He was laughing. He was hysterical. His eyes flickered with the wicked light of hate, and he began to swing her. He was having fun—first one way and then the other, building momentum, back and forth, back and forth …

But just before he slammed her into the wall, Kenny's eyes went wide. Megan had swung Hope's softball bat up between his legs, solid contact. He dropped his daughter and doubled over in uncontrollable pain.

Hope fell to the floor, stumbling over to land in front of her closet door. She was weeping. She cried for her broken life and her broken dog; she cried for her broken daddy. She could see her mom reaching for her. Hope held out her hand. As their fingertips met, the knob on her closet door began to turn.

Six

The three odd beings entered the forest. The boys draped two of them like heavy jackets slung across their backs. Youthful fingers gripped the leafy shirts the creatures wore, and young legs wrapped around their small waistlines.

Josh began to get his bearings. They were headed deeper into the trees. Deeper into the overwhelming light collage of sparkling leaves and away from his neighborhood—away from old man Robbins' house. Away from Hope.

"Gavin, where are we going? That old Robbins dude lives the other way!" Josh called out. *Did Gavin lie?* A mist of doubt arose in Josh's mind. *Did we fall for a trick?*

"Why would we go there?" Gavin replied. "We are going to rescue your friend." He brushed aside a fluorescent shrub and rushed through luminescent grass as he spoke.

Josh was confused again. "But that's where Hope is! Mister Robbins has her in his basement. Stop. Stop, please!" He was suddenly conflicted. *Are we going the right way? Do these things really know where Hope is?* It suddenly occurred to him that perhaps this is what had happened to Hope. Perhaps he and Danny were being … taken.

The group paused under the brilliant rays of an old elm. Josh and Danny looked at one another. They could see the fear in each other's eyes as they clung to the backs of their tiny rides.

"Where did that odd idea spring from, Joshua Gillis?" Gavin asked. "Hope is not there. Mister Robbins is a strange human; that is certain. Still, he did not take your friend."

"He didn't?" Danny asked. "Are you sure?"

"We are sure. He is quite innocent. It is others who have Hope. Others, who are many times more dangerous than that unusual old human." Gavin noticed the doubt and fear in their eyes. "I sense that you are now uneasy with us. Please be assured that we do not have her. We are only here to help you. We wish to rescue her."

Josh and Danny were quiet for a few moments while they considered Gavin's words. They had been on the wrong track, and that meant that the sheriff and Trooper Anders were on the wrong track too. Danny was distressed because he had supplied the information that had pointed at Robbins. Now the boys knew that the insinuation had been all wrong. They were now the only chance Hope had left—them and these three strange creatures.

"Smakal," Danny asked, "since we don't know where she is and you do, how much farther before we reach her?"

"We will run for thirty groves, and then we will need to move more cautiously," Smakal answered.

"How far is a 'grove'?" Josh asked. "We don't know what that means."

"We are in a quandary, for we do not know how to explain it in your terms," said Gronek. "It will take us much longer than the time we have already run, but I cannot define it fully so that you will understand."

"Well, let's get going then," said Josh, and the group began to move once again.

The small group moved with remarkable speed through the forest, leaping streams and bursting through brush that was aglow with the full spectrum of the colors of life.

As they ran now, they were quiet—thoughtful and introspective. The boys began to look around at the sights in the forest. It was like nothing they had ever imagined, so very alive and yet so very quiet. Now that they were in the trees, the aura broke down into individual sparkles emanating from each leaf. Here and there, a leaf would fall from a branch. It would sparkle and blink a few times before going dark as it descended to the ground. Seen through the undergrowth, the falling sparkles looked like showers of light.

On the forest floor, the light revealed thousands upon thousands of flowers blinking and twinkling—flowers that did not exist in their own realm. It was fall in their home dimension, but here it seemed that spring had sprung again. Red, blue, yellow, green, orange, purple. All twinkling and glowing like a humongous floral Christmas display.

As they ran, Josh noticed that they would occasionally dodge some rather odd-looking clumps of glowing wildflowers. The blooms emanated a red aura that fluctuated from dim to bright and then back to dim again. They ran through most everything else, but they would go well out of their way to miss those particular blooms. Once, they swerved so abruptly that Danny nearly flew off of Smakal's back.

"Why do you keep dodging those flowers? Are they dangerous?" asked Josh.

"Not dangerous to one's life," explained Gronek. "They contain the pollen from which we make the Slumber Dust. In small concentrations, it cannot affect us, but if we stir up a full breeze, we will all be asleep in seconds, and Hope will be lost to us."

Danny had finally moved beyond his fear of these three and was beginning to be overtly curious about who and what they were. In his nature, he was more of a bookworm than an athlete, and at school he was very much the nerd. At the movies, he loved monsters. In books, he loved fantasy, especially the stories of Tolkien and C. S. Lewis. A bit mesmerized, he found himself staring at Gavin and Gronek while Smakal carried him along. He noticed their slightly pointed ears, their large eyes, and their slender fingers. Their faces were angular, and their eyebrows made him think of Spock from Star Trek. They reminded him of beings from the fables he had been told when he was little. They looked like elves. *That's what they are*, he thought. *They have to be!*

He also noticed that they didn't seem to have trouble speaking while they were running. *I'd be gasping for breath and holding my side.* Since they had no such issues, he decided to ask some questions. *Why not?* he thought. He often used his curiosity to distract him from his anxiety.

"So ..." he hesitated. "Um, what are you guys?" he asked, not directing the question to any one of them in particular. "I mean, I don't want to insult you guys, but you call us 'human,' and you don't quite look the same as us. You're smaller but stronger. You've got extra-long fingers and pointy ears. I'm just curious."

The three all laughed in unison, but it was Gavin who replied. "You already know, do you not? You are the reader."

"Hey! I can read, too," Josh objected, but they all ignored him.

"Are you elves?" Danny asked timidly.

"That is one of the words that you humans have used for us. We are known by other words, as well. Some call us elves. Some call us trolls. Some of our kind from across the sea are called leprechauns."

"Trolls are dangerous," Danny said, "and leprechauns are sneaky and greedy. You seem to be kind. Are they, you know, the same as you?"

"Are all humans nice?" Gavin asked. "Are all humans loving, honest, and good creatures?"

"Well, no," Danny replied.

"So it is with us. Most of our folk are good, as we are. We are normally timid and keep to the forest. We are kind and concerned, and sometimes we even do helpful things for the humans we see through the shimmers. But there are others—mostly those who dwell in the cities—who have been tainted. They have fallen in their inner selves."

"But they are elves?" asked Josh.

"We call ourselves no such name, but those fallen ones are of our same kind. We call ourselves by a name that does not translate to your tongue. It is—"

At that moment, all three together made a sort of whirling sound that ended with a sharp "elf" at the end.

Josh chuckled. "Sooooo, we'll just stick with 'elf.' Okay?"

"If it pleases you," said Smakal as he leapt over a log. "Others have found that to be much simpler than our true name."

Josh continued, "You may be elves, but I'm gonna call you bandits." He smiled like he had been very clever, but the faces of his new friends suddenly sank. Their smiles turned to frowns.

"Bandits? Why would you insult us by calling us a name such as that?" asked Gronek.

"Yes, why?" echoed Smakal. "We bear you no ill will. We are not fallen and would only treat you kindly. We would never think to insult you as such."

Josh was stricken with guilt. "Why? Well gosh, I'm very sorry." *What have I done?* "I don't mean to insult you. Really, I'm sorry. I really am. I was just joking around. It's just ... well ... You see, it's because Gavin is wearing my new basketball shoes." The boy pointed at Gavin's feet. "And Hope said she was missing her green socks—like the ones on your legs. So I figured you swiped them from us."

"Ah, so I am wearing your shoes," said Gavin with realization. He laughed, and the smile returned to his face. "But I did not steal them. I only borrowed them."

Josh was relieved when he saw his new friend smile. *Whew!* "Well, I'm glad you're not mad at me."

"Even if you had not explained, we could not hold on to our anger," said Gronek. "It is basic to our nature to forgive. Now that we understand that you mean it only as a friendly joke, we are not offended."

"Well, good, but Gavin, you do still have my shoes on your feet. So I'm gonna call you the Dimensional Bandits," Josh said. "You know, just for fun. Just playin' around. Okay?"

There was a moment of awkward silence as the three beings considered the idea, and then Josh and Danny both burst into laughter. Eventually, the three elves joined in, and they were all laughing loudly as they dodged glowing trees, hopped over streams, and rushed through the luminescent brush.

"Did you use that Slumber Dust when you swiped— Um, I mean when you *borrowed* my shoes?" Josh asked Gavin.

Gavin turned, looked over his sloping shoulder, and gave Josh a devious grin. "I did, at that. But, Josh, you would have had them back in a day or two. I do not steal. As I said, I only borrow as the fancy strikes me. I always return what I take, although I may have to put an extra day into cleaning your shoes after this night." As he said that, Josh's right shoe—on Gavin's foot—splashed into another mud bog as they continued through the forest.

"What about that old hat you have on?" asked Danny. "It doesn't look like it came over here very recently. And what about my pajama bottoms?"

"Those items were destined to be disposed," Smakal answered. "We rescued them for our use. We will sometimes slip into your world to retrieve items that we can use that you no longer wish to keep."

After that, it was quiet again for a time. Then something from earlier leapt into Josh's mind, and he became concerned. The three beings had said that they would run for thirty groves, and then move more cautiously. *Cautiously? Why?* Why would they need to move cautiously if they were in this dimension and Hope and her captors were in the other? *Why do we need to be careful?*

"Smakal, why did you say we would need to move more cautiously when we got closer?"

The mood turned very serious as the smiles disappeared from the elves' faces. All was quiet as they each waited for the another to answer Josh's question. It was obvious that Smakal did not want to be the one to explain. He kept looking to Gavin and then looking away. Gronek just concentrated on maneuvering through the trees.

"Gavin, will you tell us?" asked Danny, his fear resurfacing.

"I will, but I must explain quickly, because we are nearing that very place. In this realm, all is normally very pleasant, as you can see. You might think it is amazing and peaceful."

Danny and Josh nodded in agreement.

"We, however, are not the only ones from other realms that can inhabit this place. There are other beings who are more transient, moving easily through dimensional boundaries. They also pass through here, and they can see us here even if they are elsewhere. Some of those beings are good, and some of them are very bad. The bad ones are often present when evil things are being done. There will likely be bad ones nearby when we approach the location where Hope is being held. The bad ones cannot hurt elves, and they cannot directly hurt you. If their attention is drawn to you, however, they can influence other humans to do you harm. Worse, you would be in even more danger if they became aware that you knew of them. They flourish most when humans are ignorant of their existence."

The three stopped running. The boys dropped to their feet. Danny looked at Josh and saw his own fear now reflected in his brave friend's eyes. It passed quickly as concern for Hope replaced the warnings Gavin had given.

"The place is just ahead. We now have the need for caution," Gavin warned. "Follow me quietly."

* * *

Rick and Sheriff Dunlap paced back and forth in Willie's living room. Willie and his buddy sat on the sofa, surrounded by a weird mix of quaint antique farm décor and classic-rock posters. Lava lamps sat on small tables at each end of the sofa. The deputies were scattered into the various corners like hesitant spectators.

"Are you telling me that you wasted all of our time getting this warrant and searching your house because you were planning to grow pot in the basement?" Rick shouted at the old man. "You've got to be the biggest freaking idiot I've ever met! There's a girl's life in the balance, and all you're thinking about is your own skin?"

"I told you she wasn't in here!" the old man shouted back. "I told you that you'd be wasting your time." He was leaning forward now, his hands on his faded, threadbare Levi's. The word "Mom" was tattooed on his right arm; "Dad" was inked into his left. "Look, I like the kid. I like her mom. But I wasn't about to go to jail."

"Now that we're in here, we're gonna find your stash," said Dunlap. His right hand was fingering his pistol, and he looked like he wanted to pull it out and knock Willie Robbins across the side of the head with it. "Don't waste any more of our time. Just tell us where it is so we can move on."

"You're not gonna find nothin'. 'Less you wanna dig through my septic tank. I used the time to clean up, so to speak." Willie looked both men in the eyes. With as much genuine remorse as he could muster, he said, "Fellas, I'm sorry. I'm sorry about the delays, and I'm sorry that you've chased down a goose. I really am. I just didn't think I had a choice. I was stuck, see?"

"Great. Just great," said Rick, frustration written all over his face. Desperation was swimming like a shark just under the surface of his composure. "Back to square one." *Oh, God!* he called out in his heart. *Help me! Help me find her!*

"Are you guys 'bout done in here now?" Willie asked. "I've got to clean up that mud you've tracked all over my floors," he said with a tone of resignation—like it was just another job that had to get done. "When I'm done, if you want, we'll come out and help search for the girl."

Anders looked down at the floor and then at his own shoes. He almost apologized, then caught himself, but not before the old man noticed. "Don't worry, Rick. We made as much of the mess as you did," the old man explained.

Rick's temper flared again. "Robbins, you just better hope that we find that girl! 'Cause if we don't, you're gonna have more trouble from me than a little bit of mud!"

The sheriff stepped in front of Rick. "Relax Anders. Give it a rest." Turning to Willie Robbins, he said, "I guess we've got nothing on you— at least nothing that will stick. If you want to help, I suppose you can. But there won't be much to do until the morning. We start searching the forest at 8 a.m."

Rick was staring at the mud on his shoes and thinking. After Dunlap stepped in, he didn't really hear the balance of the conversation going on around him. Instead, his mind shifted gears, and he was slowly letting the clutch out on the transmission of his police-trained instincts. *That's a lot of mud!*

Despite Willie's unwelcome reassurance, Rick had been the one to track in the bulk of the mud. He had picked it up while standing on the old overgrown road behind the Hicks' privacy fence. *That's too much mud.* The thing was, he couldn't figure out why there'd even be mud to step in out there. Sure, it had rained the previous night, but the road was all grown over in grass and weeds. At worst, he should have just stepped in some standing water, not gotten clumps of mud all over his shoes. Then it finally hit him, and what had been bugging him about the boys fully clicked in. The clutch was out, and he hit the gas.

Mud? There shouldn't be any mud! Something had torn up the ground and created an area of mud on the old road right behind Earl and Faye Hicks' privacy fence and gate. But what? The only thing that made sense was a vehicle, and the only vehicle that could reasonably get back there would have to be the Hicks' SUV—through their gate. *Could that be where the Hicks are? Why would they be back in the forest?*

A suspicion took root.

"Boys, let's clear out!" Dunlap shouted. "We're wastin' time in here." He turned toward the door and slapped Rick on the shoulder. "Dead end. Let's go."

Two deputies had been standing in the hallway, admiring a classic Santana poster. When the sheriff gave the word, they turned and headed out the door.

"Not so fast, Sheriff," Rick replied. "I've got a couple of more questions for Willie."

"Rick, I'm tellin' you, I don't know nothin' about the girl."

"You might know more than you realize," said Rick. "You know this area better than almost any of us. Maybe better than all of us."

Willie looked at him with quizzical eyes. "Well, that's probably true, I guess. Ask away, then."

"You've lived here longer than any of us."

"Yeah, I've lived in this house all my life. It was my folks' place and their folks before them. When I was born, it was my grandpa's house. I've had the same bedroom since I was four."

"You know the woods pretty good, too, I bet."

"Oh, yeah!" Willie was smiling now, a friendly sort of smile. "I love those woods. I used to wander up into the hills above the Notch and climb up the old oak trees." He got a wistful look in his eyes, like he was remembering a long-lost friend. "You can see for miles and miles from the top of one of those old trees."

"Do you know that old road that dead-ends behind Earl Hicks' house?"

"Sure. What about it?"

"Where does it go?"

"It doesn't go anywhere now. It's all overgrown," said Willie.

"Where'd it go when it *did* go somewhere, Willie?" Rick pressed him. He sat down to Willie's right on an old wooden rocker and leaned toward the man in genuine interest.

"It went back to my folks' old limestone quarry, but that's been closed for over twenty years now. I haven't been out there in at least fifteen or more years, myself."

"What's back there? At the quarry, I mean."

At the mention of the quarry, the sheriff's face lit up. "I know that place. Me and the boys used to hang there when we were kids," said Dunlap. "We'd dive off the huge blocks into the lake that filled up the pit and party in some of the old buildings." He looked up at the ceiling as he reminisced his glory days. "Man, we'd drag a keg out there too! It's a wonder none of us drowned."

"Come on, Willie. What's back there now besides the sheriff's old swimming hole?"

"Well, like I said, I ain't been back there in years, but there used to be an old maintenance shed, some broken-down conveyors and equipment, and the office building. Like the sheriff said, there's lots of huge old slabs of stone lying around."

"I think the old office building was our party house," said the sheriff, still lost in nostalgia. "We hauled a generator out there. Put up lights and mirrors." He was smiling from ear to ear.

Rick glanced over at the sheriff with a *What are you babbling about?* look, and then directed Willie to continue.

"That's about it. Maybe a few other small, broken-down buildings and some old oil drums."

"Can you think of any reason why Earl Hicks would be driving back on that old road?" Rick probed. He didn't want to bark up the wrong tree again. Maybe Hicks liked to hunt. Or maybe he just wanted to explore back there—maybe get away from his wife once in a while.

"Old times' sake, maybe," Willie answered.

"What do you mean?"

"Earl was the mine manager when it closed down. That's why he built his house in that spot. He bought the first lot and put his house right there because he wanted the old road to be back there. So he could remember the old days and maybe wander back there once in a while. Maybe a place to go think."

Secluded. No one around for miles. No interruptions.

Rick looked at the sheriff. Dunlap looked back and seemed to understand where this was going. The smile had disappeared from the sheriff's face and had been replaced by a look of concern. He nodded for Rick to continue.

"How far back in the woods is this quarry?"

"It's only 'bout two miles as the crow flies, but the road winds 'round a bunch of ridges and stuff. It might actually be five or six miles to get there, but why do you care? You think that girl's back there?"

"Maybe. Could be. I don't know." *I'm starting to think so.* "Sheriff Dunlap, you know how that boy, Danny, got that mud all over his pants tonight?"

"I think he said it happened when they were crawling around behind the houses."

"He said he got it crossing that old road."

"So? It rained last night."

"I live here," said Rick, "and I've been back there. The last time I was there, that old road was all overgrown like Willie said. All tall grass and brush and the like. There wasn't any open ground there for mud to be on. You could barely tell where the old ruts were."

Rick was pacing now, scattering more mud on Willie's floor. He didn't notice and wouldn't have cared if he had. He was weighing his suspicion. Considering the facts, the evidence, the scenarios. *Please don't let this be another goose chase!*

"Well, just before we got the warrant tonight," Rick explained, "I took a little walk behind my house and ended up on that old road." He stopped there. Thinking. Still rolling it around.

"And?" the sheriff prodded.

"Look at my shoes. I've got mud all over 'em. Something had to have torn up the ground enough to make it muddy—something that went through there since it rained last night."

He paused again. Scratched his head through his short hair. "There's an interesting thing, Sheriff. That old road isn't just *behind* Earl Hicks' house; it lines up nicely with the gate on the back of his privacy fence: a gate wide enough to pass a truck through. It's the only privacy fence in this neighborhood, and we haven't seen or heard from Earl and Faye Hicks all evening."

Lights were starting to come on in Dunlap's eyes; Rick could see the man's wheels turning. The big man turned to the closest deputy and barked some orders. "I've gotta get back on the horn with Indianapolis! I've gotta find out how soon that chopper will get back down here!"

Rick's adrenaline was pumping now as his pacing picked up steam. Hope was back there, he knew it. He knew it like he'd never known anything else. He could feel it. *I'm gonna come get you, Hope!*

"We can't wait for the chopper," Rick said. "That'll take at least two hours. We've got to get back there now!"

"I've got a four-wheel-drive department vehicle," the sheriff replied. "But it's in the shop with transmission issues. That's the only one in the county fleet, and it's out of commission."

"Have you got anything else besides your squad car that might be more maneuverable at night on an old overgrown road?" Rick asked. "If the Hicks are back there, they surely drove, but they know the road, and it was probably still daylight."

"We've got two ATVs in the equipment shed," said a nearby deputy. "They're equipped with halogen headlamps."

"Let's go, then," Rick said excitedly. "You and me, Sheriff—let's go get her!"

* * *

"Earl, how are you coming along with the knives?" Faye asked and then took a long drag on her slim white cigarette. Her smoke was creating a fog that billowed around and above her face. She was wearing a light-green scrub shirt that made her look like a stern older nurse. There were a few coffee spots on the front.

"We're almost ready, dear," her husband answered. "Is the water boiling in the pots yet?"

He was again honing the edge of a long, thin knife on the grinder; sparks were spurting lightly from the blade. As he spoke, he paused for just a moment to take a sip of coffee from a nearby mug. He grimaced. *Her coffee is as bitter as her mouth,* he thought.

"It has been boiling for nearly ten minutes," his wife responded with her usual impatient tone. "I'm ready to get this over with. I hate this part!"

"I know. I hate it too." *It's not the only thing I hate.*

It wasn't really that Faye hated the acts that they were preparing to commit. Rather, she hated all the work that went with those acts. Hunting was always a lot of work. Sure, tracking the prey is fun, but then you've got the killing, the dressing, the butchering, and finally, the cleaning up. The cleanup was the biggest hassle. They didn't dare leave any traces. They would have to wash the old place down thoroughly with bleach. They were experienced, though. This wasn't their first hunt, and they were getting it down to an art. Years of practice had paid off. Besides, she was there to make sure that he took every precaution.

"Faye, do you really think we should have taken *this* girl? I mean, she's our neighbor—so close to where we live." Earl slowly dragged a fillet knife across the grinding stone. Light reflected off of the shiny blade. In the background, the generator rumbled a monotone melody.

"Of course I do! First of all, she's a little snot. I don't like her one bit. But she's also strong and lean. Did you get a look at her legs and thighs? Those'll be some succulent steaks, I tell ya." *He better not be going all sentimental on me!*

"But so close to home! Somebody might've seen us pull through, and they'll suspect something."

Earl was eager for the meat; that was for sure. After forty years, he'd developed a taste for it. But he was also starting to worry. They had never taken their chances like this before. Usually, they'd drive over to Terre

Haute or Columbus, maybe even Indianapolis before making the grab, but then Faye had seen Hope walking alone down the road and had demanded that they jump at the chance.

"Nobody saw nothing," she reassured him. "Anders was at work. Nobody was outside. Nobody on the road. We were careful. Stop your fretting."

"What do you want to keep this time?" he asked as he set the fillet knife aside and reviewed his cutlery to see if he'd missed anything. "A tooth? Maybe some hair?" She always kept something. She had a whole box of 'memories' stashed up in the top of their bedroom closet and a grotesque pin board in the basement. He just wanted to forget. But that was impossible.

"I don't want anything from this one."

"You sure? You always keep something. She didn't have any jewelry except for those little gold studs in her ears, so how about an ear? Or maybe an eye? You haven't kept an eye before."

"An eye?" Faye retorted with a glare. "Are you losing it? We need the eyes for the soup."

Earl ignored the glare and the attitude. He nearly gagged at the thought of that nasty eye soup she made. He'd grown used to the attitude. After all, he'd been married to Faye for over forty years. But the soup? Well, the soup was something he had never been able to stomach. The image of Hope's pretty eyes staring up at him from a spoon made his stomach churn.

"You must want *something*," he said. "It's time to decide, because I'm done with the knives."

"Oh, okay. I suppose you're right. Lemme think for a minute." Faye took a quick puff and blew out the smoke. "I think," she said, pausing between each word, "maybe … this time … I'll keep an ear. I like her earrings." Faye smiled. "Yep, an ear will fit nicely on my memento board as it dries out."

"Okay, then. Go get her while I slip on the butcher jacket and the gloves. Be careful, though. I think she could be a feisty one."

"Oh, Earl. You stupid old fool. She ain't gonna fight," Faye smugly answered. "They never fight. You know they get too scared and too weak. It's more likely I'll have to holler for you to come help me carry her in. By now, she probably can't even walk."

"I suppose you're right." *As usual, your majesty.*

She always seemed to be right. Earl had learned a long time ago that Faye was always right. Even when she was clearly wrong, she was right. Or at least it was best for Earl if he said so, anyway.

He walked over to a plastic tote that had been placed just inside the entrance door and pulled out a long, white jacket and two heavy rubber gloves. As he struggled with the twisted sleeves of the jacket, he stared through one of the four small window panes into the night. The moon was shining and bouncing off the limestone blocks scattered here and there. In contrast, the lake was a black hole in the midst of the stones. The water, being twenty feet below the cliffs, was too low to reflect the moon into his line of sight. The wind had been blowing hard when they drove up, but now things seemed to have calmed down.

He turned back just as Faye was twisting the doorknob. With her right bony hand on the knob and her left bony hand on the slide bolt, he could see her grinning to herself as she paused to take in the moment. He'd seen that same grin before. Every time.

"Faye."

"What, Earl?" she snapped. The grin disappeared, and a snarl appeared as she turned to look at him.

"Do you want some sausage for tomorrow's breakfast?"

Faye tightened her grip on the small metal knob with her right hand and pulled the slide bolt aside with her left. The grin reappeared. "Sure. That sounds wonderful! I might sleep in a bit, though. Maybe we could have a brunch?"

* * *

Gavin, Gronek, and Smakal led the boys up a steep hill and out of the trees. The group slowed as they strolled into a clearing. Up ahead, the boys could see an open expanse, but from this distance, they couldn't tell what it was. It was like a huge box of nothingness surrounded by the fascinating aura of the forest.

Here and there were the telltale signs of buildings—rectangular depressions in the ground where no plant sparkled, geometric shapes without foliage. Large boulders were scattered about, stacked on top of one another like a race of giants had arranged them for lawn furniture.

"What's that big, open space?" Josh whispered.

"Probably some wormhole through the time/space continuum," Danny reasoned. He was starting to get more comfortable traveling through dimensions, and his imagination was fully engaged. Josh just stared at him.

"I do not know about wormholes or continuums, but *that* is a lake," Gronek explained. "You humans used to cut the rocks out of the earth here. An enormous hole was left behind, and now it is full of water."

"Wow," said Danny. "I never knew this was back here." Stepping a few feet forward, he said, "I don't see any water."

"There is a large drop down to the water's edge, so you cannot see the lake from here. This place is a long distance from your home," said Smakal. "It would be a very long walk, but many young humans have come and played here over the many years since it closed down. Now, only the evil ones come here."

Gavin motioned for them to continue. The place where they were walking had very little plant life. It was mostly slabs of stone, with various plants growing in the cracks and crevices. There were just enough plants sparkling around them, combined with the moon and the overwhelming shine of the forest, to provide a clear view of their course. Gavin placed a finger across his lips to remind them to remain quiet.

"We are at the place," he said. "Do you see the depression there by the great ancient tree?"

"Sure do," said Josh. He walked to the edge and looked down to see that the depression was only maybe a foot deep, but the corners were sharp, and the angles, square. He could see better here since the forest acted like a massive lantern and the sky had cleared enough to add the shine of the moon.

"Yep," said Danny. The chubby boy trotted up next to his friend and kicked a bit of dirt up as he stopped. The dirt looked like it would fly into the depression in the ground, but instead, it bounced off of nothing and fell back along the edge.

"Your friend Hope is inside the building that stands in that place," Gavin announced. "Unless we are too late."

"I don't see one of those shimmers," said Danny. "How do you know she's in there?"

"We must climb the tree, and you will see," said Smakal, pointing one slender finger skyward.

"We can't reach those first limbs," said Danny. "And I'm terrible at climbing trees. There's no way I can get up there!"

"We will help you," Gavin replied. "Climb back on, and we will get you up there."

Smakal and Gronek crouched down to allow the boys to remount. Both boys stood there for a few seconds, as if considering if the elves were serious. *To carry us as they ran through the forest was unbelievable enough*, Josh thought. *Now they're going to somehow get us up twenty feet in the air to the first great limb of what looks like an incredibly old oak?*

Josh looked at Danny and shrugged. Then he climbed back on the elf's back. Danny did the same. After all, stranger things had happened this night.

The boys were staring up at the limb when it suddenly seemed to race toward them. Just when they thought they would smash into it, they swung above, and their friends landed softly on top. Gavin landed in between and carefully helped each boy down onto the tree's branch.

Even though Josh had often climbed trees and was quite comfortable doing so, Danny felt a little unsteady and needed to hold on to his new friend for balance. The branch on which they stood was huge, nearly wide enough for two of them to stand side by side. Still, Danny was nervous. "It sure is high up here," he said.

"Sit down," said Gavin. "You will feel better that way."

After they were seated, Gavin pointed over a few feet to where the limb overhung the depression in the ground. "Look!" Just five feet below and about ten feet over was a shimmer. It was faint, but it was there, like a plate of dim light floating in the air.

"We must slide over," explained Smakal. Then he began to scoot his bottom across the rough tree bark, his feet dangling over the edge. "Come on. Simply do what I do."

"The limb will sag," said Gronek. "But it will hold us." He then plopped down and imitated his friend, sliding along the surface of the oak.

The boys followed, and Gavin brought up the rear. Almost as one, they scooted over on their bottoms until they were positioned immediately over the top of the shimmer. The branch bobbed in the air just a bit but held their weight easily. The light that came through the shimmer was very faint, but they could see inside.

"Hey! There's—" Danny started to yell, but before he could get much out, Gavin quickly covered his mouth with a strong right hand. The odd little man's two thumbs wrapped around Danny's face like a clamp.

"*Shh*. You must be quiet," Gavin insisted. "There are others here, and they must not notice you! Follow my direction very closely, and I will show you what you need to see. Do you understand, young Daniel?"

Through bulging eyes that stared out between Gavin's splayed fingers, Danny gave a look of complete comprehension and agreement. The boy nodded.

Slowly, Gavin released his grip.

"I can see her," Danny whispered as he leaned over to Josh.

"Where?" asked Josh. "Is she okay?"

"She's over there to the left." He pointed. "I can just make out a door, and she is crouched down beside it. She kind of looks like a pile of clothes."

"Oh, yeah! I see her too. Let's go get her, Gavin!" Josh was whispering but in a very urgent tone. *Hang on Hope! I'm coming!*

"You cannot go in," Gavin said in a quiet but firm voice. "It is much too dangerous."

"Too dangerous," said Gronek.

"Much too dangerous," agreed Smakal.

"We have to! Now that we've found her, we've got to save her." Josh was having a hard time containing his voice, but he somehow maintained the whisper despite his rising anger. He was staring down at Hope, and his heart was burning.

Gavin was patient but unmoved. "I want you to look beyond Hope. Do you see the door?"

"Yes. So what?"

"Look beyond the door. Do you see the dark shape just to the far side?"

"Yeah, that large shadow?"

"Yes, the shadow. That shadow is why you must be quiet—and the primary reason that you cannot go in. In truth, it is much more than a shadow."

Suddenly, it shifted. The shape moved in a circular motion around the room. Ribbons of darkness fluttered behind it as it changed positions. The body seemed to be whirling. They could see what looked to be a head atop an amorphous body, but they could not distinguish any facial features. It stopped directly across from the door above what looked like a smashed wooden chair. It was difficult to tell for sure, but it seemed to be staring directly at Hope.

"What is that thing?" whispered Danny with a tiny, frightened voice. "Is it a ghost?"

"It is worse than a ghost, my young friend. It is a specter, or as you may know it, a lesser demon."

"A demon!" both boys said, nearly shouting.

"Oh, crap!" Josh exclaimed. "What does it want with Hope?"

It was Gronek who explained: "It is not Hope in particular that the specter is interested in. Rather, it is the joy that it derives from the evil intentions and actions of her captors. It feeds on the negative actions of one person against another, drawing energy from their evil deeds. Hope does not know that it is there, except that she may feel cold—or perhaps she may sense a foreboding feel to the room. More than likely, considering the situation that she is in, she is not even slightly aware of its ominous presence."

"However," Smakal continued for his friend, "the specter must not become aware of your knowledge of his presence. So long as it does not realize that you know it is there, you are safe. If it notices that you can see its presence, however, you will be forever in danger."

"Much danger," agreed Gronek.

Danny and Josh stared at one another, clearly frightened. Being frightened was fairly normal for Danny but something fairly unknown to Josh.

Oh, Hope! Josh's fear was less for himself than for his friend. His heart was terrified for her, and it only hardened his determination to save her.

Gavin finished the explanation: "If the specter becomes aware that you know of its existence, it cannot directly hurt you. It will, however, work to hurt you by influencing others to do evil toward you. It whispers into their ears and places ideas into their minds. It plays with their emotions and manipulates their secret fantasies. You will become its target until you have perished."

"So what are we gonna do?" asked Josh. "How are we gonna save Hope? What is your plan?" His teeth were clenched as he stared into the eyes of the wisest of the three elves.

"We have shown you where she is." Gavin stared back and took Josh by the shoulders. "You must memorize this place." Pointing down and away from the shimmer, he said, "Do you see that road there, leading off into the trees?"

"Yes," both boys answered.

"It leads back to behind the house where the old couple lives—the ones who have taken her."

"What old couple do you mean?" asked Josh. "They live down that road?"

"The older human couple that lives in the place that is between Daniel's home and the home of the police officer. They are the ones who have your friend, and that road leads back to their home."

Josh was shocked, and he stuttered out a question: "But, um, wh-wh-wh-wh-y did they t-t-t-take her?" He was suddenly shivering. Goose-bumps rose on his arms. "Why would they want to hurt Hope?"

Smakal gave the three-word answer: "To eat her."

The boys were shocked into silence. The phrase seemed to hang there in midair like the shimmer below them. They stared first at their odd friends and then at each other. As the reality of what the words truly meant began to hit home, it was Josh who spoke first.

"We can't leave her alone," he reasoned, wearing his heart on his face. "Not when we have finally found her." He was almost in tears. "We just can't."

Danny had an idea: "Maybe one of us could stay here with one of you, and the other could go back for help. You know, to sort of keep an eye on her. In case she needs help real fast. What do you think? Could that work, Gavin?"

Gavin scratched his hairless chin and thought for a few seconds. "Yes, young one. I believe that is an excellent idea. Which one of you will go, and which one of you will stay?"

"I will stay!" Josh blurted. "Danny is better with directions, and I can't leave Hope down there alone." *I've found you, and I'm not leaving you!*

"He's right," said Danny. "I am really good with directions."

"Very well," Gavin said. "Gronek and Smakal will escort you back, and I will stay with Joshua. You should not delay, but go now. I sense that the time of her safety is coming to an end. See how the shadow dances below? Go now! Go swiftly!"

Acting as one, Gronek and Smakal grabbed Danny and leapt to the ground and were off down the old road.

Gavin placed his small but extremely strong arm around Josh's shoulders. He squeezed the boy to him and tried to provide some com-fort to the distraught young human. Josh was tough on the outside, but inside, he was struggling to keep his fears in check. He appreciated the gesture and leaned into his new friend. Together, they gazed down into the shimmer. No sooner had Danny and the others rushed out of sight than the doorknob just to the right of Hope's head began to turn.

* * *

While that doorknob was turning, Sheriff Dunlap and Trooper Rick Anders were standing outside the command post. Dunlap was fingering the mic clipped to his collar.

"The tires are flat," said the voice over the radio. The sheriff had sent a couple of his deputies to retrieve the ATVs from the equipment barn.

"What?" Dunlap replied into the mic. Rick echoed him.

"I said, the tires are flat, Sheriff."

"Well, pump 'em up," ordered Dunlap. "We need those vehicles over here right now!"

"We don't have a pump," the frustrated deputy replied.

Sheriff Dunlap uttered some choice words aimed at the wind. "Isn't there a compressor there?"

"Not working."

"I've got a bicycle pump somewhere in my garage," said Rick. "It's for my son's bike. It'll take longer than the compressor, but if I can find it, it'll work."

Dunlap looked at Rick with a bit of surprise. He wasn't aware of Rick Anders' son. "Didn't know you had a boy, Anders."

"Lives with his mom" was Rick's only reply as his already concerned face seemed to darken just a bit. He didn't want to talk about his boy, and the look on his face said so.

Dunlap paused for a moment and looked at the young trooper. He knew the type well enough. Dedicated. Long hours. Stuffed emotions. Broken marriage. He had nothing to say to Rick—at least, not right now. "Well, go find that pump. I guess we're gonna need it." Then he barked an order into the radio: "Get the four-wheelers on the trailer and get them delivered to Basketball Court, flat tires and all."

SEVEN

S till in her nightmare, Hope was confused by the turning knob on the closet door. That hadn't occurred the first time. That first time was still vividly etched into her mind. She remembered the broken body of her dog. She clearly recalled her dad holding himself and moaning on the floor with blood flowing across his face, the smell of beer, sweat, and tobacco oozing from his pores. She had jumped over her dad into her mother's arms. Together, they had rushed out through the front door. The police had been called from a neighbor's house.

When the police had arrived, they'd found Kenny stumbling out the front door with the softball bat in his right hand and a fresh beer in his left. He was cursing and slurping as he staggered across the lawn, swinging the bat wildly over his head. He even took a swing at a squad car, smashing a flashing light bar off the top. Finally, he took a homerun cut at one of the officers. He was lucky they didn't shoot him on the spot. Instead, they tazed him, cuffed him, and hauled him off.

While Kenny sat in the reformatory, the same lawyer who had handled the divorce also had Hope's last name changed to match her mother's new identity. Once the names had been changed and the papers had been filed, Maggie and Hope Spencer moved to the other side of the state and off the grid—to hide.

Disconcerted, Hope now stared at the knob. Her semiconscious mind struggled to make sense of dream and the turning knob, but the sound of the sliding bolt jarred her fully awake as it clicked loudly into the open position. The bedroom containing her screaming mother, her injured but dangerous father, and the body of her best canine friend Bart dissolved and was replaced by the terror of her new reality; the odor of her father's sweat- and beer-drenched shirt was superseded by the stench of her own human waste.

Seated with her back against the wall, she looked up at the turning knob on the old oak door that was her only option for escape, and adrenaline shot into her system like a rocket. She jumped to her feet. Quickly, she placed the stick from the wooden chair between her teeth and then hoisted the bucket from the potty chair, left hand on the handle, right hand on the bottom. Locked and loaded.

She was afraid. So very afraid. But with the dream fresh in her mind, she knew she could fight. Her mother had fought for her. Her dog had died for her. Now she would fight for herself. *Please, don't let me miss!*

As the door cracked open, a chill brushed across Hope's neck and then moved away. Goose pimples rose on her right arm, and she shivered.

She knew she would only get one shot. She had to focus. Visualize. She had to score on the first attempt. There would be no rebound, no put-back. Her legs were bent at the knees and spaced several inches apart to give her good balance. She watched the door swing wide; her eyes locked in on the target. She could feel every muscle come to attention as she coiled for the strike.

Again, the chill brushed across her neck.

A figure stepped in. The target, she could see, wasn't much bigger than herself. *A woman? Dad's new girlfriend?*

The captor didn't see Hope at first but stopped in her tracks at the sight of the broken chair.

* * *

"What the—" Faye Hicks began to say as she stared at the debris in the center of the room. The stench was overpowering.

"Over here," whispered a voice from her right.

"Huh?" Faye turned to the sound by reflex, and as she did, Hope brought the toilet bucket up and stopped abruptly just short of Faye's head. The waste inside flew out and hit Faye squarely, washing completely over her face. It entered her open mouth and plugged her nose. It got in her eyes and ran into her ears. Soiled paper clung to her as brown liquid stained her gray hair and dripped to her shoulders.

Faye Hicks was a confident woman, a woman who was always right. She had captured so many victims that she had become oblivious to her own pride—careless. This time she was taken completely by surprise. She stood there frozen, diarrhea running down her arms and dropping from her fingertips. She was shocked into inaction and couldn't make a sound because of the mess on her face.

Before Faye could recover, Hope pulled the chair rod from between her teeth. Using her right hand, she drove it with all her might directly into the neck of the villainous woman—the woman who she did not yet realize was also her neighbor.

* * *

Faye went down to her knees and collapsed on the floor. She was holding her neck, spitting and gasping for air between soiled lips.

Hope stepped past the flailing woman to the open door. *There were two of them. Where is the other one?* She crouched, leaned forward, and peeked into the other room. He was over by the door, pulling on a long white jacket. His back was turned. The left sleeve was twisted, so he was struggling to get his arm through. The man was whistling the tune from some old TV show that Hope recognized but couldn't name. He didn't seem to be aware that the circumstances had changed. *That's not my dad.*

She glanced about at the old furniture, the desk, the large pots of boiling water on the wood stove, and the various knives that were laid out in a row on a small work stand. *Where am I?* Nothing looked familiar. *Looks like they were going to cook dinner. Oh!* An understanding of their apparent plans struck her like a slap in the face.

As the man finished putting on the jacket and began to pull on some gloves, Hope closed the door softly and slipped into the room. It was much brighter in that room, so there weren't any shadows to hide in. She moved around the plastic-draped desk to the wood stove. Heat radiated from the fire inside; she could feel it warming her cheeks. There was the smell of smoke—wood smoke—and something else. *Cigarettes.* The pots boiling over the fire were too hot and too large for her to handle.

From there, she moved quickly to the knives and selected a long one with a thin blade. It looked like her grandfather's fillet knife that he used to clean fish. A sudden longing for her grandfather washed over her.

Granddaddy! I wish you were here to help me! She grabbed up the weapon and looked at the man's back, considering what to do next. *Hide and wait? Stab him and run?* She still didn't know who these people were, but she realized that the back of his head looked a little familiar. *Who are you? Do I know you?*

A loud -*plop!*- sounded from the other room, and the man began to turn. *Time to move!* Ignoring the sound and with a panic, Hope rushed at the man. He had turned toward the other room, so she was now to his right side. Catching movement in his peripheral vision, his head began to swing toward her. Before he could react, Hope stuck the knife into his side and shoved him hard. Knocking him against the wall, she made a move for the door that she thought had to be an exit. She hoped with all her might that it was an exit. There was no time to contemplate it, no time-outs.

When she reached the door, it was latched, and it took a couple of seconds for her to figure out how to open it. Just as she popped it open, a bony hand grabbed her arm. She whirled around, screamed, and viciously placed a kick. Her foot came up between the man's legs with as much force as she could muster. The effect was immediately apparent.

Earl Hicks went down holding himself, blood oozing through his white butcher's jacket. Hope finally saw his face and recognized him: It was the face of the old man from the neighborhood—the man who lived with his wife in the house next to Danny's place.

Was that her? His wife? Hope's mind flashed to the glimpses she'd had of the man mowing his lawn. He would glance over and wave as she passed by to visit Danny or Josh. He'd had a nice smile. The old man had seemed nice enough, but you never know. Sometimes monsters are real people.

* * *

For once, his wife had been wrong. And careless. If circumstances had been different—and if Earl hadn't been bleeding and squirming in pain on the floor—he might have gotten some satisfaction from Faye's obvious mistake.

He watched the girl run out through the door and across the gravel toward the lake. *Go on! Run,* he thought, and part of him rose up in the hope that she would make it—but just a part. That part that he hid inside. That small, irritating voice that still fought against what he had become.

* * *

As Josh and Gavin watched from above through the shimmer, they saw Hope sitting very still next to the door. They saw the specter fluttering back and forth in anticipation. They watched as the knob turned and the door opened. They saw Hope lurch to her feet. From overhead, they watched the old woman step into the room and stop to stare at the broken chair. They could not hear Hope call for her attention, but they did see the woman turn toward her.

When Hope attacked, Josh grew tense, and every muscle in his young body stood at attention. When the bucket emptied it contents into the old woman's face, he threw his fists into the air but managed to stifle his shout. As Hope drove the rod into Faye's throat, however, he could no longer contain himself. Gavin had no time to react to hold him back. All of Josh's pent-up emotion burst forth through his lips.

"Hope! Yes!" he screamed. "Go, Hope! Go!"

Below in the room, Hope did not hear him. She had struck and started for the door. Even so, Josh had been heard. As the door opened, the specter had rushed forward to place what looked like a dark kiss on Hope's face before fluttering back to the center of the room. There, it stationed itself in anticipation. When Josh called out, the evil presence turned its attention upward, and two red pinpoints shrouded in darkness were directed at Josh Gillis.

"You don't scare me!" Josh said to the apparition.

In response, just below the red eyes, a black mouth formed into an oversized scream, and the specter flew directly toward the boy, disappearing as it exited through the shimmer. A wind caught the boy's hair, and Gavin grabbed him to keep him steady. In the forest, a screech erupted from among the otherwise silent trees and echoed off of the neighboring bluffs.

To his credit, Josh was not shaken. His determination to help Hope—and the adrenaline that had shot through his bloodstream as he'd watched her attack below—now gave him the courage to ignore the ominous potential of the dark spirit. Without turning his head, he said, "Gavin, I've got to go down there. She needs my help." Leaning forward, he prepared to jump.

"But you must not!" Gavin responded, grabbing his arm. "It is too—"

Before he could finish, a great, deep voice sounded from behind and around them. The huge old oak spoke again, overruling Gavin. "Send him to his friend," it said. "The specter will be no more danger if the boy goes there than if he stays here. The girl, however, will need assistance."

The elf looked up and around at the overhanging limbs and huge trunk of the old tree. It was these old trees that had drawn him and his two brothers here: drawn to serve them, to protect them. "Of course, ancient one. You are wise." Turning to the boy, Gavin—despite his reservations—said, "Josh, you may go. You need only drop through the shimmer from this side. You do not need my touch to reenter your own dimension."

"Are you coming with me?" The boy had turned to look at his odd friend. A light breeze was brushing Josh's hair about his face, and a combination of anxiety and courage was showing in his eyes. "Can you come?"

"Yes." Gavin turned his head toward the sky. Looking back and forth, he studied the stars for only a moment. "There is still time. Let us be off. Let us save your Hope!"

Josh needed no further encouragement. He jumped off the limb. Slipping through the shimmer as if it were no more than a curtain of light, he landed hard with a -plop!- on the floor below. Thankfully, his young body was still quite flexible, because his knees came up hard and one popped him on the jaw. Ignoring the sudden pain, he scrambled back to his feet.

Gavin landed quietly just to his right, as if the being had no more than jumped off a curb.

"*Eww*! What is that smell?" Josh exclaimed as he covered his face with the crook of his elbow.

"Human excrement, I suspect."

"Poop? Seriously? *Ugh!*" Josh glanced around the room in case the specter had returned, but being back in his own realm, he realized that the spirit would be invisible to him if it had. Even if it was there—and he thought it probably was—it didn't matter. Regardless of the screaming mouth, fluttering darkness, and boring red eyes that he would probably see every night in his dreams, Josh still needed to find and help Hope.

Faye Hicks was moaning and crying on the floor, the stuff from the bucket smeared around her. She was snorting and spitting as she held one hand on her neck and wiped at her eyes with the other. Josh and Gavin jumped over her, opened the door, and showing no hesitation, ran through to the other room.

Across the threshold, they stopped to look for Hope and assess the situation. They spotted Earl in the doorway, holding his crotch and rolling back and forth on the floor. There was blood oozing through the long white jacket he was wearing. A bloody knife was lying on the floor beside him. "Faye," he mumbled. "She's gone out … Getting away."

"Wow! She took 'em both out!" Josh said with amazement. Pride in his friend welled up in his heart and joined hands with the part of him that had fallen in love with her.

"She is a tough one, your friend," Gavin replied. "But she is not yet safe. Their injuries are superficial. Let us find her."

"Right," Josh replied. Grabbing Gavin by the arm, he pulled him toward the door. "She must be outside!"

Earl looked up in surprise and reached for them, but before he could say anything, Josh placed another kick in the old man's groin. Calling out in pain, the old man doubled over again and rolled out of the way. The two would-be rescuers stepped over him, pushed open the door, and hurried out into the moonlit night.

"Which way?" asked Josh as he stopped short. He was anxious, and the options seemed limitless. "Which way did she go?"

With his oversized eyes, Gavin Allwind of the Trees glanced around. He studied the corners of the old building. He examined the tree lines to each side, the various out-buildings, the broken-down equipment, and the giant rectangular boulders piled upon one another. "There!" he said. And he pointed.

* * *

As Hope fled from the building and away from the people who had kidnapped, drugged, and planned to kill her, she could see fairly well, despite the fact that it was well after dark. Having been knocked unconscious and then held in a darkened room, she no longer had any concept of time, except that the sky was black and the moon was up. She guessed by the light of the moon that it was very late, but how late was unclear.

Her eyes, adjusted to the dim light of the room she had been held in, had not had time to readjust to the brighter room with the knives and boiling pots of water. That fact, combined with the bright moonlight, allowed her to see her surroundings with remarkable clarity. There was an SUV parked just outside the door. Across a driveway was a pile of odd, very large slabs of stone. Scattered here and there were what looked like parts of industrial machines. Beyond it all was an open expanse that looked like a huge pool of oil.

She ran away from the doorway and angled to her right. She hurried across a gravel drive, passed the vehicle that she recognized from her neighbors' driveway, and headed toward the huge, rectangular stone slabs. Her heart was pounding as she reached the angular boulders that reminded her of a giant game of Jenga that had collapsed from a careless pull. *My life is a giant game of Jenga*, she thought as her mind raced wildly. *One wrong move, and I'm lost.* The shape and size of the massive stones, combined with her general state of mind, were disorienting, and she was completely at a loss as to where she might be. Nothing made sense.

Darting into a hidden crevice in the shadows between the stones, she stopped to try to catch her breath. *Why? Why would they do this to me?*

With her carefully planned escape now in the past, she was no longer sure what to do. Hyperventilating, she struggled to control her breathing. She needed to think, but her mind was racing nearly as fast as both her heart and her lungs. *What do I do? Where do I go? Which way? How do I get away? Could there be help nearby?* She didn't think she would be safe for long, and she had none of the answers to those questions. She needed to plan her next move—and she was so very tired. *Move! I've got to move!*

Despite her need to move, Hope sat down in the darkness under an overhanging limestone roof; her back rested against the coarse surface of the adjoining stone wall. "I can't stay here," she said to herself. "This is the first place they'll look, and I need to figure out where I am." Even so, she closed her eyes and let her head fall back against the hard wall. A jolt of pain jerked her back forward when the lump on her head struck the cold stone.

She could feel the energy draining from her limbs as the weariness worked its way back in. Hungry and dehydrated, she edged back deeper inside, away from where she had come in. A slight breeze was blowing through from that direction.

She found that the back side of the stones opened up just a few feet from an abrupt cliff. Below her, about twenty feet down, the moon was being reflected off the rippling surface of what looked to be a good-sized lake. The sight of water made Hope lick her chapped lips. *I'm so thirsty.*

Her eyes scanned along the edge of the cliff to the right and the left. In both directions, about one hundred feet apart, there were metal stairs with metal handrails made of pipe leading down to a lower ledge at the water's edge. The lake casually lapped at the sharp shoulder of that second level. Both sets of stairs ended at old wooden docks jutting out into the water. The one on the right had an old rowboat tied up to a weather-beaten support all the way out at the end. The boat slowly rocked in the water, and it aroused a faint memory in Hope of being rocked to sleep.

She was tired to the core. Weariness, like an anchor, was hanging from a chain slung around her heart. She missed her mom. She missed her friends. Josh, with his attitude and snarky smile. Danny, with his timid heart and nerdy obsessions. And she missed Bart. *I still love you, ole buddy.*

Farther along to the right at water level, she saw a metal shed-like structure with an entry door on the side and two large metal doors dangling above the lake. The water was lapping at the bottom of the double doors, and rust had eaten them away, leaving a jagged smile of metal teeth that seemed to be biting at the water as each new ripple passed underneath. Just beyond the shed, the cliff and ledge took a hard left turn and headed off into the darkness provided by the shade of overhanging trees.

She decided to make for the rowboat. The only other option seemed to be the trees, but with no knowledge of where she was, there was no telling what she would encounter. A barbed-wire fence. A hidden drop off of a rock ledge. A wild animal. She would be lost, blind in the darkness, and there had been recent reports of cougars in the area. If she could get into the boat, however, and if it was sound, she could cast off into the lake. A few strokes with the oars, and she would be out of reach, safe. The lake was large enough, she reasoned, that she could row across to a remote place and her captors would not be able to find her in the dark of night. When morning broke, she could get her bearings and then maybe figure out which way to go.

As she started to move, she heard something scuttling in behind her. Turning, she jerked away in fear and put her fists up, ready to defend herself. Fresh adrenaline surged again into her brain, clearing away the fog of weariness.

"Hope! It's me! Don't hit me!" A figure was there in the dark with both palms extended. A second figure shuffled in behind the first.

Hope was confused. It had to be the crazy couple, but it sounded like Josh. *Here? How? Did they capture him too?* "Josh? Is that you?"

"Yeah. It's me. I'm here to help you!"

Hope's eyes were darting. She wanted to believe her ears, but could it be true? "Josh, is it really you?" She forced her eyes to focus as the form edged into view. It *was* Josh. On the back of the adrenaline, relief now coursed along through her arteries and surged into her heart. In that moment, Josh became more than her friend: He became her hero.

Josh came closer so that Hope could clearly see him. She threw her arms around him and hugged him hard. She sobbed, and tears flowed freely over her freckled cheeks and dripped onto Josh's shoulder. "Oh, Josh! I am so glad to see you. Where are we? How did you find me? Never mind. Tell me later. Right now, we've got to get outta here!"

As she spewed out the series of words, the other form stepped into view. The person she assumed to be Danny emerged, and Hope's eyes beheld the first real, live elf that she had ever seen. She pulled back from Josh slightly but held on to him as she looked at Gavin over the boy's shoulder.

"Um, Josh, who is that?" she asked.

He looked sort of weird in the shadows. His ears looked pointy, but he had a friendly grin, so she wiped her eyes and face on her sleeve and took a second look.

"I can fill you in more later, but let me introduce you to Gavin. He's an elf."

"A what?"

"An elf. Look, I don't have time to explain right now. Later, okay? Right now, I think you're right: We've got to get to a safer place before the Hicks get themselves together." The boy looked at his friend—with her wet face, tired eyes, and matted hair—and he thought he'd never seen anything more beautiful. "We've got to move!"

"There's a boat down there," Hope pointed out. "I'm thinking we could get in and row out into the lake."

"I do not—" Gavin started, but Hope interrupted.

"We'd be outta their reach. They couldn't get to us, and we can go hide on the other side." She was snuffling and still wiping her face as she spoke.

"There is a prob—" Gavin tried again.

"I like it," Josh interrupted, not even noticing the elf's attempt to speak. "Let's go!"

"But, it is a mis—" Gavin began, but before he could get his words out, the two friends were already moving. The little creature peered back out of the stone cave toward the ancient tree. "Oh, Great Oak, what have you gotten me into?" he mumbled as he turned back and rushed out after them.

Just as they reached the metal stairs and began to descend, they heard the sound of gravel scuffing behind them. As one, they turned to look, and Earl Hicks was crossing the driveway, quickly closing the distance between them. He had a large, shiny chopping blade in his right hand. His left hand held his side where Hope had stabbed him. Faye Hicks was trailing behind her husband, barking orders and carrying a butcher's blade that glistened in the moonlight.

"There is no choice now!" Gavin shouted. "Quickly! Down the ladder!"

Hope went down first, followed by Josh. Gavin leapt down and landed quietly beside Hope. She stared at him in disbelief, but he simply flashed a quirky smile and motioned for them to go quickly to the boat. "Hurry! Hurry!" he said.

Their footfalls echoed over the lake as they ran down the wooden planks. The sound seemed to bounce back into their faces like gusts of wind. The dock was longer than it had appeared and seemed to stretch out farther the more they ran. The boat sat at the end like a trophy at the end of a tournament.

When Hope finally reached the boat, she hesitated, as if unsure of what to do. Josh came up from behind and jumped into the boat, rocking it back and forth wildly. "Come on!" he exclaimed. "Jump in!"

Gavin came up beside Hope. "Miss Hope, we must move quickly," he said. "They are on the ladder."

Hope glanced to her right and saw Earl descending, with Faye taking the first step down. The large knife was clenched in her teeth. That was all the motivation she needed, so she promptly leapt into the boat behind her friend.

"Untie the ropes, Gavin!" Josh yelled.

Gavin looked, and the boat was tied up with two one-inch nylon ropes—and knots he was not familiar with. There was one rope at the bow and one at the stern. He got the one at the stern, farthest from the ladder first, and it quickly came loose. When he began to work the knot at the bow, however, it would not easily untie. Struggling, his eyes darted toward the ladder; Earl was at the bottom, turning toward them. He was only twenty-five feet away ...

The knot would not give. Fifteen feet ...

Urgency overcame finesse, and Gavin grabbed the rope with both hands, giving it an enormous, sudden jerk. Ten feet ...

The rope broke free, and he leapt into the boat.

Josh pushed the boat away from the dock with an oar just as Earl was reaching for the boat rim. It slipped from the old man's fingertips and drifted smoothly away. The old man teetered on the edge of balance and almost fell in, but finally pulled back upright—uttering some choice words all the while.

"We got away, you old fool!" Josh screamed at the man. Hope huddled behind him, peering at her captors over her hero's shoulder. Gavin sat upright and quiet in the bow.

Faye Hicks ambled up beside her husband. She had an odd smile on her face. It was almost as if she were having fun. The moon reflected off the streaks of white skin that appeared through the mess on her face.

"So it seems, son," Earl answered as he calmed down. "But we will see." He had a similar odd smile. "We *will* see."

After a few moments, Josh and Gavin switched roles, and Gavin began to row. Cutting through the calm surface of the lake, they moved swiftly away from the dock, and the two geriatric killers faded into the darkness. The lake was quiet, and the moon reflected brightly off the water. When they had moved well out of sight and under the shade of the overhanging trees, Gavin stopped, and they drifted silently on the ripples. A cool breeze rushed at them from their right, causing goose bumps to grow on their arms. From the dock, they heard a woman's laughter.

"Hide if you can for now, but we will find youuuuuu!" Faye's voice boomed across the water. "You cannot get away!" She laughed like a witch mounting a broomstick.

"That is so creepy," Josh said. "She sounds like a ..."

"A witch," Hope finished his sentence.

"That may be so," replied Gavin, "but she is also correct. We cannot get away. We are in a trap, and the spring has been sprung."

"What? What do you mean?" Hope blurted out.

"I was trying to tell you before. This is not a natural lake. It is man-made. Men dug the huge stones out, leaving a large hole that filled with water. There are no sloping shores. The sides are all high cliff walls. They are at least twenty feet high on all sides, and the only way out is one of the two docks that we saw before. They will be watching those. Our current safety is only a temporary illusion."

Josh and Hope stared at one another in disbelief, their despair growing with each passing moment. They now sat side by side, and Hope had latched onto one of Josh's arms. The boy turned to Gavin. "What do we do now? There has to be something we can do!"

"I am unsure," the elf answered. "Perhaps we should move to the far edge of the lake and pray to the Almighty One that we can come up with a better idea before the sun returns."

"What happens when the sun comes up?" Hope asked. She was shivering, and Josh had his arm around her, trying to keep her warm.

"We will be visible to them, and I will be trapped in this world."

They fell silent for a time as the dire nature of their predicament settled into their minds. The only sounds were the water lapping as the oars moved back and forth and the low roar of the cicadas in the trees. Time passed, and the moon edged its way across the sky. There was nothing to do—and none of the three felt like talking.

Hope's mind drifted back to the Monster Night in Muncie. She remembered sitting on the neighbor's porch, wrapped in a blanket while her mother spoke to the police. She could see her father leering at her through the window of the squad car. Angry eyes, filled with hate. It made her heart hurt. The memories were all pieces of a jumbled-up jigsaw puzzle coming to her in bits and all scrambled. *He had me trapped in my room, but I escaped,* she thought. *Then, those crazy people trapped me in that other room, but I escaped again. But now, I'm trapped again. And this time, there is no more escape.*

Then Hope remembered what the elf had said. Wondering, she started to ask Gavin what he had meant by being "trapped in this world." She opened her mouth to speak, but before she uttered a word, she was interrupted by the creaking sound of metal doors being swung open. Hope and her friends looked back toward the dock and the few lights that marked its location. Lights were bobbing around inside the metal shed.

"What are they doing? Josh asked.

The sound of the creaking metal doors was soon followed by a roar as an outboard engine sprung to life.

EIGHT

ronek and Smakal returned Danny to the shimmer that led into Josh's bedroom, and without even saying a word, they tossed him headfirst back into his own world. Danny rolled off the dresser and landed hard on the floor, knocking Josh's comic collection down in the process.

He looked up at the mirror, and Gronek's head poked through the center. "Be safe, Danny, and hurry!" the being said. Then he quickly popped back out.

Smakal's head poked through on the left side of the mirror. "I am honored to have met you," said the other elf. "Perhaps we will meet again someday."

Then they were gone, and Danny was left on his own to determine what to do. He had paid close attention on their journey back, but the elves had moved with incredible speed. They used the road the entire distance so that he could see the route, stopping at each fork so that Danny could be sure to note the proper turns. He tried to log each key point in his memory. Not much was said in between stops, because they were moving so fast that the sparkling leaves became a blur of tiny lines rushing past them on each side, and the boy had been overwhelmed and left speechless.

Getting to his feet now, Danny looked at the mirror from which he had just entered. Once again, it was only a simple mirror, with his reflection alone peering back at him. There was no sign of his new friends. For some reason, he thought his face looked older. He *felt* older.

Glancing around the room, he considered what he should do next. Despite the fact that he suddenly felt more mature, he was still a kid—a kid who had recently been banished to this very room for the night. Grounded. And the woman who had done the grounding was probably still asleep on the other side of his friend's bedroom door. *Should I wake Mom?* he wondered. *Probably not,* he decided.

The house was very quiet; apparently, the mothers were still asleep under the influence of the Slumber Dust. He could hear the floor creak as he stepped around the foot of the bed. Somewhere, a clock was ticking. Fear welled up inside, but he pushed it back down. He couldn't afford to entertain his fears now—a realization that had spawned from his newly found maturity.

He went to the bedroom door, leaned his ear against the fake wood, and listened carefully. No sound came from the living room except for the low rumble of the TV, so he opened the door and cautiously stepped through. As he pulled the bedroom door closed behind him, he could see that the lights were still on where the hallway emptied into the living area. He paused again to listen, then hurried down the hall and stepped into the illuminated room.

The sofa was on his left. All three mothers were reclined on it, folded together like a triple-decker sandwich. Apparently, the women had been sitting together when Gavin had hit them with the Dust. Hope's mother was in the middle. Josh's mom was lying across her lap, and Maggie had fallen forward on top of her. Danny's mom was the top layer. She had slid sideways across Maggie's back. Her mouth was hanging open, and a slender stream of drool was dangling from her lower lip.

Danny had seen a lot of strange sights that day, but *this* had to be the funniest. He stopped long enough to take it in, laughing and holding his mouth to stifle the sound. He wished he had a camera, but he had to keep moving. He needed to get help for his friends, so he trotted over to the door. He was still giggling as he grasped the doorknob.

"Daaaannnny?" his mother mumbled sleepily. "Wherrree arrre yoouuu goinnnggg?" The string of drool dripped down into Maggie's dark curls.

"I'll be right back, Mom," he said and quickly opened the door and stepped out. It wasn't quite a lie. He didn't know if the sheriff would even listen to him, and for all he knew, he'd be escorted back to the house. Besides, "right back" was a relative term.

Outside, the night was bright but cool. The wind had calmed, and the moon was shining. Most of the houses were dark, except for the Robbins' place, and the moonlight reflecting off of the dark panes reminded the boy of the shimmers he had seen from the other side. Danny felt a little bad for having blamed the old Robbins dude—but only a little. He still thought the guy was creepy.

As the breeze brushed over his face and made the normal-looking leaves rustle, it carried with it the sound of men moving around at the mobile command post. He stepped off Josh's porch and did a quick scan of the neighborhood. Looking at the Hicks' house, a feeling of dread mixed with vengeance entered his young heart. They were hurting Hope, and he wanted to hurt them. If he hadn't been on a mission, he would have picked up a rock and tossed it through one of their front windows. He was still thinking about doing just that when he saw Rick Anders step out of his garage with something in his hand. As he watched, the man began to jog back over to join the others.

"Rick!" Danny called out. "Mr. Anders! Wait! Wait just a minute!"

Rick didn't hear him call, so Danny took off running, angling his plump body to catch the man before he reached the trailer. Danny was calling out as he ran, and Rick finally heard him and stopped.

"Danny, what are you doing out here?"

"I ..." He paused to catch his breath. "I know where ..." Another breath. "I know where she is." He bent over, put his hands on his knees, and took a few more deep breaths. It wasn't just the exertion; it was also the excitement and the urgency. His timid soul was being pushed far beyond anywhere it had ever gone before.

"You need to get back in the house. You're getting in the way, and we've got work to get done." Rick looked him over, but then turned back to the command post. "We've got a lead, and I've got to get back now."

"But," Danny continued, "didn't you hear me? I know where she is!"

"Danny, I know you want to help—" Rick began, but the boy cut him off.

"She's at an old quarry out in the woods behind the Hicks' house!" he blurted out. "They're the ones who have her."

That stopped the state trooper in his tracks. Rick, dumbfounded, stared at the boy. *How? How could he have figured that out?*

Unaware of Hope's escape and Josh's attempt at rescue, the boy struggled to add, "They are planning to kill her!"

Putting his hand on the boy's shoulder, Rick asked, "How could you possibly know all of this, Danny?" The more Rick got to know Danny and Josh, the more he liked them. They had spunk, and they were loyal to one another. He needed more loyal people in his life—or at least one.

"I saw the quarry, and I saw Hope. They've got her in some sort of old building beside a lake." Danny wanted to share more, but he knew it would sound too crazy.

Much of what he was saying corresponded to what Rick had learned from Willie Robbins. It also matched up with his newly formed suspicions. "Come with me," Rick said. He ruffled the boy's shaggy head, and they walked on toward the command post.

Just as they reached the basketball court, a small trailer with a large, flat back door was being backed into the far end, beyond the mobile headquarters. Two men in sheriff's department uniforms jumped out. They quickly unlatched and lowered the door to form a ramp. Inside, Danny could see two ATVs lined up, one in front of the other. The tires were flat as pancakes.

"Anders, did you find the tire pump?" asked Dunlap from over his shoulder. He was standing with his back to them, watching the men open the trailer, but had heard them approaching.

"I did," Rick replied and handed the pump to one of the deputies. "But I also found something a little extra. We need to talk."

Sheriff Dunlap turned around to meet Rick but stopped short. He glared down at the boy in disbelief.

"Before you say anything, J.B.—" Rick started.

"*What are you doing here, boy?*" the sheriff shouted. He took an angry step toward Danny.

Rick stepped in between them with his hands palms-up in front of the big sheriff. "Hold it!" he said. "Hold on, Sheriff! Danny might have some good information after all."

"You've got to be kidding me, Anders! What could he possibly know that he hasn't already told us? Another goose chase?" The veins were standing out on the sheriff's neck, and spit was flying from his lips with every word. He was swinging his arms around so much that he knocked his own hat off. It fell off the side of his head, hit his shoulder, and flopped top-down onto the ball court.

When he had finally gotten the big man's attention, Rick absently wiped his sleeve across his face and said, "Well, all I can tell you is"—he paused for effect—"that he just told me ... that Hope was being held in an old building ... beside a lake ... at an old quarry ... in the woods behind Earl and Faye Hicks' house. And that the Hicks are the ones who have her."

"Well, geesh, boy," said Dunlap as he picked up his hat and scratched his head. His flared temper had been reined in. "How'd you come by that information?"

"I was just out there and saw. Josh is still there watching. He's keeping an eye on Hope."

"What?" Rick asked. He turned and looked at Danny. "Josh is still out there? Why didn't you tell me that before?"

"But hold on there," said the sheriff. "That place is way back through those woods. How'd you get out there and then get back here to tell us in such a short amount of time? Seems like it was just a little while ago that we took you home."

"There's a road—" Danny started to explain but Rick cut him off.

"Sheriff, we don't have time to clarify all those details. He obviously knows the fastest route. We need to get out there!"

The sheriff stared at them for a few seconds, shook his head, and said, "Fine." Then he turned and yelled at his deputies to see if the ATVs were ready.

"Almost, sir" was the reply. "Maybe another five minutes or so."

"Okay, Anders. Let's get this show on the road. We need to gear up."

"What are you guys doing?" asked Danny.

Rick explained that they were going to take the ATVs down the old road behind the Hicks' house to the old quarry. He said that he hoped there would be a helicopter on the way soon, but that it was going to be awhile before it would arrive, maybe hours. They thought the ATVs were a better choice for maneuvering through the woods. "Is that the best way, Danny?" he asked. "Down that road?"

"Uh, yeah. But I want to go!" Danny insisted.

"Nope. No way. We'll take it from here, son," said the sheriff. "You've done your part. Go on home to your momma."

"Hey! I ain't no momma's boy!" Danny shouted. *Not anymore, anyway.* "And besides, there's a bunch of forks in the road. You could get turned around real easy," he reasoned, "and I know the way. I can help you get there faster."

"You sure 'bout that? I don't remember any forks," said the sheriff.

"Well, there's a bunch of 'em, and if you don't remember 'em, then I better go, or you'll get lost. We've got to hurry!"

"I hate to say it, J.B.," Rick said, "but the boy does make some sense. If there are forks in the road out there and you don't even remember them being there, we just might get lost and not find the place for hours."

The sheriff stood there for a few moments. He seemed to be thinking it all over.

"Ahhh, come on!" said Danny.

"Fine. Get the boy a helmet!" he shouted to one of his crew. "Anders, he's riding with you. You can be responsible for him. You got that?"

"Roger that. Now let's get going," the trooper replied.

After they were all geared up, they loaded up on the two all-terrain vehicles—Dunlap on one, and Rick and Danny on the other. The boy sat behind the trooper, arms wrapped around Rick's waist. They keyed the engines, which came loudly to life, then flicked on the headlights and accessory spotlights. They lit up the whole neighborhood. Danny could see all the way into the kitchen of his own dark house.

"Sheriff, you better send a deputy over to inform the mothers that we're taking Danny with us," Rick suggested.

"They're all asleep," Danny informed them.

Rick considered that for a moment. "Okay, well, maybe have your guys wait a bit, but if we aren't back in a couple of hours, they should let them know."

Sheriff Dunlap motioned for the nearest deputy, gave him the suggested instructions, and then they started moving. They drove carefully between Rick Anders' home and Earl Hicks' house, crushing the rest of the landscaping that Rick had spent the summer working on, and turned behind the notorious privacy fence. The bright lights caused shadows to move eerily across the forest before them. They stopped briefly where the old road opened up into the woods. Rick pointed out the oversized gate and the muddy ruts. Then, with the brilliant full moon shining down from overhead, they roared off into the trees, Rick and Danny taking the lead and Sheriff Dunlap following.

* * *

"Oh, crap!" Josh blurted. "They've got a boat!"

Hope looked at Josh with weary and frightened eyes. "What do we do now?" she asked. "We're trapped, and it's all my fault!" *It's always my fault.*

"Do not blame yourself, dear one," said Gavin. He had stopped rowing when they had moved well out and away from the dock. They were now deep into the shadows and away from the moonlight, so the elf turned to face the two young humans. "Your name is 'Hope,' and we will take that to heart. As long as we can stay away from those evil humans, your name will guide our faith."

As she looked at her odd new friend, a renewed strength seeped into her. Somehow, this being had a way of looking past the despair. His huge, beautiful dark eyes only seemed to look forward into a favorable future. His gaze injected her with new determination. The fight that was at her core returned.

"Do you have any ideas, Gavin?" she asked. She was holding on to Josh, her arm around his waist, his arm wrapped around her shoulders. As she spoke to the elf, she lay her head over onto her friend's shoulder. She was shivering, but she was unsure if it was from the danger or the cool air that drifted softly over the water.

"I have one that provides us a slim chance. There is an island," he began to explain. "It is on the far side and toward the northern end. It was formed when the miners piled the topsoil they removed to get to the stone. If we can make it to that side, we will be able to hide by always staying on the opposite side of the island."

"Can you outrun them?" asked Josh. The boy's mind was wrought with conflicting emotions. He was eager for a fight—like so many teenage, invincible boys—but he was also frightened by the unrelenting danger of the situation. Intertwined in all of those emotions was the exciting and inexplicable joy of having his arms around Hope. He was looking at her hair, the shape of her nose, her eyelashes fluttering when she blinked—even as he spoke to Gavin.

"Outrun? That is unlikely. However, they do not know where we are at the moment," explained the elf. "That will give us the advantage for a short time. We will stay in the shadows for as long as possible, but we will eventually need to move out into the moonlight. That will be our time of greatest risk."

As Gavin spoke, a small spotlight appeared in the distance. It was not pointed directly at them, and it was not nearly strong enough to reach them where they were currently floating. Still, as it bounced like a child on a trampoline and swung from side to side, there was the risk of the beam reflecting off some metallic surface, revealing their position.

It was time to move, and the elf began to row. He rowed quickly and smoothly, making very little noise as the oars sunk into the water and then pulled out again, only to whip back around for another dip. He was fast—but not as fast as an outboard engine.

Across the lake, their enemies' craft angled slightly toward them, but Gavin and the kids could tell that the trajectory was wrong. Their paths would not intersect. So far, the plan was working.

After a couple of minutes, the outboard engine stopped. As the rowboat slipped silently through the water, still hidden in the shadows, the three companions could see the spotlight sweeping the water much like the eyes of an owl might search a grassy field for mice. Back and forth. Back and forth. Starting in close, then moving away.

"I will find you!" a voice called out and echoed across the lake. "There's only one way out of the lake, and no one else knows you're here."

Gavin kept moving. The island was not far now, maybe another tenth of a mile and across that dangerous bridge of moonlight. Night birds were swooping down and snagging insects from the surface of the shiny water. The chorus of cicadas still resounded from the forest above them.

"You can't get away! Ahahahahahaha!" Faye's cackle skimmed across the water at them and then echoed off the stone cliff beyond. "Ahahahahaha!"

"That is just so freakin' creepy," Josh whispered a bit too loudly. "That old woman is messed up."

"*Shh!*" Hope urgently whispered in return, putting her finger to her mouth. Josh covered his own with his hand, fearful embarrassment evident in his eyes.

The light continued to sweep back and forth. They could see its reflection across the rippled surface of the water. Earl Hicks was being methodical; he was sweeping in ever-widening arcs. Eventually, if the three didn't get behind the island soon, he would see them.

"I have another one, you know," Faye boasted loudly. "We don't really need you. We'll just sink you in the lake and be done with you."

Hope's eyes widened. She looked at Josh and frantically whispered, "Did she just say they had another one?"

Josh nodded.

"Does she mean another girl? Another one like me?" Hope hadn't thought she could get any more terrified than she already was, but that had just been proven false. And that extra terror was peppered with a renewed anger. *I've got to go back!*

"You can't get away!" Faye yelled across the liquid chasm. "You've got no other way out!" The last word bounced off the far quarry wall again: "Out ... out ... out ... out ..."

"Josh, we've got to help that other girl," Hope urgently whispered. "We can't let them hurt someone else."

"Please do not speak," pleaded Gavin. "They must not hear us. Before we can think to help someone else, we must first escape, ourselves."

"Gavin," Josh whispered, "did you know they had another one? Is it another girl?"

"I did not know," he replied. The little elf's heart ached. *If only he and his brothers had acted before,* he thought. *If only we could have stopped them earlier.*

Gavin could sense the island approaching. His large ears could hear the water lapping on its sloping shore. Glancing over his right shoulder, he could see its silhouette against the far wall of the lake. Soon, they would be in position to pull across the brighter water and around the island to the relative safety of the other side. If only they could cross that dangerous strip without being seen, they could hide behind the shield of the island's overgrown brush. With that advantage, they could simply continue to row around, keeping out of the beam of the spotlight until the old humans tired of the search and returned to shore. Once that happened, they could work on the next step in the plan. *Time.* They needed time.

The island began to rise up as a dark blob sitting in the middle of the reflected moonlight just to their right as they looked back toward the scanning beam. They had just moved out of the protective shadows and were not quite in position to turn into the shield of the island when Josh was suddenly overcome with a sneeze. It came out of nowhere and overpowered him. Before he could raise his hand to stifle the noise, the air burst out of his lungs and rushed through his nose and mouth at the same time, whistling loudly into the darkness.

The sound pulled the spotlight beam like a magnet, and they were at once engulfed in a flood of light.

"Aha! We have you now!" Faye yelled. In an instant, the outboard engine again roared to life.

Gavin pulled with all his might, but the plan was shot. The evil old humans knew where the trio were and would not stop until they were caught. There was a loud -*pop!*-, and the water plunked nearby.

Hope screamed.

"They're shooting at us!" Josh yelled. "Oh no! They're gonna shoot us! Hurry, Gavin! Hurry!"

Three more shots broke the tranquility of the lake in quick succession. Two also plunked into the water, but one slammed into the rim of the boat, causing splinters to explode around them. One lodged in Josh's cheek. "*Ow!*" the boy cried out.

With all his might, Gavin pulled on the oars until they were hidden from sight behind the island. It was only a temporary reprieve; at most, they had a minute or so before the powerboat roared around and was upon them.

Once they were hidden, Gavin stopped rowing and let the boat drift.

"What do we do now, Gavin?" Hope asked. Fear glowed in the girl's eyes like two bright flares.

"We've got to fight them!" said Josh. "It's our only chance. Maybe climb up into the brush on the island. Use the oars as weapons."

"There is one other possibility," said Gavin. "But it hasn't been done for a very long time." The elf gazed across the still, moonlit lake. His hand came to his chin as he considered his idea. "Yes. That is what we should attempt."

"What? What hasn't been done for a long time?" asked Josh. "What should we attempt?" *They can't get her! I won't let them!*

"It was our original way into our dimension—before the shimmers."

"Huh?" Hope said in confusion. "What's a 'shimmer'? And did you say 'dimension'?"

Ignoring the girl's questions, Gavin continued, "Joshua, before there were so many shimmers to make passage back and forth convenient, our kind entered our dimension from yours through another means: a passage prepared by the Mighty One, himself."

"How?" Josh asked. "What other way is there?"

"Do you see the moonlight reflecting off of the water?" The elf had again turned to face his two human friends, and he waved his arm out in a sweeping motion toward the lake.

"Yeah," both kids responded in unison.

"When the water is still, as it is tonight, and the moon is full, its light will reflect from the water, creating a mirror effect. Do you see the way the light of the moon is bouncing off of the surface? In essence, it is a natural mirror and a doorway to our world."

Hope was totally lost. She had no idea what Gavin and Josh were talking about. In the urgency of their escape and the extreme danger of their situation, she had given very little thought to the strangeness of being in the presence of a real, live elf. But now, this talk of shimmers, doorways, and dimensions had her completely bewildered.

"Guys! They're almost here!" she urged. "We've got to do something."

"Each of you, take one of my hands." Gavin positioned himself between Hope and Josh, with their backs to the port side of the boat. "We will fall backward over the side as easy as possible. If we rough up the surface too much as we tip the boat, it will not work. I will fall first, and you will follow. Do not let go of my hands."

Even as Gavin spoke the last couple of words, the motorboat screamed around the side of the island, and they were again flooded in the light. "Gotcha!" the old woman yelled as the beam from the spotlight reflected off of their eyes. As the three fell into the water, Earl Hicks got off one more shot. They heard the -pop!- before they hit the water. Hope felt it whiz through the hair hanging down under her head. Then the lake enveloped them like a grave.

* * *

The two ATVs roared to a stop at a dark, brush-lined intersection, and they killed the engines. The moon was being blocked by the overhanging limbs of the large maples, oaks, and sycamores that ringed the clearing like stolid sentinels. There were three choices, and Danny wasn't confident of the right one this time.

"Which way, Danny?" Rick prodded.

"Um … I'm thinkin' maybe …" He started to point and then dropped his arm. "Well …"

A couple of minutes went by as Danny studied the roads, the trees, the rocks, and the various bushes and brambles. He got off the quad and walked first to one road and then to another—thinking, considering. *Which way? I'm an idiot! Which way?*

"Come on, kid," urged Dunlap with an angry edge in his voice. "You said you knew the way. So which way is it?"

"It looked different before."

"What do you mean 'it looked different'?" asked Rick. "You were just out here a little while ago. Right?"

"Yeah, but … Well, I could see better then."

"It was dark then; it's dark now," said the sheriff. "It couldn't look that much different."

Danny couldn't tell them that when he'd been through here before, the whole forest had been alive with the light of its own aura. Gronek and Smakal had rushed him through, and he had paid close attention, but there were a lot of intersections. Apparently, Earl Hicks had built a network of roads for some unknown reason, and while Danny had remembered most of them clearly, this one was escaping him.

"Maybe the ATV headlights are throwing him off," reasoned Rick. "They're lighting up some areas real bright and throwing dark shadows everywhere else." He clicked off the lamps on his machine.

"Maybe," Dunlap replied. He clicked his off, as well, and the whole spot fell into a deep darkness that could almost be cut with a knife. A moment later, the sheriff snapped on a Maglite from his utility belt. "That's better," he said, flashing it from road to road so the boy could take a look at each.

"Well, I know it's not the one on the left," said Danny.

"How's that?" asked the sheriff.

"Well, that one goes up that really steep hill." It shot up like the first hill on a roller coaster and disappeared into the shadows of the tree limbs. "We didn't go up or down a hill quite like that one. Not one that steep." *Okay, two left. Which one? Think! Think!*

"Okay. Good. That narrows it down," Rick encouraged. "So just focus on the other two. Which one looks right?"

Danny examined the ruts in the roads. The men angled the quads and clicked the headlamps back on; one ATV illuminated the road on the right, and the other illuminated the one just to the left of it. Both roads had seen recent traffic from some vehicle, so there was no clue to be found there. The trees looked the same. The rocks looked the same. Nothing stood out. Nothing marked the way.

Think! Think! Danny was beating himself up on the inside. His friend was in imminent danger, and he couldn't remember which way to go to help her. His mind diverted to his memory of Hope huddled in that little room, back against the wall, and desperation nibbled at his heart.

"I ... I just can't remember," Danny choked out. From where he stood, the men couldn't see that tears had begun to trickle down his chubby cheeks. Before he could force back his emotion and say more, a shot rang out in the distance. It echoed back and forth, disguising its origin.

"Anders! Which way did it come from? Could you tell?"

"I'm not sure, Sheriff. I think it was from the general direction of that road on the right."

"Listen then," said Dunlap. "Let's see if there are more." They all got quiet, and soon, more shots were heard in the distance. Three loud - pops!-. Again, they echoed back and forth: *Pop ... pop ... pop ...*

"It's definitely coming from the right," Rick said. "Let's go that way!" He was sure of it, and he could see in the light reflecting in the sheriff's eyes that the big man agreed too.

"Roger that!" Dunlap said.

The ATVs roared back to life and headed down the road that angled in the direction of the gunfire, brambles grabbing at their sleeves as they rumbled through. At first, Danny was relieved that his dilemma seemed to be resolved. Then he realized that he was rushing headlong in a direction that would lead him to where someone dangerous was shooting a gun. That did not sound good, not good at all. As he considered the situation, however, he found that he truly was more concerned about whether those shots were meant for his friend than whether he might be racing toward his own dangerous encounter. It occurred to him that the newfound maturity he had glimpsed in himself in the mirror in Josh's room had been more than a simple reflection in a dim light ...

They hadn't gone far, maybe a half a mile, when Dunlap's ATV came to a quick stop. Rick noticed that the sheriff's headlamps had dropped back, so he slowed and turned around to retrace the distance to the big man. Danny's face and arms were scratched by some thorns as Anders maneuvered a little wide and drove slightly off the road. A trickle of blood mingled with the salty tears still drying on his cheek.

"Why'd you stop?" Rick asked the sheriff.

Dunlap didn't immediately respond. A shaft of moonlight was shooting through the trees and illuminating the sheriff like a spotlight on a park statue. He was off the machine, bent over and looking at the left rear wheel. After a moment, he stood upright, rested his gloved hands on his utility belt, and stared with frustration up through the shaft of moonlight at the lonely bright light in the night sky. He exhaled, and a mist of breath plumed from his mouth. Shadows formed under his eyebrows, giving him a ghoulish leer as he lowered his head to look over at his companions.

"What is it?" Rick asked again.

"I've got a flat," Dunlap explained. "There's a stick poking through the tread, and I can't go any farther."

"Can you get a deputy to drive another one up?"

"Don't have another one."

Rick was quiet for a moment, thinking. "How about commandeering one from a neighboring farm? I see kids driving them all over the place these days."

"That might work, but it will take some time," Dunlap said. "I'm gonna be stuck here for a while, and I'm not sure that we can afford the delay, considering the shots we just heard."

Danny was anxious to get moving. It was all he could do to sit there as his imagination, fueled by the gunshots, considered any number of terrifying scenarios for Hope. Maybe for Josh too. *Come on! Let's get going!*

Rick Anders could feel the boy fidgeting behind him, and he quickly considered Dunlap's concern. His mind flashed memories of Maggie's pretty, sad eyes and the sounds of Hope giggling with her friends as they goofed off in the middle of the cul-de-sac. He used to stand at his front window and watch the kids roughhouse and play ball. They reminded him of his own boy, and as he'd stood there watching, he would yearn to spend time with his son, his heart aching. Dragging his mind back to the present, he came to a conclusion. "We're gonna have to go on without you."

"I'm not sure that's a good idea," said the sheriff. "You've got the kid, and you've got no backup. We'll just have to wait for a replacement ATV, or you can give me your ride, and I'll go on up there."

"Sheriff, you said it yourself: We can't afford the delay. We can't wait." Rick's words were bursting forth in spurts. "And I'm not sitting here while you go. I know that girl. She's my neighbor. I've got to see if I can help her. I'm going! As for Danny, he can stay here with you."

What? No! "Hey!" Danny said. "I don't want to stay here!" He heard himself say it but couldn't believe that the words had really come out of his own mouth. He still hadn't reconciled his newly found courage with his normally timid spirit. "I want to go, and you need me. I'm back on track with the directions now."

"Are there more turns in the road, Danny?" Rick asked.

"Yep," he lied. "A couple more." He now knew that this road led right up to one last fork that sat below the ridge overlooking the quarry, but he was not about to give Rick any reason to leave him behind.

"Okay. You can go, but when we get close, I'm dropping you off. You'll need to stay back at a distance."

"Anders…" the sheriff started.

"It's no use arguing, Sheriff. We're going."

At that, Rick fired up his ATV and headed back up the road. Danny glanced back over his shoulder at the large man as they rounded a slight curve and disappeared into the trees.

* * *

Sheriff Dunlap stared after the duo as they sped off into the woods, shaking his head at their determination. Smiling a little to himself, he walked around the ATV, kicking at sticks and slapping at overhanging limbs. He took a seat on the machine's saddle and scraped at his thumbnail with his Buck knife. The smile slipped away. After giving them a couple of minutes, he calmly folded the blade and placed it back into its holster on his belt. He slid his right leg back over and casually stood up. Reaching back to his utility belt, he snapped his radio to "off" and started walking—following the trail that the other two had just blazed.

* * *

"Did you get 'em?" Faye hissed.

"I dunno," said Earl. "They're in the water! I think that last shot may have gotten one of 'em."

The old man was conflicted. He was in too deep to let the girl get away, but there was still a part of him that liked Hope. She was friendly, cute, and funny. He could still remember her timid smile as she'd opened the door the day he took over a plate of cookies. It was the day she and her mother had moved in. She had seemed almost afraid of him, and now he had fulfilled that fear. Still, he was trapped. Damned either way.

Faye was in the stern, driving the boat. Earl was handling the spotlight and rifle up in the bow. It was a small motor boat that Earl used for fishing—and waste disposal. There were a couple of aluminum benches that connected the port side with the starboard. It was powered by a very old marine engine actuated with a throttle on a handle that projected from one side. His Zebco rod and reel was clipped to the starboard rail, and a net was tied to the port.

"I want that girl!" Faye demanded. "I don't care about the other two, but I want that girl alive! She's gonna pay for what she did to me tonight!"

Earl took his eyes off the water long enough to glance back at his wife. Her normally curly grey hair hung limply over her ears, with brand-new brown "highlights" showing like dark turds lying in frosty, moonlit grass. She was steering with her right hand, and the fingers of her left hand curled around the wound in her neck.

Earl could see the familiar, bitter gleam of hatred in her eyes. "Well, steer over to the right of the rowboat, and let's see if we can fish her out." He had a sudden image pass through his mind of pulling Hope to safety and tossing Faye in the lake as an exchange. The girl would throw her arms around him and hug him, thanking him for saving her life. He would be a hero. He would be loved.

He shoved that thought away. It wouldn't work that way, he knew. *I'd get a hug, alright. They'd hug me around the neck with a rope.*

Faye gave a little chuckle. Then she laughed out loud.

"What?" Earl asked. "What's so funny?"

"Well," she smiled at him, "this is your fishin' boat, but I bet you never thought I'd get you out here fishin' for people."

Earl had put the rifle aside and was using the spotlight to scan the water around the boat. His left hand was holding pressure on the spot where Hope had stuck him. A small amount of blood was oozing past his fingers. With all the moving around, the wound wouldn't stay closed long enough to clot. He didn't laugh at Faye's joke. He didn't think it was funny. Instead, a chill went down his spine as he recalled a story from Sunday school—a story from his childhood—of Jesus telling his disciples that he would make them "fishers of men." Earl was so far away from the innocence of those days, so far away from the Jesus that his grandmother had seemed to love so much.

"Do you see them, Earl?"

"*Shh*! They're in the water. They'll have to make some noise to stay afloat and not drown."

"Don't you shush me!" Faye shouted at him. "Don't you ever tell me to shut up!"

The old man lowered his head and drooped his shoulders. Glancing back at her again, he said, "Faye, I need to be able to hear them, and I can't do that if you're talking. I'm sorry about the shush, but if we are going to find them, we need to listen."

Faye killed the engine, and they drifted up beside the rowboat. "Fine," she said, needing to get the last word. "But don't you ever shush me again! You understand?"

"Sure. I understand." *I understand that you're a crotchety old bat!* Still scanning the water, Earl motioned for Faye to grab the tie-down line hanging from the tip of the rowboat's bow. "Tie it off on our boat," he whispered, quickly adding, "please. They can't stay down much longer." Then he forced a smile across his mouth. "Okay, honey?"

After tying off the line and without saying another word, Faye sat back down near the engine. She was holding her neck with her left hand, and her eyes darted from one side of the boat to the other. As with Earl, a small amount of blood oozed through her fingers. Despite the throb in her neck, she was determined to join her husband in scanning the water and listening for movement.

A minute passed in silence, then two. The only sound was the return of the cicada chorus from the ancient forest. Ripples in the lake rocked them from side to side, and their metal boat clanged as it bumped up against the rowboat.

"Where could they possibly be?" asked Faye. "No one can hold their breath that long."

"I know," replied Earl. "Maybe their clothes drug them down." He scratched his chin whiskers. After a moment he added, "They're young. They might be able to hold their breath a long time. Let's watch a bit longer to be sure."

Another two minutes went by. Thin clouds drifted overhead, illuminated by the bright moon. Faye shivered.

"Could they have made it over to the island?" the old woman asked.

"I've been checking. There hasn't been anything moving along the shore or in the water near the island." His side was starting to throb like a jackhammer was pounding into his kidney, and he needed to pee. After another thirty seconds, he said, "I must have gotten them, or maybe they just drowned."

"Good riddance, then!" Faye exclaimed. "Let's get back to the shack and do the other one. This has cost us a lot of time, and I'm hurting." She turned to fire up the engine again.

"How do you suppose those other two found her here?" Earl wondered out loud.

"Who cares? They're gone now."

"But if they found her, maybe—"

"They were just brat kids. If the police had been with 'em, we'd be in cuffs, not out here drifting in the lake." She shrugged at him, giving him a look of impatient criticism. "Let's just be done with our work and go home."

'Brat kids'? Earl considered that. He had seen Josh, felt the boy's foot connect with his groin. Josh had been one of the 'kids' without a doubt. But Earl had also seen the other one—the one who had untied the rowboat. Earl had seen him jump into the boat just before he could grab him. That one ... was different. That one was weird. "I dunno, Faye ..."

Faye no longer cared what Earl had to say, and she didn't wait for his okay to go. She was tired. Her neck ached and was seeping blood. She had crap in her hair and caked in the curl of her ears. She needed a cigarette. She was done—well done. Ignoring her husband, she fired up the engine and turned the boat in the direction of the dock. They headed for shore with the rowboat in tow.

Hope may have been a waste of time, but their hunting expedition to the mall in Greenwood had been successful. There was still work to be done this night. A lot of work.

NINE

avin had been the first to hit the water, and he was also the first to reach the surface, followed quickly by Josh and, finally, Hope. When he opened his eyes, he knew at once that they had been successful. The boats were gone. The island, twenty yards ahead, sparkled with thousands upon thousands of twinkling lights.

His ear hurt.

Hope surfaced, expecting to see the motor boat upon them. She was thrashing and trying to swim away. Josh grabbed her arm and pulled her to him, instinctively treading water with his feet and one free arm, just like he had been trained at summer camp the previous year. Hope was disoriented but soon began to calm down. After a moment, Josh was able to release her to tread water on her own.

As the panic subsided in Hope, another emotion emerged: wonder. She jerked her head back and forth, looking around, and her mouth fell wide open. The glow. The sparkle. The colors. "Oh ... oh ..." She could manage no other words. It was as if she had surfaced in a lake surrounded by a Christmas wonderland.

"We must swim to the island," Gavin urged, straightening the soaked baseball cap on his head.

As if in a trance, Hope complied. She and Josh swam side by side, trailing Gavin by only a few feet.

The elf was the first to reach the shore. He shook the water out of his suit of leaves, clambered up a few feet, and sat down to watch his human friends crawl out of the lake. A few moments later they were all sitting together on a sandy shore that was peppered here and there with smooth stones. The lake in front of them was no longer dark. Instead, it had a phosphorescent glow and seemed to vibrate. As the human friends looked closer, they could see that the water contained multitudes of minute lights. It was aglow with plant life.

"It is algae," Gavin explained as if reading their thoughts. "As with all else, it shares the energy of life."

"Gavin, where am I?" asked Hope. "Am I dead? And why are you green?" She was a smart girl, good at math and science, but with all of the stress of the last few hours, this surprise was nearly too much. "Is this heaven?"

A sympathetic smile brightened the elf's face with a grin that reached nearly from pointy ear to pointy ear. He reached over, and with his long fingers, he gently pushed her wet hair out of her face.

"No, my sweet girl. You are not dead. You are quite safe and very much alive. It is my aura of life that you see in the green glow of my skin, but dear one, the aura of your life force is the brightest light of them all. The purity of your inner self would challenge the sun for dominion."

Josh could see that it was true. He stared at her face—at the bright-white glow that emanated from her skin and the sparkles that glittered in her hair. He knew at that moment that his friend was special. He had heard the word "soul" before. He wasn't exactly sure what it meant, but he thought he might be seeing one in the aura around Hope's face.

"But … I … um … I don't understand," Hope said. Her hands were trembling.

Gavin looked at her as he contemplated how to explain the reality of what must be an overwhelming experience for someone who had not been prepared beforehand. Over Hope's shoulder, he could see that Josh was mesmerized by the girl's wondrous life force.

"You are in the same place. This is simply a different layer of reality. You see, our world is both physical and spiritual. All that you have ever known is the one physical layer in which you reside. That one layer is dominated by animal life and devoid of much of the spiritual realm. We are in another layer; one that is dominated by plant life. This layer also connects to a realm of the spiritual that you do not see in your dimension. It overlaps and intertwines to an extent that you have never experienced."

Hope placed her elbows on her knees with her chin in her hands. Her sneakers were sinking in sparkling sand. She didn't really understand, but as young people are so good at doing, she accepted the explanation. "So there aren't any animals here?" she asked.

"There are some," the elf answered. "Mostly those of my kind but some others too. Special ones."

"Gavin, your ear!" Josh exclaimed. "The tip of your ear is gone!"

Gavin's hand flashed to his left ear and felt the spot where one of Earl Hicks' bullets had removed some elfin flesh. A look of embarrassment enveloped his face. His aura changed to a pulsating red, and he turned away from his new friends.

"Are you okay?" asked Josh. "Is it bad?"

"I will live," said Gavin. "But I am humiliated." The elf's eyes welled up with tears.

"But why?" asked Hope. "You just rescued us. Why would your injury embarrass you?"

"It is not my injury in itself that embarrasses me. It is the loss of the tip of my ear that brings my humiliation. Elves are simple creatures. We take pride in very few things. Our ears are one of those, and now I have lost a part of one of them. My folk will stare and murmur. The young ones will point and laugh."

"Is it dangerous for you?" "Can it grow back?" "Will you get sick?" "Why would your people stare and talk?" The questions were popping out of both Josh and Hope's mouths at the same time.

"I will be fine. It will hurt for a time, as any injury will, but it will heal. I will, however, never have my same beautiful set of ears again. My ears were considered most beautiful among my kind, and now they are marred, deformed, scarred ..." A single tear escaped an oversized eye and dripped off his round cheek.

Josh chuckled. Gavin flushed again and turned away, so Hope pushed Josh over into the glowing loam and put her arms around her new friend.

"Wha'd I do?" Josh protested. The elf was just too funny, sitting there in the wet sand, wearing a Reds hat, holding his sore ear, and glowing the same color as the ball cap. "I didn't mean nothin' by it. I'm sorry. I couldn't help it."

"Gavin, you can be proud of your wounded ear. You gained that mark by saving my life. I will always be grateful, and I love you for what you have done."

"Yeah," added Josh, trying to make up for his rudeness. "In our world, scars are a mark of pride for guys. It shows we've done cool stuff."

Gavin's shoulders straightened, and after a moment, his aura settled back into its normal dull-greenish color. "That is correct," he said. "I have done a gallant thing. It has been many, many years since another elf has done as much." His big grin returned, and a sparkle glittered in his eye. "Others will envy my ear! Thank you, sweet Hope. You have given me new perspective."

All at once, Gavin grabbed Hope by each of her ears and planted a big elfin kiss on her forehead. It left the afterglow of his green aura, which was quickly overwhelmed by her own bright glow.

"Now, we need to get off of this island!" Gavin shouted. He jumped to his feet, sinking Josh's shoes, which Gavin still wore, deep into the sand. "We have another rescue to perform!"

* * *

Rick brought the ATV to a stop at yet another fork in the rutted road in the woods. It had been a bumpy ride as the trek had taken them through creek beds, around rock outcroppings, and over ridges. His back was aching a bit, and his legs were stiff, but he thought they had to be getting close.

"We're close, Mr. Anders," Danny confirmed. "It's just over that ridge there." Danny leaned into Rick's shoulder and pointed to their left, where two wheel ruts crested a large hill that sloped at an easy angle and rose about a hundred feet.

Rick flicked off the headlamps and killed the engine. At once, they were enveloped by the darkness of the ancient forest. Somewhere up in the trees, an owl hooted. A cacophony of cicadas on the other side of the ridge was singing its late-summer song, only to be answered by another swarm clinging to the limbs of other trees nearby. Slivers of moonlight slipped between the fluttering leaves and struck the underbrush around them.

"Why'd you shut it off? Aren't we gonna go get 'em?"

"*Whooo?*" the owl in the tree above seemed to ask.

"We are, Danny," Rick replied. "But we've got to go in quiet. I don't want to spook them before we get there. I only hope we didn't alert them already."

As he explained his thinking to the boy, he suddenly went still, and his head cocked to one side like a dog who had just heard a rabbit in the brush.

"Are we gonna—" Danny started to ask.

"*Shh!*" Rick demanded. He lifted a finger to his mouth to emphasize his instruction. The cicadas fell quiet, as if in response.

"What?" Danny whispered. "What is it?"

"Listen. Do you hear it? From over there." Rick pointed to where the road crested the nearby ridge. The sound was a low, mechanical buzzing—like a gas-powered hive of honeybees.

"Yeah," Danny answered. "What is it?"

"A small engine. Maybe a boat. Maybe a generator."

"There is a lake over there. I saw it earlier."

"Come on! Let's get to the top of that hill." As Rick said this, the noise of the engine ceased, and the woods were again very quiet until the cicadas resumed their nocturnal praises.

* * *

The wounded old criminals didn't bother putting the motorboat back inside the metal shed. Instead, they simply docked it at the same open pier where the escaping trio had commandeered the rowboat. They needed to clean and bandage themselves and then get busy with the work at hand. They were hurt, which would slow them down, and they had lost time chasing those kids around the lake. Time was quickly slipping by, and they weren't as young as they used to be. Weariness was creeping into their joints.

As they approached their makeshift butcher shop, Faye asked Earl if he was going to put the rifle back in the Ford.

"Nope. Keepin' it with me." The old woman was just ahead of him, and he was suddenly struck with a vision of a bullet passing through her skull. He shivered. He wasn't sure if it was from the violent thought or the chill in the air. "It's starting to get nippy out here."

"Why?"

"I dunno. Probably a front coming in."

"No, you idiot," Faye growled. "Why are you keeping the rifle with you?"

"I'm just uneasy 'bout things now. I feel better with it handy, is all." Again, almost like watching a movie, the image of a shot to his wife's head popped into his mind. It was like he was standing aside and watching himself do it. Goosebumps formed on his arms, and he felt a cool wind on his neck. *Interesting idea.*

Faye said, "Okay," then pulled open the door to their workshop and stepped inside. The smell emanating from the room where Hope had been locked up struck Faye in the face like the back of her mother's hand. She grabbed her nose with both hands and gagged.

"Oh, that is rank! Earl, you've got to clean that up before we can do anything else. It's rotten." She choked the words out between her clenched fingers.

"You clean it yourself," Earl said defiantly. "You caused the mess." *Where'd that come from?* The old man chuckled inside. *Felt good, though.*

"What did you say?" Faye turned to face her suddenly bossy husband with a fierce look in her eyes that could have made a rattlesnake think twice before striking. This was the part of Faye that she reserved for her husband. To everyone else, she was sweet. Kindly. Helpful. A volunteer at church. A pillar of the Cutters Notch community. But when they were alone, she morphed into something else. Something strange and dark.

"I said, 'You clean it yourself.' After all, I told you to watch out, but you got over-confident, and that girl got the jump on you. So, you clean it up yourself." He was unexpectedly feeling sort of gutsy, pushing limits that he'd avoided for many years—decades. *Maybe I should've started carrying a gun a long time ago.*

Faye was dumbfounded for a moment. She had never before had her husband stand up to her like that—at least, not for a very long time. Sure, he had been a foreman out here at the mine and had been the boss to the men who had worked here, but she had always run the roost at home. This sudden assertiveness was disconcerting and made her feel a little uneasy. It set her back on the defensive for a bit—but only for a moment. After all, she was in control. She was going to get what she wanted, and no old man was going to stand there and give her orders. She had watched her mother cower before her father, and she swore to herself that she would never do that—not before her domineering father and not before this squeaky mouse of a husband who sometimes shared her bed.

"Earl," she said as a smile crept across her face, "are you trying to grow some manhood in your old age?" She walked past the desk to retrieve her cigarettes and lighter from the workbench. As she slid a long, white smoke from the pack, she added, "I know where you sleep. Do you remember that?" She casually lifted the cigarette to her lips and lit up. "You do need to sleep sooner or later, you know." She took a deep drag and blew out the smoke. "Now, you can clean that stinkin' mess up and sleep easy, or you can make *me* clean it up and wonder each time you go to bed if I'm going to stick a hot fireplace poker up your rear end. Your choice, sweetie." She took another puff and let the smoke slip out between her toothy grin.

When she had finished speaking, she leaned back against the old workbench, let the smile fade, and waited. Her eyes were boring into his, and she knew the effect her eyes could have. She also knew that he'd cave—but wondered how quickly. She didn't think it would take too long. He was weak. Putty in her hands. That was why she had picked him so many years ago.

Faye's eyes revived a memory into the old man's mind. Earl thought about a time forty years ago—the first time he had stood up to his wife. The only other time. They had been newly married, and she had changed. Before the wedding, she was sweet and seemed so innocent, but after the vows, her true nature emerged like a she-bear out of hibernation.

He had put in a twelve-hour shift at the mine and was dog-tired. There had been broken machines and lost production. A man had shown up drunk and had to be fired. Earl was stressed out and came home, dragging himself in well after dark. Faye was sitting in her easy chair watching some TV show—which one, he didn't recall. There had been no dinner for him. Instead, she had demanded that he go back out and drive into town to get her some wine at the store. He said, "No." He was exhausted, he explained. Too tired. She demanded the wine anyway. *The eyes! Oh, the eyes!* He declined despite how she looked at him. Finally, he made himself a sandwich before crawling into bed. A couple of hours later, he awoke as she poured a pot of hot water on his crotch. *She was laughing. She was laughing as I screamed ...*

"Oh, alright," he said now with a bit of a pout. "I'll do it. Just be more careful next time." He leaned the rifle against the desk and pulled the mop bucket from a corner. He felt another cold wind on his neck and glanced at the door. It was closed.

"That's better. I'll check in on the other one to see how she's coming along. She was pretty weak when we got here, but I'm not taking anything for granted."

"I'd guess not," Earl said with a hint of sarcasm. He poured some cleaner in the bucket, glanced at his gun, and imagined a small hole in his wife's forehead.

"Shut up and get to work," Faye ordered.

TEN

avin trotted away from the small beach toward the center of the island, pushing aside small trees and brush as he went. The two friends followed close behind, the thorns grabbing at their clothes and scratching the skin on their hands and necks. Their wet clothes hung heavy on their arms and legs. The aura of the foliage lit their way as they reached an open area at what they sensed must be near the middle of the tiny islet. The moon had shifted farther across the sky.

"How are we gonna get off this island? Swim?" asked Josh.

Hope groaned. "I don't think I can swim that far right now."

Gavin chuckled. "Swim? Joshua, you are full of humor."

"Well, how then?" he asked again. "Do you have a boat somewhere?"

Gavin laughed out loud this time. He pulled the old baseball cap off and let his laughter float up into the bright moonlight. Spreading his arms out wide, he spun in slow circles, letting the moon bathe his face in the cool light of night.

"How would I get a boat here? Do you think I could pull one through a large mirror somewhere?"

"Oh. I see what you mean." Josh began to laugh too.

"Not that something such as that has not been done before. I have seen it in my many years. But, sadly for us, it was not anywhere near this island."

Gavin pulled a small device from inside his baseball cap. Putting it to his lips, he blew into it. Even though the other two couldn't hear anything, the elf blew it like it was a whistle. He took another deep breath and blew again. Each time, there was one long blow followed by three very short bursts. When he had finished the second series, he replaced it in his hat and slapped the cap back on his head, pulling it down so that his ears poked up along the sides.

"What was that, Gavin?" Hope wondered aloud. "A dog whistle? I couldn't hear it."

"A dog whistle?" The elf chuckled again. "No, not a whistle for dogs. But it is similar in that it makes sounds outside of your hearing range. It is a special whistle that I can use to summon some friends to help us."

"More elves?" Josh asked.

"No. These are different friends." Gavin once more removed the cap and blew into the whistle. This time there was just one very long blow. "You will see very soon. It will not take long for them to arrive."

"How do you know they heard you?" Hope asked.

"They just replied, and I acknowledged. They will be here in the twinkle of an eye."

When he had finished speaking, he sat down on a rock and motioned for Hope and Josh to join him by patting the stone on either side of him. Once they had found their seats, he began to turn his head, scanning the sky from the northwest to the northeast, as if looking for geese flying south for the winter. Even though they had no idea what they were looking for, the kids joined in the search.

"Gavin, how old are you?" Josh asked. *I bet he's at least as old as my dad.*

"I am still quite young. I am only 256 years old."

Josh was shocked, and his open mouth betrayed the fact. Hope just smiled. She was staring at Gavin and taking it all in, as if she were simply learning about geography or world history.

"And Gronek and Smakal?" asked Josh as he got a grip and re-found his tongue. "How old are they? Are they related to you?"

"They are my brothers." Gavin was fingering the broken tip of his ear. He winced as he spoke. "Gronek is 242. Smakal is the youngest at a mere 197. He only gained his apron 47 years ago."

Hope had been sitting quietly, but now her curiosity began to take the reins.

"What does it mean to 'gain an apron'?" she asked.

Gavin chuckled again. "That is when an elf finally becomes fully separated from his mother. She gives him her apron and expels him into the world to make his own way."

"So there are more of you?" Hope asked. "I mean, more than just the three of you?" She now completely shared Josh's curiosity.

Josh was quiet again, studying Hope's glowing eyes as she spoke. The excitement provided by the boat chase and the dive into the lake had begun to wear off and was being replaced by the raging hormones of a twelve-year-old boy. He was struggling to focus on what was being said, but his yearning for Hope was winning the battle for the control of his mind. *Love. I love her. I think I really do.*

"We are many but not nearly as many as your kind," the elf explained. We mostly stay in the forests, but we have some who have made homes near your cities." He continued to scan the northern horizon. "I do not understand why they would want to live in such places. They miss so much of the aura of life. All of your buildings leave our world desolate, very much like a desert."

"You told Danny and me that you and Gronek and Smakal are what we call elves," Josh said as he rejoined the conversation. It took a great effort for him to drag his mind away from Hope's mesmerizing glow. "Do you know of our stories? We have books and even movies about elves."

"Absolutely." The elf straightened up into a more proud posture. "Most of them are based in truth; although your Tolkien made us much more valiant than we have ever truly been. We are by nature very timid creatures."

"You have read *The Lord of the Rings*?" Josh asked.

"I have my own copy. It was given to me by my friend, the great man himself."

At this, Josh was astonished. He was not an avid reader, and the only books that he had read were *The Hobbit* and *The Lord of the Rings*. They had completely captured his imagination the previous winter. He even had a poster on his wall and some action figures in his closet.

"You met J.R.R. Tolkien?" he asked.

"I did." Gavin gave Josh a pleasant, wistful look. "I spent one very warm summer sharing stories with both Mr. Tolkien and his friend Mr. Lewis. I shall always cherish the memories. We would walk together in Mr. Tolkien's garden in the cool of the evening, talking and sharing stories. That was the last time I spent time with those from your realm—until tonight."

"Do you mean C. S. Lewis?" Hope followed up.

"That is the name he placed on the book he gave me."

"Was it *The Chronicles of Narnia*? Do you have that too?" She was amazed. "Given to you by C. S. Lewis himself?"

"I have those and others, as well. *Mere Christianity* is my favorite. Both of those humans brought a great deal of enjoyment to me. I miss them dearly." Gavin's joyful face turned melancholy. A tear produced a light-green sparkle on his cheek as it trickled down to his chin. "I journeyed across the great sea to visit their remains and to pay my respects to my beloved friends, when each of them passed on to their reward."

Before Hope or Josh could ask any more questions, Gavin pointed to the sky to the north of them. "Our assistance has arrived," he announced.

There on the horizon, just above the glow of the trees, were three figures approaching very quickly. They made no sound, but each glowed brilliantly against the night sky with an aura to challenge the stars in brightness. As they neared, Josh and Hope could see flailing legs and what looked to be ragged horns jutting into the bright sky.

Gavin urged them back to the edge of the clearing, nudging them to get the mesmerized young humans to move. Just as they managed to get out of the way, the creatures swooped down and landed near where the three of them had just been standing. Bursts of mist shot from their nostrils. They were a fearsome and joyous sight to behold.

"Oh my!" said Hope. An excitement that she had not known for several years welled up inside; a shiver shook her from toes to fingertips. She had to sit down, placing her hands to her cheeks.

"Whaaaa ...?" Josh tried to form a question. "Um. I mean ..." The words would not come.

"Do not be so surprised, my young friends," said Gavin. "I know you have heard of flying reindeer." His elfin smile had returned.

* * *

It took several minutes of steep climbing, but Danny and Rick reached the summit of the hill. They followed the wheel ruts in the trail, hugging the edge and skimming the forest, so that they could dash into the brush if the need arose. But there had been no need, and all was now silent in the woods. Even the previously incessant cicadas had ceased their song.

As they crested the hill, Rick used his left hand to restrain Danny from going any farther and carefully concealed himself and the boy behind some large slabs of stone. The huge rectangular boulders marked each side of the trail like medieval gates or monolithic teeth. They appeared ready to slide shut at a moment's notice, blocking any chance of escape.

Edging his way around the corner of a limestone slab, Rick peered down into what was obviously an old quarry. The moon, acting as a glowing bulb, hung in the cosmic ceiling, reflected its rays off the lake and illuminated the whole scene. Here and there were more large rectangular slabs of limestone piled in haphazard stacks—some neatly arranged, some in broken heaps. Interspersed among the slabs were rusty, dilapidated pieces of equipment, many of which were unrecognizable after years of neglect. Rick could see the remnants of an old conveyor with a broken rubber belt flapping in the wind. Below it sat an ancient fork truck with its wheels sunk into the soil.

Rick's eyes followed the cut of the trail to the edge of the lake where he saw the Hicks' vehicle parked near a building that had probably once been the mine office. It was constructed of limestone blocks covered with a sloped roof. Behind the building stood the largest oak tree he had ever seen. Towering above all the other trees, the great oak's branches spread out in every direction like protective arms, overhanging the building, the SUV parked next to it, and many more stacked slabs of limestone.

Rick was carefully scanning the clearing, trying to get his bearings and look for potential threats, when he spied two figures ambling up away from the lake. The taller one was in the rear and carried a rifle. The smaller one was leading the way and looked to be holding one hand on its neck. The two figures walked past the parked SUV to the far side of the building, disappearing from view. Rick figured they had gone inside, but he couldn't be sure from that angle.

Motioning for Danny to follow, he slipped across the trail and followed the crest of the ridge, trying to get a better view. The brush was thick, and the going was difficult. Stickers were snagging on their legs and arms. Finally, unable to penetrate the foliage to gain a better look, he surrendered to the painful natural forest fencing and retreated to the path.

"Danny, I'm going to make my way down there to get a better view." Rick was brushing broken stickers from his sleeves and pulling cockleburs from his pant legs. "If I can get the jump on 'em, I'll go in. If not, I'll try to find out where Hope is and keep an eye on her until backup arrives."

"She was in that building right there. The one they just went in." Danny was pointing with his right hand and pulling a thorn out of his neck with his left. "When I was here earlier, she was in a room right under that big limb on the giant tree. You see it? It's so big you can actually stand on it."

"I think I see a window," Rick said. "I'll check it out."

"It looks kinda high up on the wall. You can hold me up, and I'll tell you what I see."

"That's not gonna happen, Danny." There was an immovable quality to Rick's voice this time, a quality that told the boy that he had gone as far as he would be going. A few hours ago, he would have been relieved, but now … Well, now he was different. On this particular night, Danny Flannery, the frightened and timid boy, had begun his transition into becoming a man.

"I know I'm a little heavy, but—" He had to try.

"You're not going down there," said Rick. He looked the boy in the eyes. He could see determination there. Courage. The trooper had newfound respect for the kid. He seemed different than he had earlier.

Still, he was just a boy, and Rick couldn't take him any farther into this dangerous situation.

"But—"

"There's no 'but' about it, son." Rick put his hands on the boy's shoulders. "I heard the shots earlier. You did too. And I just saw one of 'em carrying a rifle. You're not going down there. You're going to stay right here, and you're gonna watch for Sheriff Dunlap. You can help me out by filling him in when he gets here."

At that, Rick seemed to remember that he had a radio. He pulled it from his waist and fingered the mic.

"J.B.," he said in a voice just above a whisper. No response. "Sheriff Dunlap," he tried again with a touch more volume. The only response was the rattle of static. *Maybe the battery is weak*, he thought. Checking the radio, he could see that the indicator light claimed to be at nearly full power. He tried one more time. "Sheriff. Sheriff Dunlap." *Maybe it's his battery that died.*

Rick turned back and looked at the once-frightened boy, who seemed to have added years of maturity in just the last few hours. Eyes that once were unsure and unsteady now glared with determination. Rick would have to trust him.

"I can't reach the sheriff." Rick clipped the radio back on his belt. "So I'm going to have to rely on you to tell him where I've gone and what we saw. Okay?"

"No problem," the boy replied. "I'll watch for him and tell him which way you went."

"I'm telling you, Danny: Don't come down after me." Rick looked straight into Danny's eyes again, but this time he glared—hard. "I can't work on rescuing Hope if I'm worried about you. Do you understand?

"Yessir."

Rick could see sincerity in the boy's face as he responded.

"Is Josh down there too?" Rick asked.

"I guess so, but I don't know where. We were down there together, and I ran for help. He's probably around there somewhere. Maybe in that big tree."

"Okay. I'll look for him, but don't make me worry about you too. Okay?"

"Okay."

He patted Danny on the head. He liked this kid. Danny made Rick think of his own boy. Danny was older, of course, but he brought Rick's son to mind anyway.

Along with the thought of his son came a wave of sadness, yearning, and maybe a touch of self-doubt. *When this is over, I'm going to go find him. I'm gonna find him, and I'm gonna hug him. And hold him. Hold him for hours, maybe days.*

He patted the boy again. He was patting Danny but seeing his own son's face. After a moment, he gave Danny's shoulder one more squeeze and started working his way down the hill.

* * *

The henpecked Earl Hicks watched as his wife headed off toward the other girl, unbuttoning her soiled green blouse as she walked. Again, he considered the rifle leaning against the desk. He saw himself lift the gun. It was as if he were looking over his own shoulder. He could see the stock against his own arm and see his head lean to one side to line up the sights. His imagination heard the loud -*pop!*- and saw Faye's head explode in a bloody mess against the far wall.

I could. I could do it! The idea excited him, but instead of taking action, he shook his head to clear out the—*interesting*—images and then filled the bucket with water. The vision of his wife's head exploding continued to flash in front of his eyes as he soaked the mop in the bucket and rolled it into the nasty, noxious room.

A few minutes later, he had finished his chore and was sitting on the ancient sofa, picking at some loose stuffing, when his wife reentered the room with their next year's food supply in tow. Faye had taken some time to clean herself up in the bathroom sink before retrieving their prey from a room on the other side of the building—a room that had once been his office. She was no longer wearing the soiled top she'd had on. Now her torso was only covered by her plain white bra. Her pale, loose skin made her look even older than he remembered. She looked weak, shriveled. But looks could be deceiving.

She had bandaged the small wound in her neck. A nasty bruise had formed, turning the entire area deep blue and bright purple. Wet hair was lying straight down the sides of her face from where she had washed out the neighbor girl's diarrhea.

Looking at his ancient, vicious wife, there was a part of him that was impressed with what that girl—*her name is Hope*—had done. Considering how disoriented and weak she had to have been, she had shown remarkable ingenuity and resilience. He felt a pang of remorse. *If only I'd been stronger. If only I'd been able to tell that woman "no."* But, regardless, what was done was done. There had been no turning back from the moment they had snatched her off that bridge ...

While he had been waiting on the couch, he'd inspected the wound in his own side. It was a nasty cut. The girl had sliced clean into the muscle but had missed anything critical, and it had already stopped bleeding freely. He had covered it with a clean handkerchief that he kept in his pocket and then taped it down with some duct tape, but each time he moved around, it would break the scab and more blood would flow. The handkerchief was turning red from a small amount of blood that was oozing out, and it stung like a hornet.

Earl stood as his wife entered. He grabbed his side in a vain attempt to stem the sharp sting, and his groin throbbed from the shots it had taken earlier. The pain seemed to resonate throughout his aging body. *I'm gonna hurt for a month.*

"She's out of it," Faye advised. "She won't be any trouble."

"Let's get her up on the desk and get this done with, then."

"Come over here and grab her other arm. Help me get her turned."

"You know, Faye, I was thinking." He couldn't tell her what he'd really been thinking. *Or maybe I could tell her. I wonder what she would think if I told her that I was daydreaming of blowing her brains out all over the wall?*

"Thinkin' 'bout what?" She drew out the "what" in a sort of sneer, like she didn't think he even could think. Like she thought he was an imbecile. *Maybe—instead of slicing up this little girl—maybe I'll lock her back in the room and tie Faye down on the table. Take the fillet knife to her scrawny little throat.* Again, a chilly breeze seemed to caress the back of his neck, and he shivered.

"Well, if those three kids out on the lake are all dead," he said, "then maybe we can fish them out in the morning. Maybe we could just drag them in here, and we'd get two bonus prizes." That was the last thing he really wanted to do. He was simply too tired, and the truth was, he was finally losing his desire for human flesh. It was too much work, and somewhere packed down deep in his subconscious, there was a seed of guilt. He thought, however, that maybe the idea would coddle the old woman into forgetting about his earlier poorly chosen words. Maybe she would let it go, and he could sleep in the relative safety that had been his life for the last forty years. *Maybe.*

"You're just stupid," she replied. "Where would we put 'em? Two is all our freezer'll hold. Besides, I'm just about wore out already. No, if we find 'em, we'll just weigh 'em all down in some garbage bags and sink 'em in the lake. One will have to do this year."

"You sure?"

"Yeah, I'm sure. We just need to get rid of 'em." Then she smiled at him. It was almost warm. Almost loving. Almost affectionate. Almost. Still it was enough to give Earl Hicks the relief he needed. She had moved on.

As they spoke, they turned the girl around and laid her on her back on the desk. She had short brown hair. The mascara she wore was smeared all over her face. Her skin was blotchy, pale. She had on a T-shirt that was a couple of sizes too small, and it was bunched up just below her chest. A silver bar pierced her navel. The word "Faith" was tattooed across her tummy. She'd been wearing jeans when they'd snatched her, but those were gone now. She had apparently discarded them when the Hicks' special concoction had worked its wonders on her bowels. The buttons likely had been too much trouble to mess with as the cramps hit her.

Earl smiled at her and laid a small towel over the lower half of her body to add to what little coverage her undergarments provided. *As bad as I am, I'm not a pervert.* A single tear seeped from the corner of one of the girl's eyes, and he gently wiped it away with the back of one of his calloused fingers. Her skin was soft and smooth; her lips were full. It reminded him of the way Faye had looked when they were still only dating: young but maybe a little wild; untainted by the effects of time but with some innocence already forfeited to the desires of youth.

As he stared down into the frightened, youthful eyes, the image in his mind changed. Suddenly, the girl's face was gone. It was replaced by Faye's wrinkled cheeks and plucked eyebrows. And her eyes. Those vivid, evil eyes were staring up at him. Not in fear but in rage. Her scrawny lips parted, and two rows of jagged teeth emerged through an enormous, wicked smile. Again, he was looking over his own shoulder. He watched as his right hand used the thin, sharp knife to slice through the tendons in her neck. Blood spurted sideways in both directions as that wicked smile left her face and the light finally went out of those eyes.

The girl moaned, bringing him back to reality. He blinked. His eyes were moist. *Tears.* Whether they were tears of disappointment, joy, or guilt, he was not sure. Regardless, the image of his wife's dying eyes faded off into the netherworld of lost dreams. He shook his head to discard the remaining tendrils of the vision and then looked again at the young girl lying on her back across the ancient oak desk.

"It'll soon be over, my dear," he said with a touch of comfort in his tone. "We won't prolong it now." As he said that, he started tying the girl's arms down on each side while Faye did the same with her feet.

"Why are you even talking to the little wretch?" asked his wife.

Why not? he wondered.

ELEVEN

"Are you freaking serious?" Josh exclaimed. "Flying reindeer! Oh my gosh." The boy was so beside himself with excitement that he nearly forgot about their predicament.

Hope was dumbstruck.

The eyes of the reindeer were bright, glowing orbs surrounded by thick brown fur. Antlers rose high above their heads and curled around on each side. They had white fur under their chins and down their necks that reminded Josh of long white beards. Encircling them was a glowing aura that gave the beasts the appearance of standing inside a bright bubble of light.

"Come, my young friends," Gavin said as he motioned them forward. "They are here to give us a ride off this island." Then the elf trotted over to one of the majestic creatures and spoke quietly into its ear while calmly stroking its flank. When finished, he turned and motioned Josh and Hope forward. "Do not be shy. They are quite friendly."

As they approached, all three reindeer turned as one to look at the boy and girl. They snorted, and mist again blew from their nostrils. The one in front bent its forelegs, lowering itself to allow Hope to climb aboard. With Gavin providing some support, she lifted her right leg and straddled the great animal, wrapping her arms around its thick neck.

The animal was warm against the chill of her still-damp clothing, and the texture of its fur was soft and comfortable. The girl stroked her mount's neck and snuggled up close. Somehow, it made her feel safe.

After assisting Hope, Gavin turned to help Josh, but the boy had already mounted one of the other reindeer on his own. So the elf turned to the third reindeer and smiled. "It is so good to see you again, my old friend." The deer nodded and snorted loudly. "Thank you for coming to our rescue. Please take us across to the far shore." Jumping atop the majestic animal, Gavin pointed toward the great old oak that towered above all the other trees. "Take us there," he said.

"Gavin," Hope said as she snuggled against the neck of her ride, "of course we've heard of flying reindeer, but this is really wild. Are you sure I'm not dreaming?"

"As I told you," he answered kindly, "most legends are based on some reality."

"But seriously, Gavin," Josh said. "Flying reindeer? I've got to know—how do they fly?"

"This realm is deeply affected by the spiritual realm it adjoins. The reindeer are high-spirited animals with auras that are, as you can see, brilliant. It is their spiritual nature that permits them to fly within this dimension." Gavin looked at Hope's incredible aura and wondered about what gifts her aura might provide her in his dimension. *Perhaps one day I will find out but not this night.* "Now, we must act. Time is getting short."

"But—" Josh started and then hesitated for just a moment. His hands were holding a leather strap strung with jingle bells. "Does this mean ... I mean ... um ... is there really a ... is *he* real too?"

Gavin gave a sly sideways smile. "Let's go! We have another to rescue."

The three reindeer each took three great strides, and suddenly, they were flying. The great beasts rose high above the water, and the two young friends were again awestruck by the aura of light that emanated from the forest all around. There was a general glow, but inside there were hundreds of millions of smaller, sometimes twinkling, multicolored sparkles of light. As they rose higher, they could see the glow stretch out in every direction, broken occasionally by what must have been the small human towns where most of the trees had been removed in lieu of houses, stores, and factories.

With each breath, the flying reindeer snorted out plumes of mist that drifted back past the three passengers. Once airborne, their flight seemed almost effortless, with only a soft undulation as their legs moved back and forth. It was as if they were simply running somehow on the air itself.

Quickly, the view reached its crescendo, and they began to descend. The ride had been short but spectacular. The trio landed above the shore near the ancient oak, and soon the friends were on the ground. Gavin gave each animal a quick pat on its hindquarters. The creature on which he had ridden nuzzled him with its massive snout. Before anything more could be said, the reindeer were again in flight, heading back into the northern sky.

"Gavin?" Josh looked at the elf with the question still in his eyes. He had to know. *I'm standing here with an elf, and I just flew on a reindeer. He must be real. Is there a Santa Claus?*

Hope stepped over and took Josh's hand, and all thought of reindeer and Christmas legends evaporated. His questions disappeared and were instead replaced by the warm rush of blood as it surged into his flushed face. *She's holding my hand.* An uncontrollable smile filled his face.

"Quick!" the elf interrupted. "I sense that there is not much time."

Gavin embraced their waists, and before they could react, they were airborne again. Carried in the arms of a leaping elf, they landed on the oak's great limb. Josh had been there before and now quickly grabbed ahold of a branch, but Hope was unprepared. She stumbled, unsteady, but Gavin held her tight until she had her balance.

"Why'd we jump up here?" she asked. "Jeez!" She had a startled look on her face, but it was mixed with something else—a bit of a smile, born of a love for adventure.

"Hope, look!" Josh pointed at the shimmering square of light floating in midair just below them.

"What's that?" She shifted for a better view and scraped some flecks of tree bark loose. They drifted down onto the forest floor below. Josh and Gavin helped her move out over the shimmer so that she could see more clearly.

"That's the doorway into our world," Josh answered, as if he were suddenly an expert on this whole business of interdimensional travel. "It is how the elves go back and forth."

"Where are the buildings?" She recognized the lake, and she remembered the great oak towering in the moonlight. "If this is the same place, how come we don't see the dock, or the metal shack, or that building I was in?"

"It is all there, dear Hope," Gavin explained. "But it is all manmade. Materials that have been fully changed and manipulated out of their natural form are only present in your dimension. Here, we merely see the impact they have made on the natural world. Indentations. Imprints. Places where plant life cannot abide. See below? There is the depression in the earth where the building where you were held still stands in your realm." The elf pointed with one long, slender finger to the ground below.

Hope looked down and saw a large rectangular hole below where the shimmer hung in the air. The hole wasn't very deep, but no leaves gathered there. No broken limbs had fallen inside. It was purely bare earth.

"Okay. But where'd that shimmering thingy come from?"

Josh, eager to make an impression, answered for the elf, "On this side, it's a shimmering light, but on our side, it's a mirror. Over here, it's kind of like a window." He was so excited to be able to sound smart. "Go on. Look through it."

As she looked again, Hope focused on peering through the light, and when she did, she gasped. She remembered now. When she had been held in the room, through the fog of the drugs, she had looked up and spotted a mirror on the ceiling. She was now looking through that mirror from the other side. "This is crazy. I know I keep saying this, but are you guys sure I'm not just caught up in some weird dream?" She couldn't shake the surreal feelings that were swimming in her mind.

There was the chair that she had broken and the privacy screen hiding the potty chair. She could see the little lamp in the corner and the puddled mess on the floor where she had thrown the contents of her waste bucket on Faye Hicks. Soaking in the middle was the piece of wood she had jabbed into the old woman's throat.

"Did you guys see me down there? Were you watching me?"

"Yes," they answered in stereo.

"And you were awesome," Josh added. "I couldn't believe it when you stuck that thing in her neck."

"Jeez," Hope said. She was then quiet for a minute, staring into the room where she had been drugged and duct-taped to the chair. It was only a little while ago, but now, from this vantage point in a whole different dimension, it seemed like ages ago. A lifetime ago. Or maybe a different life altogether.

She was still staring through the shimmer into the room below—that cage with the wooden chair—when she spotted movement. "Look! There's Earl Hicks," she said as she pointed. "What's he doing?"

As they watched, Earl rolled a bucket into the room. It had a mop handle sticking out of the vessel, and he was using it as a steering rod to guide the wheeled bucket along. With his left hand, he held on to a spot on his side.

"I stuck him in the side with one of his knives," Hope explained. "Must be hurtin' pretty bad."

"You shoulda stuck it in his neck," said Josh. "Like you did ole' Faye."

"I would have, but I was in a hurry to get out," the girl explained. "He was in front of the door." Hope glanced at Josh and smiled. "But I did put a good kick in his nuts too."

Josh laughed out loud. "Me too." He placed a hand on Hope's back, and another rush of blood hit his brain. It forced his lips into another uncontrollable smile.

When the old man got inside the room, he stopped for a moment and covered his mouth with his free hand. Then he pulled his hand away and gagged. Bending over, he retched, but nothing flowed, a dry heave.

"Must stink pretty bad, huh?" said Hope.

"I hope the dude falls down and wallows in it," said Josh.

Unaware that he was being watched, Hope's former captor pulled his shirt up over his nose. He then pulled a bottle of some kind of cleaner out of a pocket on the side of the large yellow bucket and poured it on the messy floor. Finally, he pulled the mop from the bucket and began to soak up the waste. His shirt slipped off his nose, but he ignored it and kept mopping.

A dark shape drifted into their line of sight, hesitated near Earl's ear, then fluttered through the door and out of their field of vision.

"Danger still lurks," said Gavin.

"What was that?" asked Hope, glancing quickly at Josh and then at Gavin. "Some kind of ghost or something?"

"Something like that," said Josh. This time, he was in no hurry to explain. It was best if she didn't know. "Nothin' I can't handle." Outside, he kept up the façade of courage, but inside, he remembered Gavin's warnings, and a thread of fear began to work into the fabric of his mind.

The trio in the tree watched until Earl completed the chore and left the room. Down below, some leaves rustled, and a twig snapped. "It is likely just a raccoon," said the elf. "Or perhaps a skunk." After the old criminal had been gone for a couple of minutes, they were confident that he was finished with the nasty job.

"What do we do now?" asked Hope. "We need to help the other girl. But how?"

"I dunno," said Josh. "I guess we need to go back in there and see if we can rescue her."

"That does seem to be the task before you," said Gavin. "But it is not without much risk to you." The elf rubbed his scruffy, slightly green chin.

"How do we get in?" the girl wondered aloud.

"You can go through the shimmer," Gavin explained. "But I do not think it wise for you to do so." This time he fidgeted with his wounded ear.

"Gavin, you sound like you're not going with us," Josh said with a question in his tone.

Their small, amazing friend looked at them with oversized, sad eyes. Then he dropped his head to look at Josh's borrowed and muddy shoes that were still tied to his own feet. "I cannot go in again tonight," he explained. "I am injured and cannot risk exposing my open wound to the infections present in your world. Also, the morning is drawing near, and should this take too long, I would be trapped by the sun. I cannot risk it." The elf shook his head from side to side. "No, I cannot go."

"Don't we need your help to get through?" Hope asked. "We need to be touching you, right?"

Josh put his hand on Gavin's shoulder and answered for him. "No. We can go right back through on our own. We only need him to come from our side to here." Then he lifted Gavin's elfin chin and looked at him. "It's okay. We can do it alone."

"It's kind of a long way down there," Hope pointed out. "I'm not sure I can jump that far."

Josh looked down again. It *was* a long way. He hadn't considered that the first time he went through. He rubbed his chin as he considered it now, and he realized that his jaw ached a bit from when his knee had struck it on his previous jump. Earlier, he had been so worried about Hope that he'd just flung himself down. Now, though, when he had time to think about it, it definitely was a long way. Rational hesitation overcame his headlong bravado.

"We can help," a pair of voices said in unison from above them.

Gavin, Josh, and Hope all looked up together and spotted two more elves on the limb overhead. One of them held a large rope that was tied off on the limb on which they were standing.

"Gronek! Smakal! You're back!" Josh yelled. "Where's Danny?" He looked around for his other friend.

"We deposited him back into your home, and it is our hope that he has secured your authorities. Perhaps he is leading them to this place at this very moment."

"Great! Guys, this is Hope. We saved her." Josh indicated the open-mouthed girl on the tree limb next to him. "Hope, meet my other two elf friends."

"Hi," she said and gave a little wave.

"Hello," they responded together.

"It is our honor to meet you," said Gronek.

"We are pleased for your rescue," said Smakal. "But why do you wish to go back to that place?"

"There is another young human in the evil pair's possession," explained Gavin, "who must be saved as well."

Without speaking further, Gronek, who had been holding the rope, dropped it past them. As it extended, it passed cleanly into the shimmer, emitting tiny crystal sparks as it moved through. Its bottom end stopped just short of hitting the floor inside.

Josh looked at the other elves. Then he turned and said to Gavin, "Um, why didn't you let me use the rope the first time?"

"You did not wait," answered the senior elf as he looked down into the room below. "You simply jumped before I had the opportunity to give you access."

Gavin turned toward Josh and Hope with a grave expression on his odd little face. "I am fearful for you to return to your dimension at this place and at this time. It is very dangerous. Perhaps it would be better to let your authorities rescue the other one. You should let us return you directly to your home."

"But Gavin," Hope responded, "we must go in. Who knows what will happen if we wait?"

"We don't know if the police are on their way or not," Josh added. "We don't know if Danny was able to convince them. If we wait, it might be too late."

"That is true, my young one, but—"

Before Gavin could finish, Hope grabbed the rope and swung off the limb. "We can't wait," she said as she lowered herself down. Very quickly, she dropped through the shimmering window.

"She is very much like you, is she not?" Gavin asked Josh.

"Guess so," he responded as he followed his friend onto the rope and descended with similar speed. "See you later."

* * *

Rick Anders, the weary Indiana State Police trooper, crept carefully down the hill, darting from tree to slab to rock with frequent pauses to look and listen until he was standing beneath the great oak. The massive ancient tree was even larger than it had looked from atop the hill, dwarfing the small block building. Just above his head was a limb large enough to park a sofa on, but it was so high that there was no way he could reach it without a ladder. As he stood there admiring the majesty of the old tree, looking in wonder at the size of the limbs, he was suddenly struck in the face by small pieces of bark. They seemed to crumble off the nearest limb as if scuffed free by an invisible foot.

Quickly closing his eyes, he ducked his head and began brushing the tree dust off of his face. Then he looked over to the window that he and Danny had discussed. As the boy had said, it was high up on the wall. He felt some bark lurking in his hair and on the bridge of his nose, so he gave himself another quick brush off, then jumped up and grabbed on to the frame of the window. Pulling himself up, he took a quick glance inside. Not able to see anything helpful, he dropped back to the ground, pausing under the window to consider his options.

Is she even in there?

Danny had said so, but Rick couldn't be sure. *Maybe they moved her.*

He felt a piece of bark in his mouth and spit it out into the underbrush.

He had a moment of indecision. Should he wait for the sheriff? Should he go around to the other side? Maybe he could find the door and get a better look, but maybe he'd be slipping into a trap.

He didn't want to make the decision. Often in his job, the decisions were made for him, either by his supervisors or by the situation in the heat of the moment. Left with time to think, though, he often found himself in a struggle. That tendency toward indecision was what had led to his divorce. His wife had been unhappy; he had known it, but he had been paralyzed by indecision. He hadn't known what to do about it. Should he give up his job and move her back to her hometown? Or should he work less hours and be more present in her life? He knew she struggled with loneliness as a city girl stuck in Cutters Notch ...

In the end, he hadn't been able to decide what to do, so he'd just kept going down the same road, hoping his marriage problems would solve themselves. They had. His wife gave up, found another man to meet her needs, and moved on with her life—taking his son with her.

Now he found himself alone with his thoughts again, trapped in another crisis of indecision. His mind's eye focused on Maggie's pleading eyes. He could hear her voice begging him to bring her daughter home safe. He thought about Hope's cute smile and hesitant eyes the first time they'd met. His heart ached as he missed his own son, knowing that he would see the boy again soon. *This week? No. Next week.*

His son was the one thing in his life that gave Rick hope. He couldn't imagine how Maggie would feel if she lost her Hope forever.

He made his decision. *I'm coming, Hope!*

The night was quiet now, but the moon still brightened the landscape. The bright orb had followed its course into the western sky; despite the late hour, it still hung high enough to illuminate Rick's path. With his service pistol drawn, he skimmed along the side of the building, his back rubbing the blocks, feeling the rough edges of the old limestone grabbing at his jacket. A coyote was yipping in the distance. There was no sign of Josh.

There was movement back toward the woods. He turned quickly and pointed his weapon, but it was only a skunk scurrying into the underbrush. His nerves were on edge. He had to take a moment to force his breathing to relax.

Thankful that he had not encountered the skunk in closer quarters, he turned back toward the front of the building and continued his quest. Reaching the corner, he dropped to his knees and peeked around. There was no one in view. Still no sign of the boy, either. The Hicks' Explorer was parked directly in front of him. He could see the lake framed between the building and the rear of the SUV. There were night birds skimming insects off the water's surface.

Overhead, there was a single incandescent bulb dangling above a door, and light poured down on a small stone stoop. June bugs and moths were buzzing around the light. They dropped on the stoop or landed on the screen briefly, only to fly back at the bulb again. One dive-bombed his face, and he brushed it aside. *Buzz while you can*, he randomly thought. *The cold will get you in a couple more weeks.*

Rick's heart began to pound with anxious anticipation as he moved around the corner toward the door. As he approached, he heard voices, so he paused to listen. Two people. Muffled shouts. He couldn't hear clearly, but it sounded like an argument.

"Shut up!" came Faye Hicks' voice.

Rick had heard that same voice many times; it had blared over their privacy fence and assaulted his mind as he'd tried to enjoy the quiet of the evening.

"You shut up!" That had to be Earl Hicks, but Rick had never before heard the man respond like that.

Rick tried to move closer; he tried to get his ear into a better position. Edging onto the stoop, he leaned his head against the door.

"Who do you think …"

"I'm gonna …"

"Get over …"

"No!"

Another June bug buzzed his face, and he flinched, waving his arms in self-defense. He had just settled back into a listening position when there was a loud -pop!-. The sound jolted him onto his heels, and he fell back on his rear end. Hopping quickly back to his feet, he clicked the safety off on his weapon. No more waiting. He had to move now.

* * *

Earl Hicks had been looking at the pathetic little girl on the desk. Her brown bangs were matted with perspiration across her forehead, and her brown eyes stared with terror through the smeared makeup. She was sweating profusely. The stink of her body was a bit much after the night he'd had. Despite the terror in her eyes, however, she wasn't struggling. Apparently, her strength was spent, and she was resigned to her fate.

"What are you waiting for, you old fool?" said the creature that had been the woman of his dreams so many years ago. "Let's get on with it." Faye was standing at the girl's feet, smoking. Her hair had begun to dry, and strands fluttered out like gray fishing line under the light of the incandescent bulb in the ceiling.

Despite Faye's prodding, the old man still hesitated. He wondered if he was beginning to feel some empathy for this helpless little girl. Then he looked at the fillet knife he held in his right hand and imagined it slicing through flesh. A spark of thrill rushed through his mind. No, it wasn't empathy he was feeling. Guilt maybe, but not empathy. Even so, it wasn't the girl's flesh he imagined slicing; it was Faye's.

It was then that he had a revelation. He looked up at his wife. *I really do hate you.*

"Do you want me to do it?" she asked.

"No."

"Then get on with it."

An urge swept over the badgered husband. He'd felt it before, but he'd always been too much of a coward to do anything with it. This time it was accompanied by that now familiar chill on the back of his neck. He glanced down at the knife again. Then he looked over at his deer rifle.

"Do it!" a voice somewhere inside his mind prompted him.

Finally, he looked over at his wife of so many years and so many insults—so much pain and bitterness. He could see the animosity in her eyes. *Can she tell what I'm thinking?* he wondered.

"Oh, curses, Earl. I'm tired. Get on with it. *Will you please!*"

The woman had changed him. She had taken him from a simple country-farm-boy-turned-mining-manager and transformed him into a monster. She had taken him to a place from which there was no return, no retreat. She had made him into what he was, and he desperately hated her for it.

Earl straightened up and stiffened his back. He stood there for a few moments with the fillet knife in hand, wearing his white butcher coat with his own blood drying on one side. He stood there and looked at his two-legged, forty-year nightmare, and a debate raged in his mind. *Can I do it?* "Do it." *What if I freeze up?* "Do it." *What if I miss?* "Do it!" *Okay, I'm going to do it.*

"Shut up, Faye," he said under his breath.

"What?" He could feel her eyes burning into the side of his head.

"Nothing." *I don't think I can do it.*

"Yes, you can," said the voice in his head. "Do it. Do it now!"

He was cold, shivering.

"You said something. What did you say?"

"I said for you to shut the hell up!" he answered, the words finally bursting forth like a bottle rocket from a beer bottle. There was no turning back now. He was going to do it. He *had* to.

At first, Faye was dumbstruck. She had never before seen that reaction from her husband. He was always submissive. He always cowered before her demands. Sure, there was that one time, but she had fixed that. She had trained him like she might have trained a rebellious puppy, and he had never since given her trouble. As she stood there aghast, she quickly processed what was going on. Was he so tired that he had lost his mind? Was he challenging her? Was he getting senile? Why now?

"Go on then," she finally said as she took a long drag off a cigarette. She was making full use of her vicious eyes. "Take your time and sleep well tonight." Smoke erupted from her nose and mouth with each word she spoke. "Sleep really well."

"Oh, I'll take my time," Earl replied, turning his head to look at Faye. "You can count on it," he said as a leer crossed his usually solemn face. A look entered his eyes that she had never seen before, except occasionally in her own mirror.

That strange smiling leer gave Faye pause. Her own smile faltered, and power faded from her eyes. Something unfamiliar filled the vacancy: a touch of fear.

"I'll surely sleep better tonight than I have in years." Earl then turned fully toward his aging wife. "Perhaps better than I've slept in about forty years."

Faye had been looking at the impeccable nails on her hand and holding the cigarette, trying to maintain her façade of power. When she looked over at Earl as he spoke those last words, fear swept up and over her false wall of courage. All at once, she realized how vulnerable she was. He had the knife. He had the gun. She was standing there in her underwear, and she was not the strong woman she had once been. She was old now, and all of her strength was concentrated in her words—and her eyes. Apparently, he had begun to see through all of that.

"Earl. Shut up and get busy!" she shouted as she tried desperately to resurrect the façade. With obvious nervousness, she stamped her cigarette out in an ashtray on the workbench.

"You shut up, Faye! I've had all of you I can stomach. I'm done with it all." He took a step toward her. Now *his* eyes were doing the burning.

Not one to be put in her place, the last thing Faye was able to do was shut up. "Who do you think you are? I'll make you pay, and you know it!" She was fumbling with her hands, trying to find something. Anything. Something she could use as a weapon.

"I think I'm gonna make *you* pay, you naggity old witch. Now get over there by the bathroom door." He was motioning with his hand, waving the knife around just inches from her face.

Earl backed off briefly, laying the knife on the table by the helpless girl's feet and picking up his rifle. Putting it to his shoulder, he pointed it at Faye. Motioning with the barrel, he again urged his now terror-stricken wife back toward the small bathroom in the right rear corner. She lifted both hands in front of her, as if to plead with him to stop.

Earl began to laugh. She looked funny. It was like blinders had been removed. He paused and stared at her half-naked, wrinkled upper torso. Skin sagged everywhere. This was the woman that he had subjected himself to for so many years. *Why?* he wondered. *Was it for her sensuality? If so, that reason was gone about twenty years ago.* He suddenly could not understand why he had waited so long to put an end to this … this … this nightmare.

Tears were starting to run down her cheeks, changing directions with each crease in her skin. She had backed up to the bathroom wall. There was nowhere else to go. She looked at the man whom she had dominated for nearly half a century aiming the rifle at her. The light bulb was suspended just above his head, and it cast shadows down across his face. There was a darkness there; she could see it. It was fluttering around his eyes.

"No! Earl, no! Please, no!" For the first time since she was a little girl, she was begging.

The old man stopped laughing. He lowered the rifle and took one last hard look at his shriveled-up old wife standing there, her arms now holding herself with only her bra to provide any cover. A wet stain formed in the crotch of her pants. After all they had done, that seemed fitting somehow. They had watched so many victims wet themselves, and now Faye was soon to be the victim. He chuckled one more time and shook his head in disbelief. *Time to wake up from this nightmare.* Then he raised the rifle and fired.

TWELVE

ope lowered herself on the rope through the shimmer without any hesitation, as if it were something she'd done dozens of times before. Josh followed, being careful not to drop too quickly and hit her on the head. When they were clearly in the room, they dropped one at a time to the floor, each landing in a catlike crouch. Hope looked up to see if the elves were still watching, but all she could see was her own soiled face looking back. She winced at her rough appearance. Despite being a bit of a tomboy, she still cared about looking good, especially with boys around. And Josh was a boy. It seemed that she had only just noticed that fact, but she had no time to dwell on it.

The rope, which seemed to be dangling directly from the mirror without any visible support, began to slowly rise, disappearing inch by inch into its own reflection. The two friends looked at one another. Hope placed a finger across her lips to indicate their need for stealth and then motioned toward the door.

Careful to stay out of the sightline of the next room, they moved silently to the doorway. As they did, they could hear angry words being hurled back and forth from voices they recognized as those of Earl and Faye Hicks. When Hope peered around the doorjamb, she could see Earl Hicks motioning with his rifle at his half-naked wife. His back was to them. A light bulb hung above his head, and the light was reflecting off of a bald spot that bloomed like an island in a gray sea. Faye had her hands up and was backing away toward what looked to be the door to a small room, maybe a bathroom. Loose skin hung under her arms and shook as she waved with her palms up for Earl to stop. She was pleading.

Josh tugged on Hope's arm and pointed toward the plastic-draped desk. On top was a weak-looking young girl who was alive but barely alert. They could see her chest rise and fall with quick, shallow breaths. As they looked at her, she opened her eyes and stared back. Those two windows into the young girl's soul revealed terror—terror and a seed of hope. As earlier, a tear leaked out of one of her eyes and slid quickly down, dripping onto the plastic tarp. Her hair was lying in damp clumps across the side of her face.

Hope spotted the fillet knife by the girl's feet. She pointed at it so that Josh could see and then motioned for him to follow her. Each in a crouch, they slipped into the room without a sound, and Hope quickly grabbed the knife. Acting fast, she cut through the girl's bindings on the side of the desk closest to the Hicks and then moved back around to the other side to get those, as well. The old criminals were too preoccupied with their own issues to notice.

She cut through the remaining ropes, and Josh pulled the girl down. He was a strong boy, but this was no little girl. She was dead weight, like a large sack of potatoes. He sagged under the load. *Come on. I got this.*

The unknown girl had just landed across Josh's shoulder when two things happened in quick succession. First, Earl Hicks shot his wife. Then, soon after, Rick Anders burst loudly through the entry door, gun in hand. Rick's sudden entry drew Earl's attention—and his rifle—away from his wounded wife. The three young people were now in the no-man's land between the old man with the rifle and the state policeman with the large pistol.

* * *

When the shot rang out, Hope and Josh both looked over at Faye just in time to see her grab her left shoulder. Blood began to ooze out between her fingers, and more blood was splattered on the white block wall behind her. She had a look of disbelief on her face. That look was quickly followed by another look of horror as Earl loaded another round into the chamber. He was apparently not satisfied with simply wounding his wife.

"Thought I'd give you just a taste of the pain you've been to me all these years!" he shouted. "Now, just one more between the eyes." He was grinning. He hadn't felt this glorious feeling of control in about four decades.

Earl was raising the rifle for the kill shot when he heard the door
burst open. Startled, he turned to find a scene so confusing that it put
him at a disadvantage. He saw a man charging into the room. That man
had a gun. Earl also saw three kids over beyond the desk. The weakened
girl he had been about to butcher was being held up by a boy. *Josh?*
Another girl was helping him with her. *Hope? How?* Disbelief caused him
to hesitate and lower his rifle just long enough for Rick to get the drop on
him.

* * *

After recovering from the initial start of the gunshot, Rick rushed in,
barging violently through the door without any concern for being
stealthy. Trained to quickly assess situations, he didn't need more than a
moment to figure out what was what. In the corner of his eye, he could
see Hope, Josh, and another kid. *Another one?* Across the room was the
old couple. Earl Hicks was turning toward him with a rifle in his hands,
while his wife was slumped against the wall, bleeding.

Rick pointed his gun directly at the old man. "Freeze, Hicks!" he
ordered. "Drop the rifle on the floor and step away."

* * *

Earl Hicks froze as ordered. He didn't move, but he held on to the
weapon and seemed to be considering his options. After all, he had
just found the courage to stand up to the one person who had been
terrorizing him for decades. He was so close to getting that little piece
of satisfaction, and a surge of energy was still coursing through his
system.

He had to think, and he had to do it quickly. As he saw it, he had
only three choices. First, he could try to raise his weapon back up and
shoot the cop with his .22 caliber rifle. He would be risking the likely
response of being shot with the police-issue semiautomatic pistol that
was already aimed at him by a skilled marksman. That choice would
leave him dead, and Faye would be alive. Second, he could try to turn
and put a bullet through her old, ugly skull. Again, he would likely be
shot dead by Rick, and his own shot would probably miss Faye alto-

gether. He would be dead, and she would be alive. Third, he could surrender and face whatever consequences would befall him *and her* through the court system. He dropped the rifle and stepped back. *Maybe she'll get the death penalty.*

* * *

Faye Hicks was obviously no longer a threat. Backed up against the wall next to the bathroom door, she had slipped down onto her butt, leaving a smear of blood on the wall in her wake. She had passed out from the shock of both her husband's newly found intestinal fortitude and the actual trauma of being shot. Her head was leaning to one side, and her feet were spread out in front of her. Blood had soaked her plain white bra and was running down her arm, gathering in a small pool by her left hand.

"Back up against that wall there!" Rick ordered Earl. *Maybe I should just shoot him,* Rick thought. *Maybe shoot the both of them and be done with it.* The thought seemed to form in his mind from nowhere, carried there on the chilly breeze that tickled the back of his neck. *No. That's crazy. I can't do that, and I won't do that.* The breeze dissipated as if someone had closed a window.

Earl obeyed, backing up and glancing down at his unconscious wife. He smiled. The satisfaction he gained from the shooting of his wife increased exponentially with the size of the blood pool by her hand.

"Drop down on your knees!"

Again, the old man obeyed. He wondered how his wife's blood would taste on a cracker. *Probably as bitter as aspirin.* Forty years as a cannibal was a hard habit to break.

Without taking his eyes off Hicks, Anders turned his attention to the three teenagers. "Are you kids okay?"

It was Josh who spoke first. "We're fine Mr. Anders, 'cept this girl here is awful weak."

"Who is that?" Rick asked.

Josh was holding on to the girl, but she was slumped over. With an effort that seemed to take all the energy she had, she raised her head and looked at the big policeman. She tried to raise her hand, and she moved her lips, but she still couldn't bring herself to speak. A grunt was all that escaped her mouth.

"We don't know," answered Hope. "We got away, but then we found out they had her, too, so we came back to get her. How did you find us? Did Danny bring you?"

Rick didn't answer but shifted his attention back to the old couple. As he moved around the plastic-covered desk toward Earl Hicks, he kicked the rifle against the far wall and pulled a set of handcuffs from his belt. A sense of relief swept over him. It was all but over. *We're going to be okay. I'll give Maggie her Hope back.*

"Hicks, lay down face-first on the floor and put your arms behind your back," Rick instructed. Once Earl had complied, Rick moved over the top of the old man and placed his own knee in the small of the man's back, expertly cuffing both wrists. He then lifted Earl to his feet and sat him on the ragged sofa.

"If you move, I will shoot you down quicker than you can blink," Rick said, looking Earl directly in the eyes. "Do you understand?"

The man nodded. He was still smiling. "Did I kill her? I don't think I did, but maybe she'll bleed to death."

Rick stepped back and looked at the old man. He didn't understand. "Why? Why'd you shoot your wife?"

"A man can live his whole life in a cocoon, but eventually, he has to break through the silk cage and escape."

Rick didn't know any more than he had before he'd asked. The answer made no sense. Still, he had old Hicks in custody. The man would rot in prison, likely for the rest of his life, though he didn't seem to be disturbed in the least about being caught. He just seemed happy. Giddy, even.

"Mr. Anders," Hope tried again, "how did you find us?"

"Danny led us here" was his only response. His attention was focused on securing the old man first, and then he needed to see about the old woman. Once those two priorities were covered, he would turn his mind to the kids.

Rick began to assess Faye's condition. Despite her apparent incoherence, he cuffed her anyway. The wound did not appear to be life-threatening. The bullet had passed clean through the thin, fleshy area of her shoulder and had had just enough velocity left to stick in the plaster wall behind her. Her old skin and muscle hadn't provided much resistance, not even enough to stop a small .22-caliber bullet. She was bleeding freely, so he took a clean rag, and after dipping it in the hot water that was still simmering on the wood stove, he placed it over the bullet hole and secured it with a roll of twine—the same twine that Earl and Faye Hicks had used to tie the girl down on the desk.

Having completed all that, he pulled the radio from his belt and switched it back on. He hadn't been able to raise Sheriff Dunlap earlier, but he needed to try again. He was going to need some support on scene and help getting everyone out. Before he could call the sheriff, the old woman moaned, so he put the radio aside to check on her.

The kids watched him without further interruption as he moved from place to place and did his work. Josh shifted the unknown girl to the floor but was standing next to her, letting her lean against his legs. Hope was quiet. She looked around the room, taking it all in. When Rick was nearly finished with wrapping Faye's bullet wound, Josh spoke up again.

"Danny told you where we were?"

"He sure did, Josh." The trooper walked over and leaned against the desk with the plastic tarp. When he had been working on Faye, he had re-holstered his weapon; now he rested his right hand lightly on the gun and ran his left hand across his face and through his hair. He pulled another piece of bark from his scalp and tossed it aside. "In fact, he led us here."

"Twice." Earl Hicks had turned his attention from his bleeding wife to Rick and the kids.

" 'Twice' what?" Rick asked. "What are you talking about, old man?"

"Twice now, you've said the boy led 'us' out here. But I only see you. Who is the 'us' the boy led here?"

The policeman glared at the old man, who now looked ridiculous on the beaten-up old couch. *I would have never suspected these two to be any threat to anyone.* In his white lab coat, Earl Hicks looked like an ancient doctor—or maybe a shriveled-up surgeon that had waited one patient too long to retire.

"Me and Sheriff Dunlap," Rick explained. "The sheriff had a flat tire out in the woods and is waiting for backup. He'll be here shortly."

After answering the question, he turned and thumbed the mic on his radio. "Dunlap. This is Anders. Do you copy?" *Come on. Answer.* All was silent for a few seconds, so he tried again. "Sheriff, do you copy?"

"10-4." The answer crackled the small speaker in the handheld radio. "What's your status?"

"Position is secure. Suspects in custody. Kids are safe. We have one perp wounded. What's your 10-20?"

Now that he'd established contact with Dunlap, he felt secure, even more at ease. Help was on the way. *We'll need to drop a chopper in here*, he thought. *Maybe Dunlap will do the paperwork.* He allowed himself a smile. *Unlikely.*

"I'm just outside," said the sheriff. "I'll be there momentarily."

Rick didn't see the smile that Hope and Josh saw as it crept across Earl Hicks' face. It was different from the giddy, delirious grin from earlier. This one seemed dangerous. Sly. Confused, they looked at one another. Josh shrugged. Hope gave an "I have no idea" motion in response. The old man seemed nuts.

A few seconds later, Danny barged headlong through the door with Dunlap right behind him. Once inside, the boy darted over to his friends and hunkered down, obviously afraid. His eyes darted to Rick and then back to his friends.

Sheriff J.B. Dunlap entered right behind the boy with his hands near his hips—left hand on his cuff pouch and right hand on his weapon. His face wore a familiar smile. Rick was busy securing his radio back to his belt and only glanced up when J.B. stepped beside him.

Addressing the old man on the sofa, Dunlap said, "Well, I guess you've gotten yourself into a fine pickle this time, Uncle Earl."

What he said registered immediately with Rick Anders, but it was too late. As he reached for his pistol, he felt something cold against his neck. Dunlap's weapon was pointed at the back of Rick's head.

THIRTEEN

"*A*nders, turn around and put your hands behind your head," the sheriff ordered. When Rick complied, Dunlap carefully reached down and pulled the trooper's service weapon free of its holster and secured it within his own ample waistline. "Now, pull your pants legs up."

"I don't have a spare weapon on me," Rick said. "I didn't think I needed it for a search and rescue."

"Wouldn't have done you no good anyhow," Dunlap answered, "but let me see for myself."

Rick started to lower his arms to comply, but the sheriff stopped him. "One arm at a time. And, like they say in the movies, you move real slow. Okay?"

Keeping his left arm up, Rick slowly lowered his right arm and pulled up his pant cuff. Nothing there. He could feel the cold steel of Dunlap's gun as it pressed into the back of his head. Across the room, Earl Hicks was grinning from ear to ear. "So, you were in on this whole thing?" Rick asked the big sheriff. "You're an accessory?"

"Nope. Just related's all," Dunlap replied. "Blood's blood in these parts. I've got no part in their 'hunting' expeditions."

"Well, you're part of it now."

The sheriff laughed. "Maybe so. But you won't be takin' me in for it."

After repeating the process of raising his other pant cuff with his left hand—with the same result—Rick returned both hands to their position on the back of his head. "Satisfied?" he asked.

"Yep. Now move into that room over there," Dunlap said, indicating the same room in which Hope had been held captive earlier. "Take those stupid kids with you."

Rick began to walk toward the room. Josh, Hope, Danny, and the new girl were already by the door, so he motioned with his head for the kids to go on in. Looking helpless, they stared at the trooper and the sheriff in disbelief. Somehow, they kept it together. Danny led the way. Hope and Josh followed and were on either side of the other girl, helping her walk. She was still slumped over but moving better. As Rick reached the doorway, Dunlap's boot connected with his butt and shoved him on through. Once they were all inside, the door was shut tightly behind them. They heard the slide-bolt engage, securing them in the makeshift holding cell.

* * *

Rick cursed and then looked guiltily at the kids. "Unbelievable. I cannot believe he got the drop on me like that." He bent over, hands on his knees, and shook his head back and forth. *I am so freaking stupid. How did I miss that?* Moving to Cutters Notch was like going to a new church; you never know who is related to whom.

Anders began to look around the room with his back to the door. A broken chair lying in pieces near the middle. A privacy screen in a far corner with a portable toilet just visible beyond it. A small table lamp in the near corner to his left. A window set high up in the wall on his right—the window he had glanced through earlier. He checked it now and found it secured down with nails. Concrete block walls with broken paneling and steel conduit running to outlets positioned at intervals. A tile floor that looked recently mopped. No useful weapons. No way of escape.

After assessing the situation, he turned to the kids and found Josh and Danny standing together in the middle of the room. The girls were huddled together in the far-right rear. Hope had knelt down. She was trying to talk to the other girl, who seemed nearly too weak to respond.

The boys were looking up at the mirrored ceiling. Josh was turning his head left and right while Danny was waving at his own reflection. *Those boys are just a bit odd*, Rick thought. *Still, they seem to be taking this in stride. Maybe better than I am.*

"What are you boys doing?" Rick asked as he joined them in the center of the room. He cocked his head to look up at whatever they were looking at. "Something special about that mirror?"

"We're looking to see if the elves are still there," Danny responded.

"The what?" Rick asked, dumbfounded.

"The elv—" Danny started to explain, but Josh interrupted.

"The *Ls*," he interjected. "Some kids held Danny down the other day and used a marker to put a couple of Ls in his hair. They call him Lard-butt *Loser*, and they thought it'd be funny to write that on his head. With the mirrors on the ceiling, he can sort of see the top of his head if he looks at it kinda crooked. I said the Ls were gone, but Danny wanted to see for himself." As Josh was creating the elaborate explanation, which wasn't hard to do since it had actually happened a couple of weeks prior, he was also stepping on Danny's foot—sort of hard.

"*Ow!*" Danny complained. He shoved his friend and hopped away.

"Oops. Sorry, Danny," Josh said.

I could have sworn he said "elves." Shaking his head and sticking a finger in one of his ears, Rick turned to the girls. "Hope, are you okay?" As she looked up at him, he could see her mother's features in her face, the angle of the eyes and the shape of the nose. *They are both so pretty.* He felt a long-forgotten yearning and the warmth of new-formed affection. Maggie had somehow captured his heart, but he stuffed that realization down deep inside. *Now is not the time.*

"I'm tired and weak, but I'm okay. I haven't really been hurt in any way except for the knot on my head."

"How about that girl? She okay?" he asked. The unknown girl still had not spoken, but she was moaning, rocking back and forth. Rick took his jacket off, knelt down, and laid it across her lap. He wanted to give her some cover, since she was wearing only a tiny T-shirt and panties. It was cool in the room.

"Best I can tell, she's not physically hurt," Hope said. "I think she's just tired and really scared. Rick, they gave me something to drink that made me go to the bathroom a lot." Hope looked at him with concern in her eyes. "If they did that to her, too, and she's been here longer, she might be really bad off."

"Mr. Anders," Danny spoke up, "are we gonna be okay? Can you get us outta here?"

Getting back to his feet, the trooper turned to face the boys. "I'm sure going to try, Danny, but we are definitely in trouble here." *Big-time trouble.*

"And you don't have a gun anymore, either," said Josh.

"Oh, no," Rick said quietly, "I've got a gun. Sheriff Dunlap isn't the sharpest tool in the shed, and he was sloppy. Troopers don't leave the house without a spare weapon." As he spoke, he reached back and pulled a small pistol from inside the waist of his pants. "You better believe I never leave home without this little baby. I just don't put it on my ankle. Instead, I keep it clipped inside my belt on the small of my back. We aren't quite as helpless as he thinks we are."

Rick looked down at the Smith & Wesson Airweight .38 Special 5-shot revolver resting in the palm of his right hand. It wasn't a long-range weapon, but it could be deadly up close. His father had given it to him as a present when Rick had graduated from the academy. He had only fired it a few times and had hoped he would never need it. Now he was very thankful to have it handy. *Thank you, Dad.*

He was still looking at the tiny handgun, allowing the nostalgia of the day he'd received it to give him a brief respite, when a ragged two-inch-wide, three-foot-long oak limb dropped from the mirror and landed right at his feet. Startled, he jumped back and stared at the piece of hardwood. He looked up at the mirror. He looked back at the fallen limb. Finally, he looked at the boys.

"Did that come from the … elves?" he asked. *It had to be somehow hanging up there. I just missed it when I looked before. Had to be.* "Up in the mirror?" *I must be losing it.*

"Yep," said Josh.

Hope and Danny just nodded a bit apprehensively.

Before Rick could ask the kids to explain, voices arose from the next room.

* * *

After closing the door and latching the bolt, J.B. Dunlap turned around and took a long look at his grinning uncle and his bleeding, moaning aunt. He couldn't understand how this had ballooned into such a mess. He couldn't believe that it was his aunt and uncle who had snatched the girl. He had been aware of their preoccupation with human meat. He had known they were cannibalistic kidnappers, but they always did their hunting away from home, so he had been certain they hadn't been responsible for this one. *Why?* Despite his duty to protect and serve, if he'd known the truth, he would have steered the investigation away from his kin. His father had drilled one code into him as a child: Family first, always and forever. He had not known though, and factors beyond his control led both he and Anders to the quarry.

Now he was going to have to clean up the mess. He would have to dispose of the evidence and the witnesses. He would have to get his relatives away. He would have to do it all without being discovered by his own deputies and other law enforcement officials, neighbors, and friends who were on the scene to help. *What a full-blown freakin' mess!*

"J.B. I'm sorry—" Earl Hicks started to apologize before being cut off. His grin had dissipated under the glare of his looming nephew.

"What were you thinking?" Dunlap asked as calmly as he could. "Why? Why would you hunt so close to home?" *Maybe I should just get rid of these two, along with the others. Say I lost Rick in the woods, and I couldn't find anyone else. I searched but couldn't locate anyone. Nice, clean story.* It suddenly felt chilly in the room. "Why? Just tell me why?"

Earl didn't immediately respond. Instead, he pointed over to the slumped and wounded woman sitting on the floor against the bloodied bathroom wall. The sheriff turned his head and looked at the pathetic lump. She was beginning to stir and looked back at him with dawning recognition.

"She made you do it? Is that what you're saying? Earl, don't you have any stones at all?" Even as he berated his humiliated uncle, he knew that what Earl had indicated was true. She had always been the stronger of the two of them. She had always ordered Earl around: "Get me a beer!" or "Make me a sandwich!"

Dunlap used to marvel that his uncle was so compliant. He had never understood it. If Faye had been *his* wife, he would have put her in her place the first time she mouthed off at him.

Dunlap's implication that he was less than a man got under Earl's skin just enough to turn his face red, and he struggled to sit more upright on the sofa, glaring at his uniformed nephew. His eyes bugged out, and the tendons in his neck stretched out through his gray whiskers. "You don't think I've got stones? Really? Well, maybe you're right. Maybe I didn't for a long time, but boy, I do now!" He was shouting back at the younger man. "I'm done takin' orders and being pushed around by that wrinkled-up hag over there. Who do you think put that hole in her shoulder? Huh? *Me.* That's right. I shot her, and if you'll get these cuffs off my wrists, I'll put another one right between her eyes!" He tried to stand, but Dunlap placed his hand on the old man's head and shoved him back into his seat.

The surprises just won't end tonight, J.B. thought. He had always liked his Uncle Earl and had spent many a summer night sitting in the man's backyard, talking about baseball and sipping root beer from bottles. Those days were long gone, but Dunlap sure missed them.

He wasn't as fond of his Aunt Faye. It always seemed that she just put up with him. She stayed inside watching her "shows" or listening to the police scanner. When she did speak, she called him Bucky, and it was always accompanied by a demand or a snide remark. Her eyes could cut you in half.

"Let's just start with cleaning up this mess around here and figuring out what we're going to do with the people in the other room," said Dunlap as he leaned over to unlock the cuffs. *And maybe you too.*

"I've got the answer," replied Earl. "Just let me get up and get the feeling back in my hands, and I'll explain." The old man again struggled to get on his feet. This time, J.B. started to help him.

"Bucky, honey ..." A voice smothered with artificial sweetener came weakly from the sheriff's right. "Bucky, I'm so thankful you're here. He shot me, honey. Please help me. I'm afraid of him. He wants to hurt me." Faye Hicks was regaining her wits and was awkwardly working to stand up. "Sweetie, don't unlock him. He's lost his mind. Maybe gone senile. There's no tellin' what he'll try an' do."

Dunlap stopped, suddenly conflicted. Who did he believe? He wasn't sure. He loved his Uncle Earl, and he had always known his Aunt

Faye to be a difficult woman, but she was telling the truth about the shooting. Earl had just admitted as much. *Get rid of them both.* The thought was almost as clear as another voice in his ear.

The hesitation that followed Faye's allegations prompted the cuffed old man to react. "Shut up, Faye! I'm done with your mouth! I'll come over there an' kick you to death!"

Faye cackled. "Earl, you're a coward and an idiot. Now that Bucky's here, you ain't gonna do nothin'!" She started to lift her left hand but stopped when she realized she was handcuffed, herself. She twisted to try to get her feet under her, and pain shot straight to her brain. Wincing, she cried out, "*Aaaaahhhhh!*"

Earl mustered the strength to drive his old body up and off the broken-down sofa without the use of his hands, which were still locked behind his back. He lunged toward his half-naked wife, laughing, and with murderous intent in his eyes.

"I'll show you who's gonna do something!" he screamed at her. "I'll rip your heart out with my bare hands, you hairy, old canker sore!" The laugh died away and was replaced with something more somber. "For years, I've let you order me around and coerce me into doing things I will never be able to get away from. Terrible things. Things that will follow me to my grave and probably from there right into hell. Well, maybe they will follow me to my grave, but I'm tellin' you, Faye, those things, those terrible things we've done…they're gonna see you over there first." Earl then turned toward his nephew. "Unlock me, J.B.! Unlock me right now!"

Dunlap stepped between the old man and the old woman. He placed his hands on Earl's shoulders and stooped down to look in his eyes. "Settle down, now, Earl. Just slow down a step." *I think the old man really has found his stones.*

"See, Earl. I told you he'd stop you," Faye sneered at her husband. She had managed to get to her knees but could get no farther. She felt weak.

J.B. ignored the old woman's voice. He looked down at his aunt on the floor. *She's still calling me Bucky. I really don't like her at all.* Her voice grated on his nerves in a way that reminded him of sour apples and rotten potatoes. "Just slow down, Earl. We can deal with the old woman at the same time we deal with the cop and the kids."

Earl smiled.

Panic flared in the wounded hag's eyes as the cuffs were removed from her once-cowardly husband's wrists. "No! No! What are you doing?"

"Let's dump her in there with the others while we figure out what to do." J.B. Dunlap had made his decision. One would live; one would disappear.

* * *

Gavin, with Gronek at his side and Smakal one limb higher, stood on the outstretched limb of the ancient oak peering down through the shimmer and into the room where they had first spotted Hope taped to a chair. The room was empty now, and they were anxious about their human friends. Smakal could not stand still; he roamed to and fro across the rough bark surface, showering chips of bark on Gavin and Gronek.

"They should not have gone back through," Smakal said with deep concern in his voice. "We should have insisted that they return to their homes. They are yet children."

"I agree," said Gronek. "I regret providing the rope." He was solemn. He stood still, staring intently into the room below as if willing something good to happen.

"As do I," replied Gavin. "But we could not stand in their way." He was the most worried of all. "Could we?" He had grown very fond of both Josh and Hope, and he had seen the evil in the eyes of the Hicks as they had chased the three of them down the pier. Doubt joined arms with his worry.

Some time went by, but they kept watch. The door to the room finally opened. The elves shook with excitement, hopeful for good news. Then their hearts sank as the children shuffled in, two of them helping another girl who the trio had not seen before. Lurching in behind them, as if shoved, was the man called Rick. The door then quickly closed, trapping them inside.

"Disaster!" shrieked Gronek.

Gavin was so shaken that he nearly lost his balance and fell. Gronek grabbed his arm to steady him, all the while making unintelligible sounds of disbelief himself.

"We must go in!" shouted Smakal, making his tiny, elfin voice as mighty as he could muster. "We must help!"

Though clearly upset—so much so that he was unstable on his feet—Gavin managed to hold them back. "We cannot," he said. "It is too near the dawn. We would be trapped, and we cannot risk being locked in that world during their daytime. We must instead pray to the Great One to show mercy to our valiant friends. Pray! Pray fervently!"

"Is there nothing else we can do?" cried Smakal. "Nothing at all?"

"Nothing."

When their gaze returned to the shimmer, they saw the boys looking up at them from below, turning their heads back and forth as if trying to see through the mirror. Danny was waving. They were obviously looking for help from their new friends, hoping for a rescue from above. Gronek and Smakal became so excited that Gavin began to wonder if he would be able to hold them back. They were all stunned into silence and drew back, however, when they saw the man—Rick—step up beside the boys and peer in their direction.

"Perhaps we should drop the rope back in?" suggested Gronek.

"It would not work," Gavin reminded him. "They must be touching us to exit their realm."

They saw Rick turn his head back toward the boys. A few moments later, after he had turned away, a large oak limb fell from above the elves. It passed so close that Smakal felt the bark tickle his right ear as it dropped. Inexplicably, it did not bounce and tumble off the roof of the invisible building below as limbs normally did. Instead, it fell directly through the shimmer, landing on the floor beside the man.

The human looked at the limb. He looked at the ceiling. He looked down at the limb again. Finally, he looked at the boys and said something that the three brothers could not hear from their perch. The boys simply smiled back at Rick and seemed to nod in agreement.

"That was odd," said Smakal. "Very odd, indeed."

"Agreed," replied Gavin. "I have never before seen that happen."

Gronek looked up at the great tree in amazement, moved with deep emotion. "There is much kindness and concern in you, old friend," he choked out as he patted the oak on its huge trunk.

Before more could be said, they saw Rick and the children turn their attention back toward the door.

FOURTEEN

$\mathcal{M}$aggie was still sleeping fitfully on Cindy's sofa as the nightmares came and went. Her dreams, having shifted from a pleasant day on the beach to terror in the sand, had further transitioned into a simple haze of foreboding emotions. Her heart leapt as Rick's smile came into view. She liked his smile. It was warm. Honest. But it wouldn't hold; instead, it would be replaced by Kenny's leer. Hateful and bitter. She saw Hope bouncing a basketball in the street—then she heard screeching tires and her little girl screaming. As if in a loop, the sequence of images repeated, then repeated again.

More than once she drifted toward consciousness and had the vague impression that she was sandwiched between two other people. She felt as if she were deep under the sea, surrounded by monsters and trying desperately to swim toward the surface, only to be pulled back down. It was during one of these brief periods near the surface that she heard the noise. It was loud. It broke through the fog, grabbed ahold of her mind, and yanked her awake.

Bang! Bang! Bang!

She jerked and tried to sit up, smashing one of the other mothers between her back and the sofa. "Uh, sorry," she mumbled. *What's her name again?* Somebody moaned; it was the other mother lying across her lap. "What was that noise?" More moans.

Bang! Bang! Bang!

This time, the sound drew Maggie toward the door. Someone was banging on it. *Was I somehow drugged?* Her head was spinning, but she struggled to get up. She lifted the woman off her lap so she could slide out, only to let her fall back down. The other two mothers were now positioned face-to-back, still asleep as Maggie staggered over to open the door. The TV was still on. Some rerun in the middle of the night. It was an old console. She put her hand out and steadied herself against it. Her mouth was dry. She smacked her lips.

Bang! Bang! Bang!

"Okay, I'm coming." Suddenly, her heart raced. *Hope?* She lurched to the door and jerked it open. "Hope!"

"Miss Spencer?"

It was a deputy. She didn't know his name. He was holding his hat across his chest and had a thin smile showing under his close-cropped mustache.

"Uh, yeah." She struggled to focus her eyes. "Did you find her? Did you find my baby?"

"Not yet, ma'am," he said. "They're chasing a good lead, though. Can I speak to the boys' mothers?"

Maggie turned and looked over her shoulder at the two women lying like oversized dolls across the sofa. She rubbed her face, her eyes. "They seem to be out cold right now. Is something wrong? Did something happen?"

The deputy continued to stand there with the thin smile, glancing over Maggie's shoulder and then back to her. *He probably thinks we drank ourselves into a stupor and passed out.*

"Well, no, ma'am. Nothing's wrong. I just wanted to assure them that the boys are okay."

Maggie was confused. She thought he was asking *if* the boys were okay, so she glanced down the hall to her right at Josh's closed bedroom door. "Of course they're all right. They're in bed." She realized her curly black hair was hanging in her face, so she awkwardly brushed it aside.

"No, ma'am. You misunderstand me. I need to advise the mothers that the boys are okay. You see, they slipped out again."

"Oh. Oh, oh, oh." It finally clicked. "*Oh!*"

"Anyway, ma'am." He hesitated. "Please let the boys' mothers know that they're okay. They're with Sheriff Dunlap and Trooper Anders. They should be home soon."

"Did they go somewhere? What's going on?" Maggie's emotions were driving the residual fog from her mind. "Tell me, deputy!"

"Well, a while ago, Danny approached Trooper Anders and corroborated a theory that Hope was being held at an old quarry back deep in the woods."

"Corroborated? How in the world would Danny corroborate any-thing? He was supposed to be asleep!" She was getting worked up, and she was alone in her anxiety. The other two women were still snoozing away. One was snoring, and the other was mumbling.

"I don't honestly know how," he replied. "I just know that he did. Sheriff Dunlap and Trooper Anders took him along to find the quarry."

She was beside herself. *Why? Why would they take the boy?* "So they took Danny with them? What about Josh? Is he with them too?"

"According to Danny, he was already out there waiting for them."

Maggie shook her head. *This can't be real. I must still be asleep.* "What? How would he get out there in the woods? And why would they take Danny out there in the middle of the night?"

"Well, ma'am, we couldn't get a chopper from the state police for some time yet. Some mechanical issue. So Anders and Sheriff Dunlap decided to take a couple of ATVs out there. Danny went along to show them the way." The deputy was starting to fidget. He was uncomfortable. The ridiculousness of the story was beginning to dawn on him.

Her dander rising, Maggie Spencer looked the deputy in the eyes. "You mean to tell me that two seasoned officers of the law took two twelve-year-old boys deep into the woods in the middle of the night in an effort to track down a kidnapper at a stone quarry somewhere out in the forest? All because they couldn't get a helicopter from Indianapolis?"

The deputy swayed on his feet a touch, stepped back with his left foot, and said, "Uh, pretty much."

Suddenly, she felt helpless again. Alone. Maybe more alone than she had yet experienced. Annie and Cindy were sleeping, draped over one another like folded strips of linen. Hope had vanished. Now Rick, for some reason that made absolutely no sense to Maggie, had taken Josh and Danny off on a dangerous mission into the deep forest in the mid-dle of the night.

Maggie took one more silent look at the unnamed deputy in the entryway, then slammed the door in his face.

Turning around, she strode past the snoozing mothers and picked up her purse. Fishing around inside, she slid her hand back and forth until her fingertips contacted the small piece of thick paper for which she had been searching. It was tucked in deep, near the bottom, in a tiny pocket. She pulled it out and studied the writing. The logo said WISH-TV8.

Her childhood best friend's business card. It was her ace in the hole, and it was time to play it. If Kenny had Hope, then media exposure no longer posed a risk.

Maggie glanced around the room and spotted a telephone mounted on the wall; she snatched it up and dialed a number scribbled across the bottom of the card.

It rang on the other end. Three times. Four. A groggy voice answered, "Hello?"

"Sandy? It's me. It's Megan. I need your help."

* * *

Rick's attention was drawn toward the door by raised voices and angry words. He walked over and placed his ear against the chipped paint of one panel, raising one finger to his lips to encourage the others to be quiet. Quickly, the two boys joined him at the door, listening in also. They could hear Earl. They could hear Faye. Threats. Accusations. After a few minutes, Rick had heard enough and moved away. With the boys in tow, he rejoined the two girls across the room.

"Okay," Rick began. "We're going to have to be smart about what we do from this point. I'm going to need you all to follow my lead and listen to my instructions, even if I sound crazy. Okay?"

The kids each nodded their understanding.

"The fact that I have a gun—and they don't know about it—gives us an element of surprise, but we also have a child down, and that will make us more vulnerable."

"What are we going to do?" asked Hope. She was sitting with the weakened girl, who was looking more alert, her eyes darting from face to face. She had brushed aside Rick's jacket as her hands tried to smooth out a nonexistent skirt on her legs. "How do we get out?"

"I'm not quite sure yet." *I can't let them see how worried I am.* "Whatever it is, we'll all have to move quickly, and I'll have to take out the sheriff." *I'll have to get him off his feet. No small task.* "When I do, I'll need the four of you to run. Head to the woods. It'll be harder for them to find you if they get past me." *Three against one. They will probably get past me.*

"I've got a weapon too," said Josh, holding up the rugged piece of oak that had fallen into the room. He swung it around a couple of times like a baseball bat. "This thing'll do some damage!" The lone light from the corner caused the makeshift bat to cast looming shadows on the wall over their heads.

"Yes, it will." replied Rick with forced enthusiasm. "Use it with all your might if you need to, but your first priority will be to get yourself and your friends into those woods. You understand?"

"Yes, sir!"

"Good. Now—" Rick began, but then the bolt on the door clicked free. He turned quickly, instinctively placing himself between the door and the kids.

"Josh! Hide that thing behind you!" he said. "Stay behind me—all of you!"

"Move back and keep where I can see you," ordered Dunlap as he eased the door free of the latch. His big gun led him inside, but he was dragging something with his left hand.

"You're hurting me!" screamed a struggling Faye Hicks. The door had barely been fully opened when the sheriff flung the old woman roughly into the room. "What are you doing? Let go of me!" Her hair was stringy, and her bandaged shoulder had blood seeping through from the bullet hole underneath. Losing her balance, she fell to the floor hard and lay there sobbing as the door closed behind her again, trapping her with her former prey. "Bucky, don't! Don't do this! Please!"

The formidable huntress was now helpless. Before, she had been a dangerous predator. But now ... now she seemed like a toothless, clawless, aging lioness that has suddenly found herself in the midst of a herd of vengeful gazelles. Fear flared in her eyes, where before there had been so much power and hatred, the glow of an evil mind.

With her eyes darting from the trooper to the array of kids, she slid herself away from them. Using her cuffed hands and flailing feet, she pushed herself backward until she was safely in a corner. There, she curled up in a ball, wrapping her wrinkled arms around her shaking knees. Burying her face between her arms, she began to sob.

For a few moments, the group was speechless. Hope had helped the other girl to her feet; the girl had perked up with a sudden surge of renewed strength. With Rick in the middle, the girls on his right, and the boys on his left, they stood near the center of the room, staring at Faye. Rick had not yet formed a plan, but he understood that this definitely was a new wrinkle in the situation. "Hmm."

"Yooooouuuuu!" screamed a new voice. "I'm gonna kill you!"

Before anyone could react, the unknown girl grabbed the oak limb from Josh's hands and lunged at Faye. She moved as fast as her weakened state would allow, which was not quick, but the wounded old woman had nowhere to go. The girl raised the bark-covered weapon high over her head, pausing just a moment to look at the hag, then began to swing it down. Rick snagged it before she could whack the old lady.

Pulling it away from her, he said, "Hold on there, girl."

Having exhausted every last ounce of energy left in her drained body, she swayed and collapsed toward the floor. Danny caught her. Wrapping his arms around her, he gently lowered her down and sat with her, resting her back against his chest. "It's all right. I've got you," he said. She leaned back and let him cradle her, rocking back and forth.

Giving the limb back to Josh, Rick said, "Keep a better grip on it next time. Okay?"

"Sorry," the boy replied. "I had no idea she'd snatch it like that."

"I know." The man tousled the boy's hair. "I know." As with Danny, he imagined some of his own son in Josh's eyes, and his heart ached. *I've got to get these kids out. I have to. But how? Oh God, don't let me fail them like I've failed myself. Like I've failed my own son.*

"Do me a favor," he told Josh. "Take your friends back over there by the wall. Try to rest for a bit." He indicated the wall opposite the door and away from the old woman. "Okay? I need to think. I need to think hard." *I need to pray hard, too, but God probably won't listen to me now. Not after I've failed him so miserably.* As cold air brushed his neck, a voice in his head confirmed that he was a loser.

"Sure," the boy replied. Without speaking further, Josh went to his friends and moved them back to the opposing wall. There they sat side by side, leaning on one another as if they could survive by sharing their mutual strength. Josh sat next to Hope. He took her hand in his own, interlocking his fingers with hers. She rested her head on his shoulder.

Meanwhile, Rick walked over to the corner with the little lamp. He sat down, leaning his head against the wall in a failed attempt to draw strength from the structure. Feeling the pressure of his spare gun in the small of his back, he wondered, *Will it be enough?*

He was tired, so tired. He didn't know what to do. The kids were looking to him to save them, and he didn't know what to do. *I'm so lost!*

It seemed that he never knew what to do. He didn't know what to do when his wife said she was lonely. He didn't know what to do when she told him that she had found solace with another man. He didn't know what to do when she took his son away. And he didn't know what to do now. *I just can't do this!* His knees were shaky. Despair was threatening to overwhelm him. Tapping the back of his head lightly on the paneled wall, he took a deep breath and struggled to compose himself. He couldn't lose it now. Not now. There were too many people … kids … counting on him.

A voice arose in his mind again: "Take your gun and shoot the kids," it said. "Save them from the trauma of whatever Dunlap is planning. Then shoot yourself too. Save the world from any more of your blunders."

Rick pulled the pistol from its spot near the small of his back. He stared at it. Five shells. One for each of the kids and one for himself. Glancing over at the two boys and two girls leaning on the far wall, he imagined a hole in each of their foreheads.

He shivered and shook his head violently. *No! I won't even think those kinds of things! No! No, no, no!*

The voice of despair receded.

Time passed. He wasn't sure how long. A hint of light began to filter through the glass in the window. Birds began to whistle and chirp outside, their songs bringing the lyrics of hope with their melody.

In his core, Rick Anders' resolve steeled itself. Anger gathered in his heart as if called there by the incessant warbling of the forest wildlife. He might not know what he should do, but God help him, he was not going to go down without doing *something*. He had let his family dissolve without fighting back. He had let some strange man take his place as a father without so much as a tussle. But this was different. Those stakes had been high, but here—in this place—lives were depending on him. He didn't know what he was going to do, but he would look for his opening, and he would fight. He would fight, and he would die if need be.

I will probably die.

FIFTEEN

"Josh," Rick said as he motioned for all the kids to join him. "Time is short. They'll be back to deal with us in a few minutes, but I'm not going to wait on their timing. We need to get back on the offensive."

Josh was eager and was again brandishing the oak limb like a baseball bat. Danny, Hope, and the girl joined Josh and drew near to hear Rick's plan.

"Josh, I want you to stand to the left of the door with that piece of oak raised over your head. I'm going to try to get Dunlap to talk. Then I'm going to try to lure him in here." He looked each of them in the eye. "Remember, no matter what I say, you need to trust me. Okay?"

"Yep," said Danny. The others just nodded.

"As he walks through that door with his gun raised, I want you to hit his arm as hard as you can. Can you do that for me?"

"I sure can!" Josh was grinning with excitement.

"Okay," Rick continued. "When you hit him, it will give me a chance to get the jump on him. I want all the rest of you to kneel down in that other corner over there by that little lamp—out of the way. Get low on the floor just in case a shot goes off. Make yourselves as small as possible. Got it?"

"Got it," they all said together.

"Oh, and one more thing," the experienced trooper added. "I want you to pray. Pray real hard."

The seemingly broken, frail-looking woman in the opposite corner was eyeing them as they spoke. She was listening, but she didn't say a word as she sat shivering in the chilly room with her arms wrapped around her knees. She seemed to have lost all of the gravel in her gut, so Rick disregarded her.

"I hear them out there moving around, and I don't think it's going to be much longer before they come back in here. It's getting to be morning. They need to be done with us before we become visible from the air.

At any rate, I don't think we can wait for them to make the next move. Let's do this. Are you ready?"

"Yes!" They all said it at once. Even the unknown girl had again found her voice.

The sturdy state policeman had regained his composure. His earlier bout with his personal demons had passed. He now moved with renewed energy fueled by a combination of adrenaline and resolve. His doubts were still there in the back of his mind, but he kept them at bay with a tremendous force of will. He wasn't going down. Not now and not in this way. He especially wasn't going to let that pompous, good old boy Dunlap hurt these kids, even if he lost his own life in the process.

Walking over to the door, Rick leaned the side of his face against the slab of oak and listened briefly. Then he stepped back to the middle of the room and began to call out. "Dunlap! Hey, Sheriff Dunlap!"

"Shut up in there!" Dunlap replied.

"Come on, J.B.," said Rick in a forced friendly tone. "You don't want to do this. You don't really want to hurt these kids." He started by playing on the man's sense of duty. He had sworn an oath, after all.

There was no reply, only the sounds of things being moved around and the outer door opening and closing. A broom swishing. Something scraping on the floor.

"Dunlap, come on," said Rick. "How did you get so low? Are you really going to do this to some kids? Helpless kids? Don't you have children, sheriff?" He moved on to play on J.B.'s conscience. *Does the man have a conscience?*

"Leave my family out of this and shut up," the sheriff retorted.

"They didn't seem so helpless a little while ago," said Earl. "The wound in my side says they ain't all that helpless."

"You shut up, too, Earl," said the sheriff. "Rick, I didn't want this, but Earl's my family. It's a blood thing."

Okay. I've got a little nibble. He's talking. Now to coax a full bite. "What about ol' Faye in here?" Rick asked. "She's your kin, too, right?"

"Not after tonight," replied J.B.

"Well, surely you don't really want to hurt her." Rick was working him. He had Dunlap talking, but he couldn't seem to come up with the right words to draw the man into the room. "She's cold and scared. Just sitting there, shivering in the corner."

"Not my problem," said Dunlap. "Earl's my uncle. He married the old woman, but now he's done with her. So she's nothing to me anymore."

Nothing seemed to get the sheriff worked up enough to make him want to talk face-to-face. Rick had one last card to play. "Could we make a deal, J.B.?" *I'll play on his greed. If he'll kill kids, then maybe he's dirty in other ways too.*

Things went quiet for a minute. The sheriff didn't immediately reply. Then Dunlap said: "What kind of deal are you talkin' about?" The voice was closer. Dunlap had moved up next to the door. His tone had changed just a touch too. There was genuine curiosity there.

I think I've got him. Rick winked at Josh and motioned for him to get set. "I've got an idea how we can both get out of this, and you'd be a good bit better off," he said.

"Better off how?" asked Dunlap. "What's your play?"

"I've got this money I recovered from a bank robbery over in Bloomfield last year. I found it in a duffle along Highway 37 … Ah, come on, J.B. I'm getting tired of yelling through this door. Can we just talk?"

The bolt slid over on the other side of the door. Josh nodded. He was excited and smiled at Rick, the oak limb raised high. Rick nodded back as he reached behind and withdrew his pistol. Hope, Danny, and the silent girl huddled in the corner to the right of the door. Everything went quiet. Time seemed frozen, stuck on that moment of reality. Anticipation became a palpable feature in that tiny square room.

* * *

In her corner, disregarded and unnoticed, Faye was silently watching the events unfold. She had heard every word. She had watched Josh move into position between herself and the door. She had seen Rick as he had examined his small weapon. Now she moved into a crouch, like a cat preparing to snag a juicy mouse. A certain gleam had returned to her eyes. This was her opportunity, her chance to survive.

* * *

Before he opened the door, the sheriff called in with the old clichés for Rick to stand where he could see him and to not make any sudden moves. "Don't give me any trouble," Dunlap said.

"I'm right here in the middle of the room. What kind of trouble could I be?" Again, Rick forced the friendly, conspiratorial tone. "You've got the gun. I'm just hoping to make a deal with you that will get me out of here alive."

"What about those kids you were so worried about?" Dunlap asked. There was some hesitation riding on his words. He was curious, but he was also wary.

"I'm still worried about 'em," Rick admitted. *The lie can't be too thick.* "But I'm more worried about my own skin. Come on, J.B. Do you want to make a deal or not?" *Easy, easy.* "I can see some daylight in the window. We don't have much time." Rick was hoping he didn't sound too much like the spider asking the fly over for dinner.

The door swung open, and there stood J.B. Dunlap, his large profile filling the doorframe, silhouetted by the backlight spilling in from the other room. He remained there for a moment, assessing the situation before stepping inside. With his big gun pointing out from his ample waist like a gunslinger from the Old West, he made his decision and took a step into the room.

Josh lifted the tree branch a tad higher to get a bit more momentum behind his swing. He had both hands squeezing one end, and he stood up on his toes as he reached the pinnacle of his arc.

"Watch out, Bucky!" screamed Faye Hicks.

Just as Josh was about to bring the rugged club down on the sheriff's arm, he heard movement behind him. Before he could complete his move, two bony hands pushed him from behind.

"It's a trap!" the old woman blurted. "Rick has a gun!"

* * *

The three elves stood side by side, arm hooked inside arm, staring down into the shimmer. They were terrified for the children. Gavin was wracked with guilt.

"What have I done?" he moaned. "Why did I involve the others? I have brought an end to them all."

His brothers had no reply. They loved their brother and trusted him explicitly, but tonight he seemed to have erred—and erred greatly. His shame would be great, and they would share in it. They watched the tears stream down Gavin's face, and their own began to flow.

Still, despite the hopelessness of the events, they could not turn away. They continued to watch. They watched as the group separated into corners. They watched the big human man as he sat in the corner with his head against the wall. They watched the evil old woman fidget in her own corner. They watched the specter flutter around, going in and out of room. They watched … But as the sun began to brighten the horizon, creating a pink glow behind the trees, their view into the shimmer began to fade.

"Look!" exclaimed Gronek. "The policeman is calling them together. He seems to have some sort of plan."

The light of dawn grew a touch brighter, and the shimmer faded even more. In the faint view below, they saw Josh move over beside the door. He stood there much as Hope had stood there earlier, awaiting her chance. The man took up a position in the middle, directly under the shimmer, across from the door. He was talking. They could see his lips moving. The specter's fluttering intensified. The door opened. A large man stepped inside. The old woman pushed Josh. Then the light of the new day overcame the glow of the shimmer. Their view was lost, and as it left, they began to abandon all hope.

* * *

Rick, raising his weapon in anticipation of Josh's strike, was stunned when the boy suddenly lurched into Dunlap's arms. He watched it unfold. It felt like slow motion as the sheriff grabbed the boy around the neck with his left hand and pulled him in close.

Raising the gun in his right hand, Dunlap pointed it at Josh with a sneer. "Drop your gun on the floor and kick it over to me," he ordered. "I gotta hand it to you, Anders. You almost had me. I should have known you didn't have any real stash of money. You're too straight-laced for that."

Rick kept his gun leveled at Dunlap but stayed silent. He stared at the big man, burning a hole in his forehead. He was thinking. *I could shoot him. He makes an easy target, as tall as he is.*

"Drop it, I said!" The crooked sheriff shoved his huge revolver into Josh's ear. "Drop it now, or I'll blow the top of this boy's head off!"

But what if he pulls the trigger as he's hit? I can't risk that. Resigned to the situation, Rick dropped his weapon and kicked it over to the sheriff. Dunlap stopped it with his right foot, stepped on it, and slid it behind him through the door. "Earl, get that gun behind me."

Josh had dropped the oak limb at the sheriff's feet. "Where'd you get that piece of wood, boy?" the man asked. Josh didn't answer, so he shoved him across the room to Rick.

"Time to go. Everybody line up behind Anders," J.B. directed. He was motioning with his pistol. "I want y'all to walk out here, turn right, and then go on outside. Slowly and single file. If anybody moves outta line, I'm gonna shoot 'em. Understand?"

Everyone started moving and lined up behind Rick. Danny was immediately behind him, still holding the other girl up, helping her along. Josh and Hope took up the rear. Hope reached out and took Josh's hand. Despite himself and the situation, the boy blushed.

"I said 'single file,' not two by two," Dunlap said to Danny.

"I have to help her," Danny retorted in a defiant tone. "She can't hardly stand up."

The sheriff paused to take a closer look at the girl. She was pale, with huge dark circles around her eyes. She was shaking, and he could see she was unstable on her feet. "Fine then, but you just watch that she don't try to run. Got that?"

Danny glared at the man, nodded, and slid his arm around the girl's waist.

"You too," Dunlap said to Faye. "Get in line with the others."

"B-b-but, Bucky …" she stuttered. Her newly regenerated, leering smile faded, and the gleam again left her eyes. "But I helped you. I shoved the boy and told you 'bout the gun. I … I saved you."

"Pretty stupid on your part, huh?" he replied. "Now get over there in line, and stop callin' me Bucky."

Dejected, Faye crossed her arms over her blood-stained bra and hobbled over to the others. The makeshift bandage that Rick had applied was fully soaked, but the flow seemed to have been stemmed. As she was told, she fell in line behind the kids, her fate now tied directly, inseparably to theirs.

Dunlap backed out of the room, and they all began to move through the door. Out in the main room, they could see that everything had been cleaned up and emptied out. The plastic tarp on the navy desk was gone. The boiling pots had been removed. The knives had been put away somewhere. Faye's blood had been wiped from the wall. It looked like a deserted old industrial shop again, albeit a bit too clean. The only indication that anyone had been there was the little bit of heat still coming from the wood stove.

Earl stood at the door, grinning and pointing Rick's spare gun in their direction. "Follow me, kids," he said with a smirk. "We've got a surprise for you around back. You, too, Faye, my dear old bride."

* * *

As the brightness of the morning cleared away the shimmer, Gavin, Gronek, and Smakal were left in suspense regarding their new friends. For a few brief moments, they stood gazing at the spot where the window into the realm of men had hung, but all they saw now was the rectangular crater in the earth below. The shimmer was gone.

They were huddled together on the largest of the great oak's massive limbs, holding one another. Gavin was weeping. "I failed them miserably. I have shamed myself, and I have shamed our family."

"You do not yet know that," said Gronek. "They may yet live."

"Yes," added Smakal, trying to sound hopeful. "The Mighty One may yet smile upon them." He had pulled away and was now leaning back against the trunk of the old tree. His six-fingered hands were stretched out behind him on each side and were wrapped as far around the huge trunk as he could manage. "We should pray, and perhaps our ancient friend here will join us in beseeching the Lord of Hosts."

Reluctantly, Gavin moved to join his brother where the limb joined the trunk. When Gronek made it three, they began to pray, their foreheads resting against one another as they hummed their personal prayers for their human companions. Soon, the great oak began to vibrate, and a low-pitched hum joined with their own as the tree added its prayer to the triune requests of the elves.

To their great amazement, another younger tree began to hum. Then another. And another. Before long, the entire forest was a harmonic chorus of prayer. The unity of their voices called out to the Mighty One. They pleaded that all hope was not abandoned, and that Hope and her friends would be brought safely back home.

Overhead and to their left, in the midst of the humming branches, each vibrating like a strummed guitar string, one massive limb began to shake with even greater fervor. Swinging forward and back, up and down, it reverberated as if plucked by an unseen hand.

* * *

Earl Hicks backed his way through the screen door into the clearing in front of the small stone building. Rick and the kids followed, with Dunlap bringing up the rear, poking his large revolver into Faye's back. The old man stopped and waited as the prisoners exited, then he turned and headed past his Ford. He went around the corner toward the rear, where the old oak stood at the edge of the forest among the huge stone blocks. Dunlap made sure that everyone stayed in line as they followed his uncle.

The noise of the birds filled the chilly morning air. Wisps of vapor spouted from everyone's noses, and dew had settled on all the fallen leaves. A thin layer of fog was drifting across the surface of the lake. The darkness of the night had surrendered to the first blooming glow of sunlight in the eastern sky, which was illuminating the trees, underbrush, and giant slabs of limestone. Two mourning doves were perched on a rusty steel cable that stretched from a broken crane across to a dilapidated conveyor. Their song provided the soundtrack to the parade: "*Whoo, who-a-who, who-a-whooo.*"

Together, the prisoners and their captors marched under the great, old massive tree that stood like a guardian behind the block building. With the brightening morning sky, they could see how truly large the oak was, towering high above the other trees. It spread out in every direction like a canopy, sheltering more giant slabs of stone. The tree's trunk was as big as a small bus. As they passed by, Josh reached out and patted the mighty tree. Looking up into its branches, he wondered if his elfin friends were sitting above, worrying about them.

About twenty feet beyond the trunk was another assemblage of huge stones. At first glance, they looked no different from the dozens of other stacks of slabs, but as the group approached, they could see what seemed to be an opening in the pile. Ringed by the white of the limestone, the darkness inside peered out at them like a malevolent ebony eye.

About five feet wide and maybe six feet high, the stone walls that formed the opening were capped by another thick pad of limestone laid across the top. The deep darkness inside indicated that this structure had only one opening.

Just to the side was another giant slab sitting on its end, but teetering toward the opening. It was sitting half off a small mound of smaller stones at just the perfect angle to keep it from falling. One shove in the right spot would send it over, encasing the cavity behind two feet of solid stone on each side. It was a tomb, and it was meant for them.

Earl waived the pistol at them to indicate they should go inside. Everyone stopped.

"Get on in there," said Dunlap.

No one moved. Above their heads, the leaves in the huge tree began to rustle as if the wind had suddenly picked up.

"Get in there," he said again. "Or I'm just going to shoot you where you stand."

Rick was looking for his moment, waiting for a chance to act, but nothing was presenting itself. *Two guns at two angles. We're going to die.* Soon, he would have no choice but to just take whatever risk was necessary and fight for all their lives. Soon, he would just have to go for it. *One last hopeless move.*

Dunlap shoved Faye, and she tumbled into the opening. Earl angled out so that he and J.B. pointed their guns at the group from ninety degrees apart. Slowly, the kids backed into the darkness behind Rick, leaving him as the only one who had not yet fully resigned himself to die without a fight.

"Go on, Rick." Dunlap pointed his weapon at Hope. "If you don't, I'll just shoot her now." The big man glanced above as the rustling of the leaves picked up intensity. It seemed that the other nearby trees had joined in. The entire forest began to shake as if the trees were in the midst of a mighty rushing wind.

Rick didn't move. He looked above, as well. *Crazy wind. I don't even feel it.*

"Do you really want me to blow her brains all over the inside of that hole?"

Rick inched back, considering his options. He had no choice. If he dropped back with the others, Earl would drop the stone, and they would all die of thirst, maybe suffocation, whichever came first. They would all be dead either way. If he fought, there was always a chance that they—or at least some of them—would survive.

The rustling leaves continued to pick up momentum until they blurred together in a massive, buzzing hum. The vibrations migrated down the trunks and into the ground. The three men who stood staring at one another could feel it in their feet.

"Go on now, son," said Dunlap. "Y'all have to disappear. There's no choice about it. Now get on in there. Don't make this any harder."

Rick made eye contact with the sheriff, revealing that he was not going to go easy. The big man was going to have to get actual blood on his hands. *Can he do it? The old man has murdered before.* Rick was sure of it. *But can Dunlap just kill me? Point-blank?* Silently, Rick flexed and released all of the muscles in his back, his legs, and his arms. *We're about to find out.* He readied himself. It was time to act.

As he stood there, just under the cover of the slab over his head, the vibrating hum of the forest reached a crescendo. From high above, there came a loud -*pop!*-, a series of snaps, and finally, one awesome -*crack!*- As all three men looked up, a huge limb fell from the ancient tree. Crashing through the other limbs, it fell with such speed that neither Earl nor Dunlap had time to move out of the way. The leafy end landed squarely on top of old Earl, knocking him to the ground. The heavier end slammed down as if propelled by a gigantic spring, crushing the top of Dunlap's head. The man who had been the county sheriff, sworn to protect and serve, landed in a lump. He was dead before he hit the ground.

SIXTEEN

The elfin brothers stood huddled in prayer in the massive tree as the huge limb plummeted to the earth below. When it reached the ground, the forest fell silent. In the brightening light of the new morning, they stared at an indentation in the soil beneath the heavy end of the large branch. The broken limb itself seemed to hang in mid-fall just a few inches above the ground, but it was clear that it had driven something down into the soil in the human realm. It had struck with so much force that it had driven the object well into the earth.

"It is done," rumbled the deep, somber voice of the old oak. "The young ones live."

Gavin, Gronek, and Smakal shouted with joy. Holding on to one another, they bounced around on their giant arbor perch, dancing and smiling and singing elfin songs of praise.

* * *

Recovering from the shock and good fortune of the fallen limb, Rick Anders accomplished several things very quickly. He started by checking Dunlap to confirm the man was dead, although the volume of blood and the fact that his head was pinned into the ground was clearly evidence enough. Picking up the sheriff's revolver, Rick tucked it into his belt. Glancing at Earl, he saw that the old man was pinned under the tangle of tree branches, unable to free himself. His small .38 had been thrown well out of the old man's reach, so Rick turned his attention to Faye Hicks. Dragging her out of the pile of slabs and reversing her cuffed hands to her backside, he looped the bracelets around the fallen limb. Finally, he dragged Earl Hicks from under the brush, observed that he was shaken up but otherwise okay, and handcuffed him back-to-back with his hateful spouse.

After collecting the other gun, Rick moved everyone except the fallen sheriff around to the front of the building into the clearing. The kids all sat on a stone slab while Earl and Faye sat on the ground in the open. Flies began to find the drying blood oozing through the makeshift bandage on Faye's left shoulder. They buzzed around and around, crawling across her arm and landing on her face. Despite her cries and sobs, no one came to her aid.

He was attempting to radio for help when Rick heard the distinctive thumping of a helicopter in the distance. Joy swept across the kids' faces as the rotating blades emerged over the tops of the trees and descended above the open water of the lake. The spinning blades dispersed the lingering fog, causing ripples in the otherwise calm lake as it buzzed across. Circling a couple of times, it finally came to rest about fifty yards away, in between an old broken-down flatbed truck and a rusty metal-clad shed.

A door carrying the WISH-TV8 logo flew open and out jumped two deputies and a woman with long, curly, black hair. Hope spotted her mother and jumped to her feet. Mother and daughter crossed the open space quickly, grabbing, embracing, and squeezing one another with a furiousness born of love.

Brushing the strawberry-blonde locks from her daughter's face, Maggie kissed away the tears that were streaming down Hope's cheeks. Then she opened up her arms and pulled Josh and Danny into a warm group hug. The four of them held one another, swaying and laughing, crying and dancing for several minutes. The unknown girl stood aside until Danny pulled her in, as well.

Finally, looking over their heads, Maggie caught Rick's eyes. Those warm, honest eyes. When she did, all of the anger she had felt for him a few hours earlier evaporated, and she simply mouthed two words: "Thank you." Her heart went out to him, and she smiled at the trooper.

* * *

Rick watched them holding one another as he stood off to the side. Alone.

The crisis had passed. He had succeeded. The kids were safe, and Maggie had her daughter back. Life would continue. Things would return to normal. And, he … he would be … alone.

His son was still gone. Maggie had her Hope back, but Rick's family was still broken, and his son was never around. As the adrenaline drained from his system, the shadows of depression began to edge their way back into his mind. *They're safe, but I'm still a failure.* The dark voice of doubt began to whisper in his ear again. He shivered.

Then something happened that he wasn't expecting. Maggie, the beautiful woman from next door—the one whose exotic eyes and cute smile seemed to intrude into his secret thoughts—found his eyes. She smiled at him. He caught her glance as she twirled with the kids, and she held on to his eyes with a magnetic grip. There was brightness there, a sparkle that could not coexist with his feelings of impending solitude.

Her lips moved. He couldn't hear her over the roar of the chopper blades, but he could read her lips. "Thank you," they said. His heart leapt within him, and the dark whisperer was again banished. He walked over and joined their reunion embrace. Hope pulled back and allowed him in. He was lost again, but this time he was lost within the embrace of a new family—a family created through the trials of one dark night.

* * *

Before the sun had fully risen into the morning sky, other choppers were circling overhead. An Indiana State Police helicopter was the second to arrive, followed by an air ambulance. News crews from Indianapolis, Evansville, and Louisville arrived in their own choppers and were in full reporting mode. First, the children were flown to a Bloomington hospital to be checked out and reunited with their parents. Then the state police bird was ready to gather up Rick Anders and his prisoners. He had placed them under arrest and would accompany them for processing.

Earl and Faye were raised to their feet to be led to the awaiting airlift. One trooper led the way and another guarded them from behind. Rick had already boarded. A large crow swooped down from a nearby tree. First, it dove at the old couple, causing them to duck and call out. But then it gained a little altitude and circled above, as if checking the air currents. Just before the geriatric criminals began to duck under the whirling blades, the crow swooped one last time and dropped a load of white and gray bird crap. The mess, caught by the air whisking around the chopper, was flung directly into the faces and across the bodies of the two kidnappers.

"*Caw, caw, caw,*" it added with delight as it soared back into the giant oak.

The killers began to spit and gag, but the seasoned officers joined Rick Anders in a wholehearted belly laugh. Turning to one of the pilots, Rick chuckled, "Sometimes you do reap the whirlwind."

SEVENTEEN

Over the next week, divers recovered the ATV that Rick had driven to the mine. They found it at the bottom of the lake, where they also discovered dozens and dozens of human bones—enough to keep the forensic laboratories busy with identifications for a long time to come.

In the Hicks' freezer, they found two hamburger patties that turned out to be human remains. They also found a macabre bulletin board in the Hicks' basement and a steel box of trinkets hidden in a bedroom. In the box were rings, bracelets, and other assorted jewelry, plus a toe and a little finger: Faye's mementos. The collection and the bones from the lake would eventually tie the couple to over thirty disappearances going back over a quarter of a century.

After spending a few days in the IU Hospital in Bloomington for treatment of minor wounds and dehydration, plus some counseling consultations, Hope returned to Basketball Court and her two loyal friends. The very next Saturday, they were out shooting hoops again, playing a game of Make It-Take It.

"I still think he's creepy," Danny said as he looked over at Willie Robbins' house.

"Not nearly as creepy as those two who used to live over there," Josh said as he pointed toward Earl and Faye's place. *Or that dark, fluttering demon,* he thought. He hadn't mentioned it to anyone, but he had begun to sleep with a light on. In the quiet of the night, he found that his mind would see that flutter in the shadows of his darkened room. "I'm glad they're gone!"

"Yeah, well, I still don't trust him," the larger boy said. Then he shifted gears. "I'm gonna go see Faith in a couple of days." The other kidnapped girl had finally given Danny her name during the helicopter ride to the hospital. "Mom said she'd drive me to Greenwood to see her."

"How's Faith doing?" asked Josh. "She okay?"

"She's still weak, but I've been calling her every day. She sounds stronger."

Josh looked over at Hope. *She is so beautiful.* He was still smitten, but now that the excitement had passed, he was again hesitant to let his feelings for her show. Instead, he contented himself with simply being near her and dreaming of a time when he could again hold her hand.

Hope was staying quiet, thoughtful. She took a shot that rimmed out, but she caught it on the fly and laid it back in. Retrieving the ball as it fell through the net, she said, "Do you think we'll ever see them again?"

"I hope not!" Josh exclaimed. "I hope they rot in jail for a gazillion years."

"No," Hope corrected him, "not the Hicks. *Them.* You know—our new friends."

"I sure hope so," Danny replied. "I look for them in the mirror every night, but all I see is my own stupid reflection."

"You're not stupid, Danny," Hope said. "I think you're smart, and brave, and wonderful." Before Josh could get jealous, she turned to him. "You too. You're my hero. I love you both so much." Moving in quick before he could react, she kissed Josh square on the mouth.

The boy turned bright red and found he couldn't think of anything to say. After a moment, he smiled from ear to ear, grabbed the ball from the ground where Hope had dropped it, and swished a three-pointer from half-court.

"Oh, I think they'll be around," Josh assured them as Danny retrieved the ball. "They'll be here when we need 'em. Now throw me that ball back, lame brain, so I can show you how it's done again."

When the three friends awoke the next morning, Josh had his new—freshly cleaned—basketball shoes back, Hope found her lost socks, and they each found a unique flower on the corner of their dressers, just in front of their mirrors. It was a flower they had only seen in one other place, a place very close by but also very far away. They knew then that their friends were still there. They would see them again—in this world or the next.

EPILOGUE

On the day the kids were rescued, at about 6 p.m. two hundred miles away at a broken-down house on West 17th Street in Muncie, Indiana, Kenny Burton returned home from his lousy job stocking shelves at the local grocery store. Fresh out of prison, it was the only employment he could get because of his criminal record and his limited education, not to mention the short fuse on his temper. His mother had called in some favors to help him get it. He'd gone out to the foundry to see if he could get his old job back, but the place was closed down and boarded up. Stacking up cans of peas and boxes of cereal was his life now.

It had been a warm day, but the place seemed chilly to him for some reason, almost cold. He clicked on the electric space heater he kept on the floor next to the old Magnavox television. Regardless of the temperature, it was always the right time for a beer, so he stepped into the kitchen to get a Bud from the refrigerator. A cockroach skittered across the floor and under the stove. While he was there, he pulled a TV dinner from the freezer and popped it in the ancient microwave. The whole place was "furnished," which meant it came with the essentials. In other words, it had a broken-down bed, a fuzzy couch, a fake-wood table, a couple of lamps, and a few nearly worthless kitchen appliances—plus cockroaches.

As the dinner heated up in the buzzing device behind him, he stood in the arched passage between his tiny living room and his tiny kitchen, sipping his beer and considering what he would do when the sun went down. *Maybe I'll hit the Stag*, he thought. It was a little bar on South Madison Street. *Or maybe the Island. Hmm …* He settled on the Island because he thought there might be a few more ladies to chase.

Out of the blue, he had a sudden urge to watch the news. He rarely turned on the TV, and he never watched the news, but this evening it was almost a compulsion. At first, he fought it. He wanted to shower up, shave, and get to smelling good. He wanted to finish this first beer, eat his dinner, clean up, and go chase some girls, so he turned back toward the kitchen.

"Turn on the TV, you idiot!" something screamed inside his head. It seemed so real, like someone was standing there right beside him—yelling—just like his dad used to. Stunned, Kenny looked around for the source of the voice. Nothing. No one there.

He shook his head, looked at the beer, and then shook his head again. He knew it would take more than one beer to make him loopy, but he definitely didn't feel right. Then it occurred to him that the voice was familiar. He had heard it before. It was the voice of revelation. The voice of realization. It had visited him on that night back before prison, and it had revealed to him that Hope wasn't his child. It had helped him to realize that Megan was fooling around.

"Fine," he said aloud to himself—or to whoever had screamed in his head. Then he clicked on the tube and plopped down in the lumpy chair. When the picture appeared, it was on ESPN. They were talking football. Letting out a few curse words, he got back to his feet and changed it to the local CBS channel. He wasn't sure why. "Is that the channel you want to watch?" he asked the voice.

"Yes!" it answered. It was so loud, it hurt.

He didn't much watch the news, but when he did, he preferred the ABC channel. The anchor lady was sweet-looking. She looked a little like his old lady, Megan, but hotter. For some reason, though, the voice in his head wanted CBS this time. "Good enough, then."

He wasn't sure where Megan had gone off to with that little brat of hers. The only word he had heard from her since the night of his arrest was when a lawyer had shown up with divorce papers, wanting his signature. When he'd gotten out, she was nowhere to be found. She'd skipped town and taken the kid with her. He called her folks, but they just hung up on him. He staked out their house, but she never came by. He didn't know where she was, but he wished he did. Oh boy, did he wish he did. Just thinking about her and that ugly kid of hers was making the anger well up inside him. *If I ever find her, she'll pay. Her and the kid.*

When the newscast came back from commercial break, Kenny sat bolt upright in his broken-down chair. There she was. *Megan!* Right on the TV. Her hair was different, but that was her. No doubt about it.

"I want to thank the state police," she said to the reporter. "If it weren't for Trooper Anders and the other officers …" She hesitated, emotional. "Who knows? I may never have gotten my Hope back. They're heroes, and I'm so thankful." Tears of gratitude were streaming down her face. Kenny wanted to smash it to a red, mushy pulp.

The newscast switched to the anchor. "Thirteen-year-old Hope Spencer was abducted yesterday afternoon by two neighbors for unknown reasons. She was then transported to a remote abandoned quarry for purposes that have not yet been revealed to the media. We are told that in addition to the heroic actions of Trooper Rick Anders, authorities are also attributing the rescue to the assistance of two of Hope's best friends. Hope and another as-yet-unidentified girl were rescued from an abandoned office building on the quarry site after the police were led to their location by the girl's friends."

At that point, the channel flashed a photo on the screen of Hope with a chubby boy on her left and another, smaller boy on her right. They were laughing. There was a cake on the table in front of them. It was obviously a picture from someone's birthday party.

Kenny felt the old anger rise up inside him and kick into a higher notch. It was welling up from his stomach and threatened to explode out his ears. He could feel his face turning red, and the muscles in his arms began to tense. *I wish I'd killed her! I wish I'd smashed that girl just like I smashed her stupid dog!*

"You still can," the voice in his mind said. "It's not too late. There she is. Just go get her."

His eyes shifted to the boys on either side of her, first to the chubby one, then to the smaller boy. "Josh," said the voice. "His name is Josh."

As Kenny's eyes stared at Josh, it seemed that the anger welling inside rose to an even greater fury. He could feel the blood coursing through his arteries. His neck was bulging. That kid needed to be taught a lesson. He could see that from looking at the goofy smile on the kid's face. He needed to have those pearly white teeth driven back into his throat. *I'll reach down his neck and rip his throat out through his mouth!* Suddenly, he knew he needed to do it. It had to be done.

Kenny didn't really understand why he wanted to hurt the boy so much. His hatred for Megan and Hope somehow made sense to his bungled-up mind, but he'd never met the kid. Still, he felt an intense, almost uncontrollable urge to hurt the boy. Hurt him bad.

No. That's not right, he thought. "I want to *kill* that little snot," he said to the voice in his head.

"Yes, you do," it replied.

On the screen, the anchor was repeating the details of the story. "Again, the girl, Hope Spencer, was abducted near her home in Cutters Notch yesterday afternoon. Following a harrowing night of horrors, she was rescued early this morning by Trooper Rick Anders of the Indiana State Police, who located her with the assistance of her two best friends ..."

"Cutters Notch, Indiana?" Kenny said aloud. He was growing accustomed to talking out loud to himself. "I have no idea where that is."

As if on cue, the TV explained, "Cutters Notch is a tiny community in southwest Indiana along Highway 257. It is nestled right up against the Hoosier National Forest ..."

It was Sunday evening. He was supposed to check in with his parole officer in the morning and be at work by ten o'clock, but that no longer mattered to him. Cutters Notch had to be a couple of hundred miles away. It was within reach, but he would have to be careful, take his time, plan. He wasn't going to go back to prison. Not again.

Just over his right shoulder, invisible to his alcohol-clouded vision, stood an entity. It was formless in Kenny's world, but in another dimension, it had a form—a fluttering, billowing, dark form. It moved with malevolent purpose and fed off the dark intentions of people it encountered. Yesterday, it had stood in a different room, sucking in the delicious flavors of hate and murder. It had been anticipating a feast, a banquet of evil. Its appetite had been piqued, and the anticipation had welled up ... only to be smashed to pieces by that human man-child.

It would inflict its revenge. It would make him pay. The boy would suffer, and the being would again be able to feast. It would gorge itself on the wickedness it had inspired in this man sitting here in front of it. Kenny Burton would inflict pain on the woman and her daughter, and the entity would drink deeply of their terror. Then Kenny would find the boy. The specter would enjoy that the most. Oh, yes. It would savor the boy.

Kenny absently reached up with his free hand and rubbed a chill on his neck. Despite the heat blowing from the space heater, he felt cold. He watched as the news anchor switched to a remote reporter standing on a basketball court. An old white farmhouse with tall shrubs stood behind him. Kenny was watching, but he was no longer paying attention. He was thinking, working out a plan.

"Screw it!" Kenny said as he threw his empty bottle and smashed the ancient TV. "They'll never see me coming."

CPSIA information can be obtained
at www.ICGtesting.com
Printed in the USA
FSOW01n1414071117
40868FS